100 Reasons to Celebrate

We invite you to join us in celebrating
Mills & Boon's centenary. Gerald Mills and
Charles Boon founded Mills & Boon Limited
in 1908 and opened offices in London's Covent
Garden. Since then, Mills & Boon has become
a hallmark for romantic fiction, recognised
around the world.

We're proud of our 100 years of publishing
excellence, which wouldn't have been achieved
without the loyalty and enthusiasm of our
authors and readers.

Thank you!

Each month throughout the year there will
be something new and exciting to mark the
centenary, so watch for your favourite authors,
captivating new stories, special limited
edition collections…and more!

Dear Reader

It is very exciting to have a new book out in the first month of Mills & Boon's centenary year.

I can remember, years ago, before I ever dreamed of writing for them, seeing an exhibition of Mills & Boon® covers over the years and admiring the way they moved with the times, reflecting changes in taste and casting such an accurate spotlight on how each decade saw romance.

For me, writing and reading romance is all about storytelling, sharing daydreams, exploring my ideas about how two lovers 'find' each other, and delighting in how other authors weave such variety around that theme. It seems incredible that one publisher has been able to provide that outlet for authors and readers for so many years.

I am particularly delighted that this book is coming out in this special year because it represents a real departure for me. I have always been faithful to my Regency heroes, but I have to confess to losing my heart to a man from a very different era—a Visigoth warrior called Wulfric. I do hope you enjoy my flirtation with another world as much as I enjoyed exploring it.

With best wishes

Louise

VIRGIN SLAVE,
BARBARIAN KING

Louise Allen

MILLS & BOON®

Pure reading pleasure

First published in Great Britain 2007
Paperback edition 2008
Harlequin Mills & Boon Limited,
Eton House, 18-24 Paradise Road, Richmond, Surrey TW9 1SR

© Melanie Hilton 2007

ISBN: 978 0 263 86239 3

Set in Times Roman 10½ on 12½ pt.
04-0108-87884

Printed and bound in Spain
by Litografia Rosés S.A., Barcelona

To Keith Emsall for his
constant encouragement with this book.

Louise Allen has been immersing herself in history, real and fictional, for as long as she can remember, and finds landscapes and places evoke powerful images of the past. Louise lives in Bedfordshire, and works as a property manager, but spends as much time as possible with her husband at the cottage they are renovating on the north Norfolk coast, or travelling abroad. Venice, Burgundy and the Greek islands are favourite atmospheric destinations. Please visit Louise's website—www.louiseallenregency.co.uk—for the latest news!

Recent novels by the same author:

ONE NIGHT WITH A RAKE
THE EARL'S INTENDED WIFE
THE SOCIETY CATCH
A MODEL DEBUTANTE
THE MARRIAGE DEBT
MOONLIGHT AND MISTLETOE
   (in *Christmas Brides*)
THE VISCOUNT'S BETROTHAL
THE BRIDE'S SEDUCTION
NOT QUITE A LADY
A MOST UNCONVENTIONAL COURTSHIP
DESERT RAKE
   (in *Hot Desert Nights*)
NO PLACE FOR A LADY

Chapter One

~~~
⚭⚭⚭
~~~

Rome
24th day of August, AD 410

The sound was terror made real. It was heard through the ears, and felt through the bones. It was the sound that her ancestors had heard thousands of years before as they huddled in the dubious safety of a shallow cave with only the protection of the fire between them and the things that prowled in the dark. The things that growled.

Julia stopped struggling against the rough hands that held her. The three of them, assailants and victim, turned as one, eyes squinting against the smoke that billowed from the burning shop. A pillar fell and smashed across the roadway, sparks showering. In the distance, from the direction of the Forum, screams could be heard. Here, now, after that low threatening rumble, there was only the sound of fire eating wood.

Julia sagged in the grip of the two men. In her terror had she imagined it? But the men had heard it too. It had cut through her frantic cries, through their threats and curses and coarse laughter. In a world gone mad, when barbarians sacked the greatest city on earth and respectable tradesmen tried to rape the daughter of a senator, it was no stretch of credulity to believe a wolf was stalking the streets.

Out of the corner of her eye she could see the crumpled body of the slave girl her mother had sent with her on this insane errand. The men had thrown her against the wall with brutal indifference as she clung to Julia's arm. She had not moved since. *I do not even know her name…*

'Nothing there,' the taller of the men grunted. 'Imagination.'

'She heard it too, didn't you, rich bitch?' It was the one whose face she had clawed, futilely.

'Yes. Yes—a wolf. It will be dangerous. You should run.' Even a wolf was better than these two. Fearful to run from the besieging Goths, fearful to fight, they had snatched at the chance to take what they had only been able to covet from afar. So often she, and ladies like her, had been carried past them in the street in litters, had browsed amongst the trinkets on their stalls and never noticed them. Now one of these pampered, elegant creatures had fallen into their hands. Amidst chaos they could take their pleasure and dull the terror of what was happening to their world.

But this sheltered virgin had fought back, ripping at their hands and faces, kicking at their shins, biting where she could. And the other girl, the little slave, was likely dead, and no fun at all.

The man with the bleeding tracks of four exquisitely manicured nails down his right cheek sneered back at her. 'Just some dog, chained behind the portico. No help for you there, sweetheart.' His fingers grasped the neck of her tunic and yanked downwards, his sweaty hand sliding over the bared flesh.

'*Hades.*' The taller man's voice shook, even as the second, long growl froze his friend's hand on her breast. The smoke swirled and the animal padded out less than a dozen feet in front of them. It stopped, head lowered, watching them.

The slanting green eyes set close over the long grey muzzle studied them with an aloof indifference that was more chilling than overt aggression. The curled lip revealed one long white fang. There was a low whistle and the animal walked off to the side and round the back of them. The men scrabbled to turn, dragging Julia, squinting into the drifting smoke as they tried to keep the animal in sight.

'Gone.' The tall man wiped a hand over his damp brow. 'Let's get out of here before that fire gets worse, find somewhere more comfortable to enjoy ourselves.' His falsely confident voice trailed off as they faced the burning building again and the smoke billowed, parting in rags around another figure.

A man. Tall, broad, bare-armed, golden. Light glinted off chain mail and helmet, wrist bands and belt buckle as he stood there watching them, as the wolf had done, with utter composure. There was no expression on the bearded face and there was no weapon in his hand, but a long sword hung from the wide belt that cinched his waist and for all his still-ness he exuded the promise of force poised to strike.

Julia swallowed, trying to force her spinning head to think. Trousers, long blond hair, bearded. A barbarian. A Visigoth, one of the enemy. But her immediate enemies were beside her, her own kind. Was she in more danger now, or less?

Hands tightened on her arms, half lifting her off her feet as the tradesmen began to edge backwards. She made a decision, forced herself to hang limp, making her weight a burden they must drag.

'Drop.' The big man spoke as though to a dog with a game bird and achieved the same unthinking obedience. Julia

landed hard on her heels and staggered, turned and hit the
bleeding man in the ear with her clenched fist, the sheer relief
of being free of their hands lending her anger force.

The man slapped back wildly at her, knocking her against
his friend. Then, as she scrabbled for balance, he grunted
abruptly and keeled over to the ground. She stared down at
him sprawled at her feet, the hilt of a dagger sticking out of
his throat, a thin trickle of blood curling down to his collarbone. Dead. She had not seen the barbarian move. The other
man took to his heels, then stopped, cowering, as the wolf
padded out of cover in front of him.

The barbarian ignored him, his eyes locking with Julia's.
There was no reassurance there, only the same chilling aura
of power she had seen in the wolf's eyes. He gestured towards
the tumbled figure of the slave. 'They did that?'

Julia nodded dumbly, falling to her knees beside the girl.
The barbarian took a long stride past her, she heard the scrape
as he drew his sword, then a scream, cut off on a choking sob.
A thud. Silence. She kept her head averted, searching with
her fingers for a pulse in the girl's neck. Nothing.

'Is she dead?' Julia half turned, saw him stoop to wipe the
long blade clean on the fallen tradesman's tunic and, shuddering, looked away.

'I think she must be. I can find no pulse. They threw her
against the wall when they first caught us. She was so frightened.' *She didn't want to come with me, poor little thing. She
wouldn't say boo to a goose and Mother sent her out with me
into this nightmare and I did nothing to protest. She won't be
frightened any more now…*

The Goth hunkered down beside her and she was aware
of the size of him, the smell of sweat and blood, metal and
leather. Alien, utterly male. He reached out a broad hand and

touched the girl's neck, then, with a gentleness that surprised Julia, closed the staring brown eyes.

'What is her name?'

'I do not know what she was called.' Julia gazed at the small body helplessly. There was a hot burning in her chest, her eyes prickled. *I must not cry, I must not show weakness in front of a barbarian, an inferior.* 'She was one of my mother's slaves. She sent her with me…'

…sent us both on this insane errand. And I did not insist on an escort of male slaves. I just did as I was told while she stayed behind high walls, directing the family treasures to be buried beneath the paving slabs in the peristyle. Mother always knows what her priorities are.

'I was trying to reach my father and another senator at the Basilica.' *What did Mother expect they could do about it? Stand on the threshold looking pompous in their togas and tell thousands of men like this one, this hunting wolf, to go away and stop being a nuisance?*

Two hours ago she had obeyed without question—the men would know best what to do. Her father, Julius Livius Rufus, a man in his Emperor's confidence for many years; her betrothed, Antonius Justus Celsus, the coming man in the Senate, a man who never put a foot wrong politically, who judged each opportunity with coolness and then acted correctly. Only they had been gone for over twelve hours and had sent no word. What should the women do? There were too many options. To stay or to flee? To hide or to rely on high walls and heavy doors?

The barbarian cut across her thoughts. 'But she was one of your family.' He turned, with a litheness that seemed unimpeded by his crouched position, and stared at Julia as though he had trouble understanding what she was saying. His beard was a golden brown, cut close in contrast to the paler hair that escaped from under the metal helmet and flowed over his shoulders. His eyes, intent on hers, were green, the clear green of snow-melt river water over pebbles.

'She was one of the household,' Julia corrected. His Latin was good, but obviously not good enough to understand the niceties. She found to her shame that she was trembling and stiffened her limbs. To show fear, to lose her dignity—what she had left of it—was unacceptable. 'A slave.'

'Your responsibility, then.' The green eyes chilled. He stood up, dismissing her with the turn of his shoulder, scooped the girl's body up as though she were a child and walked into the burning building.

'Stop! It is on fire!' It was a foolish statement of the obvious and he ignored her. Julia scrambled to her feet, aghast. Another beam crashed down inside the shop, which was burning fiercely now. She ran forward and saw him, in a nimbus of flame, lay the girl down on what must have been a stone counter. He smoothed down her tunic, crossed her hands over her breast and touched her head. Julia thought his lips moved. Then he swung round and strode out of the building just as the roof collapsed with a roar of uprushing flame and sparks.

'Better than leaving her in the dust for the dogs,' he said curtly, pulling Julia further up the alleyway and around a corner. It was blissfully cool there, in the shade, away from the flames and out of sight of the two sprawled bodies.

'The fire will spread,' she said, wishing she could uncurl her fingers from around his forearm and finding she could not.

'But not this way, the wind is against it.' His head was up, his nostrils flared as though scenting the breeze. A hunter, aware.

She made herself release her grip and looked up. 'Look out!' A large lump of smouldering wood, as big as her fist, had lodged on his shoulder and was sliding down onto the bare skin of his upper arm. She reached out and knocked it aside, feeling the sharp sting of the burn on her palm, the tight muscle, the warmth of his arm.

'Thank you.' He caught her hand and turned it palm up, studying it. 'That will stop stinging in a minute. What is your name?'

'Julia Livia Rufa.' He did not appear ready to release her hand; tugging was undignified and might display fear. 'I am the daughter of the Senator Julius Livius Rufus. What is your name?'

'Wulfric, son of Athanagild, son of Thorismund.' He said it without emphasis, yet she was left with the clear impression that his name was known amongst his people, that he was used to command and to recognition. He thought for a moment, then said, 'You would say King of the Wolves, perhaps.' For the first time, searching for a translation, his Latin seemed less assured, the alien rhythms of his own language surfacing.

Wolf King? *What else,* she thought, sensing her own desire to laugh hysterically, and biting it back with hard-won discipline. 'Thank you, Wulfric, son of Athan…Athanagild.' Julia managed to get over the cumbersome syllables. 'I would be grateful if you could escort me to the Basilica where I hope to find my father. Naturally, we will not be ungrateful for your assistance.'

The wolf padded back down the alley from wherever it had been exploring and sat down beside its master, tongue lolling in the heat. Two pairs of green eyes regarded her; she could have sworn there was amusement in both.

'So, you would be grateful for my escort, would you, Julia?'

'Julia Livia,' she corrected. He was a barbarian, she could not expect him to understand how to address the daughter of a patrician Roman family correctly.

Now Wulfric was openly amused. His beard was clipped close enough for her to see the lines of his mouth, which just now were curling unmistakeably. 'How grateful, Julia?'

'I am sure they will reward you suitably with gold,' she said stiffly. 'My family, that is, and also my betrothed, the Senator Antonius Justus Celsus.'

'But I can take all the gold I want,' he said softly. 'I can take anything I desire from this city. Why do you think we are here, if not for the wealth within these walls?'

'For your king, Alaric, to speak with the Emperor Honorius. I know there has been some misunderstanding over a promise of land…' Half-heard discussions between the men over dinner, debates she had only partly understood or ignored. The Visigoths had entered Rome before, demanded a vast bribe in gold, then they had gone away, leaving political turmoil. But that was all settled now. Honorius was back in control in Ravenna…

'No misunderstanding. Treachery. We fight for your emperor for many years, we hold back the Hun hordes from the east from your lands, even as they overrun ours, and he promises us land, grain, security. And gives us lies. Now we have come to take what is owing. Two years ago we entered Rome, but it seems you Romans do not learn from the past.'

He stood there, as solid as the stone pillar behind him, as alien as the wolf that walked by his side, and she could believe that he would take anything he wanted. And there were thousands like him pouring into her city while frightened, over-civilised men in togas or silk tried to talk away the danger.

Two years ago it had seemed they had placated Alaric. They had been wrong.

'Honorius is not here; he is in Ravenna.' Behind impregnable walls, equipped for the longest siege, while here the food was already running out. The invaders would find gold and silver, but they would find precious little to eat.

'We know. The time for talking is past. Come.' He turned on his heel and began to walk down the alleyway. Julia stood watching his back. Broad shoulders carrying a chain-mail shirt as easily as though it was linen, bare arms, tanned to a golden colour so different from her own olive skin, long legs in cloth trousers tucked into leather boots like a legionary's. The broad belt cinched around his waist was legionary kit too, but the tall figure was anything but reassuringly familiar. Everywhere about him was the living glow of gold and the sullen blood red of garnets. His sword hilt, the scabbard, the buckle on his belt, the gold bands that strapped his biceps and wrists, all gleamed.

He was bigger than any man she had ever been close to—as big as the emperor's German guard—and he moved with the predatory grace of a gladiator in the arena.

Behind her the burning shop collapsed across the alley with a crash. There was nowhere to go but to follow him. 'You will take me to the Basilica?' She had to run to catch him up.

'We may go there.' Wulfric stopped at the end of the passageway and surveyed the cross-street. A man peered out from a doorway, saw him and slammed the door to. Julia heard the thud of a falling bar. A woman, a child in her arms, ran past, shied away with a shrill scream and hurried on. At both ends, where the street opened out onto wider thoroughfares, there was a chaos of carts and mules and people shouting and shoving.

'What do you mean? We *may* go there?' She put her hand on his forearm and shook it when he did not immediately reply. Wulfric looked down at her, one corner of his mouth lifting, and she saw that the green eyes had lost their chill. Julia lifted her hand off his arm with elaborate care and stepped back, her heart thudding in response to the heat in that look. 'No. No…you wouldn't…'

'Wouldn't…' He searched for a word. 'Wouldn't ravish you? I do not approve of ravishing women, as you saw just now. You need not fear that. Now, come.'

Relief made her snap at him. 'Come where? I want to go to the Basilica.'

'But what you want is no longer important. Come with me. I told you we had come to take what is owing. And we need it to be portable. Grain, horses, gold, silver and slaves—we take all of those.'

'But…you want me as a hostage?' Incomprehension turned to cold fear. She had leapt from the skillet into the fire.

'No.' She had amused him again. It was perversely insulting. 'We already have the best hostage after the emperor. We have his sister. We do not need any more; hostages are hard work. They need looking after.'

'You have Galla Placidia?' A gracious lady, one who lived closer to the people than her brother. She had stayed in Rome, not fled to the thick walls and high towers of Ravenna at the first hint of danger.

'Yes. Now come.'

'Where? Why?'

Wulfric turned on his heel and studied her with the air of a tutor confronted by a dense pupil. 'With me. You are now mine. I need a household slave. You will do very nicely.'

'A *slave? Me?* You are jesting.' There was no hint of

teasing in the calm regard. 'A…' He meant it. 'No!' Julia took to her heels. Ahead the turmoil of the street, once so terrifying, now seemed to offer sanctuary. The breath tearing in her throat, she yanked up her skirts and ran. Only a few more yards, a few more steps.

A blur passed her and then stopped in front in a scrabble of claws on stone. The wolf. Julia juddered to a halt. It wasn't showing its teeth. 'Good boy, there's a nice wolf. Stay! Sit?' It regarded her impassively then padded forwards. She spun on her heel. Wulfric hadn't moved. If she could just make it to the door that stood ajar…

Something hard and wet and hot closed gently round her right wrist. She looked down. The animal had her arm between its jaws. It was not biting, just holding with a pressure that would not crack an egg, yet which had all the potential to rip her flesh from her bones.

Wulfric whistled loudly. There was a disturbance in the milling crowd and a horseman pushed his way through and into the side road, another horse on a leading rein behind him. No, not a man, a youth, she realised, sixteen at most. He had a leather jerkin over a linen shirt, no helm on his head, but a long dagger hung from his belt and he controlled the horses with ease.

He spoke to Wulfric in a tongue she did not know.

'Speak Latin, else how will you ever have it perfect? This is Julia, she comes with us. Take her up behind you.'

The boy turned interested blue eyes on her. 'The new slave? The one you said you would find to cook for us? That is good, I am tired of cooking, it is women's work.'

'I am not a slave, I am not going with you! I am a noble-woman!'

'You do not appear to be in any position to argue.' The infuriating man strolled towards her.

'You mean you would let your wolf savage me if I try to escape?' Julia enquired sarcastically. 'I wouldn't be much use as a slave then.'

'True.' He picked her up with startling suddenness and tossed her up behind the boy, whipping a leather thong out of his belt and lashing her hands to a ring in the youth's broad belt. 'Don't forget she is there, Berig,' he advised. 'You do not want her landing on top of you when you dismount. Oh, no!' He grabbed Julia who was trying to slide off the far side. 'Berig is not very big yet, but he is heavy enough. I advise you to sit still.'

He swung up onto the other horse, a rangy, ugly grey. 'Now, we go and find ourselves some more gold.'

With the wolf trotting at his heels, he forced his way out into the crowded street, the very sight of him sending terrified citizens diving into side alleys. The boy Berig followed. Julia slid, gasped and tightened her hands on to his belt in an effort not to fall off. *Sooner or later they have to untie me. That wolf can't be everywhere, sooner or later I can run...*

'*Hwa namo thein?* Er... What is your name? Are you a good cook?' Berig tossed back over his shoulder as he steered his mount in his master's wake.

'Julia Livia. And, no, I am not,' Julia snapped back. 'I cannot cook. I do not need to cook. I have slaves to do that.'

The boy gave a snort of amusement. 'Then you had best learn fast, because you have no slaves now and my lord has a good appetite and no patience if kept hungry. This is good. Now we have you, I do not need to kill chickens, or cook anything, or fetch hot water, or wash clothes or even scrub my lord's back. You can do all that.'

Scrub his back? Julia stared furiously at the broad figure in front of them. *Oh, I'll scrub his back all right—with an axe in my hands!*

As though he felt her thoughts, Wulfric turned in the saddle and looked at her steadily. She felt her flimsy defiance shrivelling. This was real. He was a savage, uncaring, immovable force and she was in deadly serious trouble. For the first time in her life her position in society, her connections, her status meant nothing. All she had to fight this man with was her courage and her strength and she very much feared that they would count for nothing against those muscles and that cool green-eyed intelligence.

Chapter Two

Courage and strength, Julia mocked herself bitterly as she gripped Berig's belt and fought for balance on the horse's rump. *And what opportunities do you ever have for exercising those, Julia Livia? Do you even possess them?* When had she ever had to stand up for herself and use her own initiative?

Shop here, wear this, go to this party, not to that one. Be friends with those girls, that one is unsuitable... Marry Antonius Justus Celsus. Yes, Father, yes, Mother. Whatever you say. He is boring and smug and he'll have two chins in five years, but it is the right thing to do to marry him. So suitable.

Being carried off as a slave by a golden giant with a wolf and a boy at his heels was *not* suitable. But how do you learn to fight if you have never had to before?

'This one?' Berig's voice snapped her out of her whirling thoughts. They had halted in front of the plain high wall and closed doors of what she guessed must be a prosperous merchant's house. 'It looks a poor place.'

'With these walls and those locks?' Wulfric leaned over and hammered on the unyielding planks. 'I don't think they want to let us in. Why do you think that is?' Julia smiled inwardly; her own home had doors and walls that were even better than these.

Wulfric edged the ugly grey horse up to the wall, and stood up on its back with a smoothness that had her gaping. He reached high, grasped the top of the wall and hauled himself up, muscles bulging with effort. With a grunt he straddled the wall, then vanished.

'You are thieves, all of you,' Julia spat at Berig's back, fury at her own reaction to that display of brute strength lending venom to her words.

The boy shifted in the saddle and half turned. Focusing on him, she saw he had a snub nose, blonder hair than Wulfric, vivid blue eyes. 'We keep our word, all of us. Your emperor is an *oath-breaker.*' He put loathing into the words. 'There is nothing worse. If you cannot trust a man's word, what can you trust? He is less than a man, he is not fit to lead.'

'It is politics. Honorius must do what is right for the state,' Julia protested. *What am I doing, debating politics with a barbarian youth while the city burns around us?*

The boy stared at her as though she had sprouted two heads. 'Do Roman women understand nothing of honour? Your emperor gave his word. He broke it, now he must pay.'

She was saved from answering him by the doors swinging open and Wulfric appearing on the threshold. 'They have fled and abandoned their slaves, let's see what else they left behind.' He whistled and the grey followed him, Berig's mount behind. Hooves cracked sharply on the expensive mosaics of the entrance.

'Where would you hide the family treasure, Julia?' Wulfric enquired, his eyes scanning the empty peristyle.

There was a muted scuffle from the shadows; the whites of wide eyes were just visible.

'You! Come out, I will not hurt you.' To Julia's amazement the slaves shuffled out of hiding, their eyes fixed on the big man like mice in front of a fox. 'Your master does not treat you well.' It was a statement, not a question. The group were thin, bruises showed. 'Perhaps you saw where he hid his gold before he ran and left you.'

They shook their heads, silent. Then their gazes slid furtively towards the big urn standing in the open space. A drooping laurel bush stuck out of the top.

'Not a good time of year to be transplanting shrubs,' Wulfric observed, strolling over and giving the urn a push. It was rock solid, taller than he was. 'Fetch me a rope, a long, strong one.'

The oldest slave, the steward perhaps, grinned suddenly and hurried off, returning with a hefty coil of hemp in his hands. Wulfric tied it round the urn, fed it round the nearest pillar, then tossed the end up to Berig before remounting. The two riders looped the rope on their pommels and began to back the horses. Craning round Berig's shoulder, Julia saw the urn rock. The grey's hooves slithered on the mosaic, there was a lurch and the marble vessel toppled over to smash on the paving.

No wonder the shrub had been drooping! It was planted in pure gold, a mass of coins that spun and flashed on the paving. The slaves hurried forward and began to scoop up the money, stuffing it into the saddle-bags that Wulfric gave them with an enthusiasm that said everything about their feelings for their master.

When the bags were full, one woman ran off and found more. 'Keep the rest.' Wulfric secured the gold behind his saddle. 'And run.'

'One of them is sure to be able to cook better than I can and they are slaves already,' Julia protested.

'Yes, but I want you.' Wulfric smiled. It was not an indication of weakness—even in her desperate state she was all too aware of that—but it held a touch more warmth again.

Something cold settled in Julia's stomach. She tried to tell herself he had meant it when he said he did not believe in ravishing women. Surely he did not think he would not have to? That she would willingly… *Oh, no, my arrogant barbarian, if you think that broad shoulders and big muscles are going to seduce Julia Livia Rufa, you are in for a major disappointment.*

They stopped again further down the street in front of an arched doorway. 'No!' she protested. 'Don't you dare, you thieving pagans! That is a church, it is sacred…'

'Yes, I know.' Wulfric swung down from the saddle. 'I want to check they have had no trouble.' He disappeared inside, leaving Julia gaping after him.

'We are Christians,' Berig said angrily. 'Don't you Romans know *anything* about anyone else?'

'I…I didn't think. But you haven't been Christians very long, have you? Some of you still worship the old gods?'

'A few, perhaps,' the lad conceded. 'It doesn't mean we would smash up a church. And I will wager some Romans still worship your old gods as well.'

Grandmother for one. Julia knew her father's mother kept the shrine to the household gods tended, despite her son's displeasure. She bit her lip. What else did she not know about these people? She recalled seeing Wulfric's lips move as he had laid the slave girl down in the burning shop. Had he been praying over her? And she, Julia, had not even thought to do so. Ashamed, she tried to fashion the words, but her mind was too muddled to find them.

Wulfric emerged. 'They are all right, Theofrid passed this way two hours ago and gave them a password.'

Julia looked about her, puzzled. This was not at all what she had expected the sacking of a city to be like. True, there was panic and confusion, smoke was rising everywhere she looked and she was with two men whose saddle-bags bulged with looted gold. But she had expected blood to be running in the street, churches and palaces to be burning, savage men, painted with strange symbols, to be dragging women off by their hair for unspeakable purposes. This was more like a particularly forceful form of tax collecting. With human coin.

'We will go to the Forum, see who else is there.' Julia's spirits rose—surely there would be soldiers, surely some resistance to this invasion was being organised? By going to the Forum they would be walking right into the hands of the emperor's men and she would be saved.

But they were moving against the tide of people streaming away from the heart of the city and her confidence began to ebb. Why were people fleeing, unless the Goths had overrun the Forum itself? Other riders, dressed like Wulfric, their hair long on their shoulders, fell in beside them.

Greetings were exchanged in the tongue she could not understand, snatches of news tossed from rider to rider. A knot of men on foot were herding a group in tunics before them. From the resigned expressions on the captives' faces, Julia guessed they must already be slaves.

Berig was calling to another group who appeared to be teasing him about his captive. Julia turned her head away from their curious stares with a haughty lift of her chin and found herself looking into the startled face of a man she knew, half-hidden in a doorway.

'Marcus! Marcus Atilius! Help me!' The young man, her

neighbour, started from his concealment, then began to back away as the riders closed up around Berig's horse. 'Tell my father,' she shouted as he took to his heels. 'Tell Antonius Justus! I have been kidnapped!

'Let me go!' Seeing someone she knew galvanised her, gave her hope. She jerked at the bonds linking her to Berig, then tried to score her fingernails into his back.

'Ouch, you cat, stop that!' He twisted round, furious, hissing with pain as Wulfric wheeled his mount alongside them.

'Stop it.' He reached out one hand and jerked back her clawing fingers. 'If you do that again, I'll sling you over the front of my saddle like a sack of grain, which won't do much for your dignity, my lady.'

Julia subsided, more shaken than she was willing to admit to herself. Somewhere, in the back of her mind, had been the thought that she would be rescued just as soon as someone in authority realised her predicament. She had expected to find all the young men of patrician birth had taken up arms and were defending Rome, while their elders met to form strategy in the Basilica.

But if men like Marcus Atilius were skulking in doorways, togas or silk tunics hidden under dark cloaks, then who was rallying the troops?

No one was the answer, she saw as soon as they reached the Forum. The heart of Rome, its pride, was overrun by the besiegers. Groups of mounted men shouted news to each other, others mustered carts laden with chests, sacks of food, barrels. Anxious huddles of slaves waited the pleasure of their new masters—and there was not a sign of resistance.

Wulfric reined in under the circular wall of the ancient Temple of Vesta. It seemed it was a prearranged meeting point, for the men already there crowded forward, clenched fists raised in salute.

Thirsty, stiff, hungry, almost beyond fear with sheer discomfort, Julia let herself lean against Berig's back, let the noise wash over her, and sank into a half faint, half doze.

'Here.' Someone was shaking her shoulder. Wearily she raised her head. Wulfric was holding out a flask. 'Drink, you must be thirsty.'

'How can I? My hands are tied.' The thought of water made her dry throat tighten with longing, but she refused to thank him.

Wulfric leaned forward and released one wrist. Julia took the flask and drank. It was watered wine, a poor thin red probably snatched from a tavern, but it went down like the finest vintage from the family vineyards. She handed it back with a stiff nod. He did not try and secure her wrist again and she realised as she steadied herself that the pommel of Berig's knife was now within reach. She could snatch it, hold it to his ribs until they agreed to take her back, or… She let her free hand drift further round the boy's side as though to secure her position.

'Berig, move your knife.' The boy shifted it round, out of her reach, and she glared furiously at the big man.

'Do you have eyes in the back of your head?'

He grinned, the green eyes crinkling with amusement. 'Of course, that is how I stay alive. That, and being able to read my enemy's mind.'

Is that what I am? His enemy? What have I done to him to deserve this?

One of the groups of slaves trudged past and she looked down at them, seeing for the first time just what a mixture they were, the people who made life in the Empire run with the smooth efficiency of a water clock. Tall, sandy-haired, light-skinned Northerners, a few black faces, the wiry stature and deep olive skins of men from the Eastern Empire, all caught up and brought back here. *What have* they *done to deserve it? These barbarians have learned from us and now we reap what we have sown.*

'Come.' Wulfric raised his voice and heads turned. 'Back to camp, we have done enough today. Alaric has called a council for tomorrow.'

It seemed Wulfric's word carried weight. That had been an order, not a suggestion, and Julia watched to see who followed him. Fifty or so men, at a rough count, and many older than him by years, grizzled old veterans.

'Who is he?' she asked Berig, once they were away from the hubbub of the Forum. The wine, thin though it was, had revived her; to escape she needed knowledge, needed to understand her captor. 'Who are all these men?'

'Our kin and some of those who would ally with us. There are many more than this, of course.' *More? A private army, then.*

'Are you his…no, he is not old enough for you to be his son.'

'I do not know the word.' Berig wrestled with it. 'My mother's sister married the brother of his mother.'

'A distant cousin?' Julia suggested. 'Why do you serve him?'

'Cousin.' The boy practised the word. 'It is the custom. I serve him, he teaches me how to be a man, how to fight. In two years he will give me my sword.'

'I see. But why do all these men follow him? They are older than he is, many of them.'

'Because he is—ah, I do not know the word in Latin! King-worthy? Do you understand? He has the way of it, to lead.'

'But you have a king. Alaric.'

'He will not live for ever.' The boy shrugged. 'Wulfric is

loyal, says Alaric is a good king, but many mutter against him. We have been wandering for years, fighting, waiting for your emperor to honour his word. There are some who say Alaric should have struck harder, sooner.'

Julia stared at the tall figure riding in front of them. King-worthy. Just what sort of man was she now the chattel of? 'What must a man do to be king-worthy?'

'Be wise in Council, fierce in battle, kill the enemy, be cunning in strategy, a law-giver and judge. Be generous to his people and lead them to much gold.'

'And Wulfric is all that?'

'And more.' The boy nodded fiercely, passionate in defence of his lord. 'He is high in Alaric's Council.'

'But so are others?' she suggested. 'He is not the heir?'

'No,' Berig conceded. 'It does not work like that. When Alaric dies there will be a fight, perhaps.' The thought did not seem to alarm him. 'Look, we are almost there.'

They had passed out of the Salarian Gate without her noticing. Now, in the distance, she could see the smoke from camp-fires, see the low lines of tents, more than the biggest legionary camp she had ever seen. As they came closer she saw that while the shelters might resemble Roman army tents, though in a wild mixture of sizes and colours, the camp seemed to be more a vast village than a military emplacement.

Women were everywhere, bustling amidst the tents, bent over fires, chasing errant children. Hurdles kept horses, oxen, pigs and sheep corralled, the tents were arranged in orderly blocks with streets between them, great wagons were drawn up in rows, banners flapped lazily overhead and mounted men circled the area, their eyes on the horizon.

'There are thousands,' she murmured, then started as Wulfric answered her. *He must have hearing like his wolf.*

'This is a people, a nation, in search of a homeland. And now you are part of it.'

'Never,' she said, as he turned away and began to make his way down one of the wide streets between the tents. 'Never.'

'You are very stubborn,' Berig observed. 'I thought Roman women stayed at home and did as they were told.'

'Do Goth women?'

'Oh, no!' Berig chuckled. 'I think you will be quite at home here.'

I very much doubt it, Julia thought grimly. There were the big things to worry about—how to escape, how to survive living with an arrogant, musclebound barbarian until she did. And then there were the trivial things. The things that made life survivable—a proper bathhouse, a proper latrine with running water, civilised food, and someone else to cook it, clean clothes. These were all the things she was not going to find in the midst of these barbarians.

Wulfric dismounted outside the largest tent she had yet seen. Women from neighbouring tents looked up from cooking pots, smiled and waved. A small child, sturdy legs pumping as he ran, skidded to a halt in front of him, tugged at the hem of his tunic and began to pelt him with questions.

Wulfric answered him patiently in his own language, then scooped the child up and deposited him, squealing with delight, on his horse's saddle and handed him the reins. Julia stared. This was the man Berig said was a possible future king, a ruthless warrior. She tried to imagine any of the senators of her acquaintance stopping to talk to a grubby child, trusting them with their horses.

He hauled down the loaded saddle-bags and untied a bundle of fur and feather that Julia had not noticed before.

'Dinner.' He handed it to her. Two rabbits and a game bird

of some kind. Even as she held them away from her skirts, grimacing in distaste, the wolf trotted up and dropped another rabbit at her feet, then sat back, panting.

'I suppose you expect me to be grateful, do you?' she demanded, glaring at the animal. It lolled its tongue out. She could swear it was grinning.

'We will eat well tonight,' Wulfric said. 'And his name is Smoke.' The creature lifted its great head at the sound of its name.

'Does he speak Latin, then?'

'Of course.'

'Well, is Smoke going to skin these, or pluck them or whatever one does with whatever they are?' She knew perfectly well what needed doing to them in theory, but she had not the slightest intention of doing it. Let him think her completely pampered, it would put him off his guard.

She expected a show of temper at her defiance, but all Wulfric said was, 'Berig will do it tonight. And tomorrow I will find someone to show you how to cook.'

Julia looked down her nose at him. 'We will see about that. And now I want to wash.'

'We all do. *Hades, was it impossible to provoke the man?* 'If you go and ask Una there…' he nodded at a young woman who was feeding wood under a vast cauldron '…she will give you hot water.' He slapped the grey horse on its rump and it walked off, its tiny rider crowing with delight and followed by a watchful Berig. Wulfric flipped open the tent flap and vanished inside.

What would happen if she just strolled away, vanished into this city of tents? At her feet Smoke got to his feet, shook himself vigorously and stood waiting. Of course, her hairy bodyguard would bring her back to its hairy master.

Julia grimaced and went over to Una. The other woman smiled. She was fair haired, taller than Julia and, it was apparent, despite her long tunic and swathing cloak, pregnant. 'Hello. Are you Una? Do you speak Latin?'

'Some. Better if I practise it.' Una straightened and rubbed the small of her back, smiling. 'You are Wulfric's woman now?'

'No! He thinks I am his slave.' They stood looking at each other. Una was obviously working out what Julia's position was. 'I need hot water. And I need the latrine.' And how was she going to mime *that*, if Una's Latin was not up to it? Her faintly desperate air must have communicated her meaning. Una smiled and pointed to a square of wattle standing alone in the middle of a clear space.

Julia approached with caution, fearing the worst. The wattle, just the height of her head, had an opening with a baffle screen set inside it, a deep hole with a plank, a bucket of ash with a scoop and a box of large leaves. In the absence of running water, it was remarkably civilised, although how one indicated that it was occupied was a problem. There was nothing for it: Julia sang.

She emerged to find Una scooping hot water into a pair of buckets. She hooked chains on them and lifted a yoke for Julia to step under. 'Enough?'

'Yes. Yes, thank you.' Julia took the weight and straightened up. It was not that it was too heavy, although she certainly had to concentrate to keep the buckets steady, it was the symbolism of the thing. She was under Wulfric's yoke now. She had accepted the first task set her—was there any going back from that?

'My name is Julia,' she said abruptly. 'Julia Livia.' Una smiled and nodded and went back to making up the fire.

Julia walked slowly to the tent, stooped through the flap and set down the buckets without spilling a drop.

'Over here.' Wulfric's voice was muffled. In the shadows at the back of the tent she could see that he had discarded helmet and sword belt and was pulling the chain-mail shirt over his head.

Doubtless he expected her to rush over and help him. Julia straightened up under the yoke, brought the buckets over and stood and waited while he untangled himself.

The chain mail rattled to the ground, pooling into a heavy mass. It had dragged his linen tunic with it, leaving him bare chested. Julia swallowed.

It was expected of Roman men of good family that they exercised, that they cultivated fitness. They were not bashful about showing off their bodies at the baths or in sport. And the city was littered with statues of naked men, in gleaming white marble or painted in lifelike colours.

But this man was bronze. A bronze god come to life. Every muscle stood out, defined, developed, powerful. His skin was golden and she had a sudden, powerful impulse to put out her hand and feel it, feel the heat, the texture, the pulse beating beneath it. He was more alive than any person she had ever seen and he terrified her.

She realised her mouth was open and snapped it shut.

'Don't you ever smile, Julia?' He was watching her, apparently quite unconscious of the effect his half-naked body was having on her.

'Yes. All the time—when I have something to smile about,' she retorted. 'I shall smile when I am rescued.'

Wulfric lifted his right hand and cupped her chin, his thumb gently pushing up the corner of her stubbornly straight mouth. 'Smile for me now, Julia.'

Chapter Three

Julia bared her teeth at Wulfric. *Will she bite?* 'Smile for me,' he said again, intrigued to see what she would do. It was like having an exotic animal, half-tame, half-wild. He had been mad to take her, he knew that. She was so far from what he needed—neither the wife he should acquire, nor the domesticated slave who would make life comfortable—that he wondered at himself for the impulse.

But how could he delude himself that it *was* an impulse? He could have let her go at any time. Something about this dark-haired, dark-eyed, olive-skinned creature called to him. It was going to be hell to teach her their ways, with her patrician arrogance and her stubborn defiance. He knew perfectly well that she had brought the water only because she wanted to use it herself.

'I would sooner smile at your wolf.' She jerked her chin, but he refused to let her go and she was too proud to continue struggling. There was fear at the back of those brown eyes, fear that he would force her to do more than carry water, despite his pledge, and that angered him.

These Romans had no concept of honour, no respect for

a man's word. Alaric, and all his people, had experienced it, year after weary year. They had fought for the emperor, learned his language, kept his enemies at bay, waiting for their reward while they were lied to and deceived. And now, what would they do? They had taken the greatest city on earth, they held the sister of the emperor, they could strip Rome of gold and slaves and treasures. But were they any closer to what they needed, their safe homeland?

Loyalty to his king told him to trust Alaric's judgement. Experience and his own imagination told him to doubt the outcome. And yet to doubt his king was not honourable.

Frustrated, he released her. 'That is your space, take some water.' He jerked his chin towards a length of striped cloth that shielded one corner of the tent.

She stepped away from him, and he watched as she wiped her hand across her chin where he had held her, as though to rub away his contaminating touch. 'This is a large tent,' she observed, as if nothing had passed between them, hefting one of the buckets and making her way over to the corner. She was stronger than she looked.

'We copied the design of the legionary tents, but bigger than the standard eight-man model. We have spent years living in them, now they are as close to a home as we can make them.' He watched her poking about in her space, amused by the feminine instinct to build a nest in the most unpromising circumstances. 'I will give you rugs for a bed and Berig will fill some sacks with straw for a mattress.'

'Luxury indeed,' she said drily, letting the curtain fall between them.

Wulfric whistled to Smoke and, when the wolf trotted in, nodded towards the corner. The animal padded behind the curtain and must have sat down. Wulfric could see its tail protruding underneath. Julia murmured something and the tail began to wag. Smoke liked her, it seemed.

Berig, it was obvious, did not. 'Where is she?' he demanded, marching in.

'Washing.' Wulfric jerked his head towards the curtain. 'Here, take some of this and make yourself decent. You stink of horse and smoke.'

'So do you.' Berig began to ladle hot water into a bowl.

'I'm washing, aren't I?' Wulfric aimed a cuff at the lad's head, watching him critically as he ducked smoothly away. He was growing up fast, too fast yet for his lanky frame to catch up with. He had a quick tongue, fierce loyalty and worked magic with horses. He was also beginning to flirt with the girls of his own age.

Wulfric cast a thoughtful eye in the direction of Julia's corner. There was splashing, but no other sound. Was he asking for trouble, introducing an attractive young woman into the tent with the youth? Probably not, not while they were squabbling like brother and sister, but it would bear watching. Berig deserved better than to fall into puppy love with a haughty Roman girl like this one.

He fished another soap ball out of the earthenware jar and went to hold it round the edge of the curtain. 'Here.'

There was a pause, then wet fingers brushed against his hand as she took it. 'Thank you.'

As though struck by an adder's bite his body went rigid with desire. Wulfric shook his head, trying to clear it. Why that fleeting touch should affect him so, he had no idea. One moment he was worrying, with the corner of his mind that wasn't thinking of Council tomorrow, about Berig's adolescent fancies, the next he found himself as aroused as though Julia had emerged naked and wrapped herself around him.

The touch of those damp fingers fired his imagination with images of her wet and bare behind the flimsy curtain and he strode to the shadowed back recesses of the tent to give himself a chance to recover. This was not why he had taken her. He just wished he did know why.

'There's a towel here somewhere.'

'No, they are all here,' Berig called. 'Una washed things for us, and they're with the tunics.'

'Una has been your skivvy up until now, I presume?' The cool voice effectively dampened his fantasies. Wulfric went back to the hot water with a grimace.

'Una's my sister, so she looks after us when there isn't anyone else,' Berig snapped. 'And she's expecting a baby, so she shouldn't be looking after two households now.'

'Then you had better kidnap her a slave too, hadn't you? Or give her some help yourself.'

Damn it, the woman had a tongue on her like an adder, as well as its fangs. 'An excellent idea, although once you find out the way of things, I am sure you can help her—she'll appreciate a woman's company,' Wulfric said smoothly. 'She will be busy when the baby's born.'

Silence. Then, 'Exactly what do you expect me to do?'

'Cook for the three of us. Keep this tent clean and tidy. Wash and mend our clothes. Fetch water, heat it for when we return.'

'Nurse you when you are sick, I suppose?'

'Of course. Or wounded.'

He could almost read her thoughts. *The sooner the better…*

'Are you both decent?'

Wulfric cast a hasty glance downwards, but the frosty exchange had cooled that ridiculous flash of lust. He was still shaken by his momentary loss of control.

Was it time to think seriously about a wife now? There

were plenty who would advise him that he should do just that. A man in his position, a leader, needed strong sons about him. Hilderic was hinting about his daughter Sunilda. It was a good alliance, it would bring many spears to his side and she was a strong woman, in mind as well as body. A woman who understood what was needed and what must be done so that all the children had a homeland to grow up in.

He realised that he must have been lost in thought when Berig replied, 'We've got our trousers on, if that's what you mean.'

Wulfric smothered a snort of amusement. 'Then put a shirt on as well,' he ordered. 'And go and do something about our evening meal.'

'I skinned and plucked the game,' Berig said, his voice muffled as he pulled the clean linen over his head. 'Una's taken them to add to a hot pot of vegetables. They'll be enough for us and for her brood. Sichar's going to be late, she said, something about horses.'

Wulfric grunted. Berig's brother-in-law had been sent by Alaric to take a count of all the available animals and their condition. They would be breaking camp soon, that was no secret—sitting outside a starving city, once they had stripped its wealth, was foolishness—but where they would go—north or south—that was what disturbed his sleep at night.

'Then stuff the straw sacks for Julia's bed.'

'She's supposed to be our slave,' the boy began to protest. Wulfric raised one eyebrow and he subsided. 'Sorry. Yes, my lord.'

Wulfric waited until he had let the tent flap drop, then smiled wryly at Julia as she emerged into the main space. 'A difficult age.' Perhaps she had experience with brothers, some link he could make to allow her to see Berig as a young man, not an enemy. Having them bickering—or sulking if he exerted his will—would not make for a comfortable existence.

'I wouldn't know,' she said stiffly, her attention apparently fixed on tying her long plait. 'I have no brothers.'

So much for that idea. 'But you must have gone through a stage of wanting to rebel, to go your own way.' It suited her, the simple style, unlike the elaborate pleats it had been in before. It made her seem older, less of a girl, more of a woman. He was aware of the clean bones of her face. 'It is good that Berig chafes at authority, tries the limits of my patience. If he doesn't try and get his own way, he will never learn the discipline of subduing his will to orders. And one day I will let go of the reins and give him his head. By then, he'll have learned self-discipline for himself.'

'I would never dream of disobeying my parents.' She looked at him down her nose. 'Roman children are not encouraged to have their head, as you put it. Their duty is quite clear, their training and career set out.'

'Possibly that is why we have defeated Rome and not the other way about,' he suggested mildly, earning a look of disdain as Berig came in, tugging two bulging sacks behind him.

'I'll go and get a frame off the cart.' He went out again, hooking up the tent flap.

Through the open doorway Julia could see the bustle of camp life as the sun began to set. Men were beginning to come back to their home fires, children running out to met them, womenfolk standing up from tending their cooking pots to wave, or to exchange a kiss with the big, long-haired warriors. So fierce, so savage looking, and yet, apparently, so domestic. There seemed real affection there. Julia could not recall the last time she had seen her father kiss her mother, other than with a cool salute on the cheek on formal occasions. She shivered.

'Are you cold?' Wulfric came up close behind her. He moved very quietly for such a big man and she felt her body stiffen as though ready to run.

'No.' She must not yield to gratitude for his small gestures of thoughtfulness, let them blind her to the full realisation that she was a captive. That way lay fatal weakness. He was like his wolf, domesticated until roused, then a killer.

'Sure? I can find you a cloak, Una would lend one.'

'No.' She struggled to suppress another shiver. It was not cold, the air still held the heat of a long hot day, yet her whole body felt chilled to the core and she knew, if she relaxed, she would begin to shake. Shock, she supposed, surprised to find herself able to analyse anything.

'Then what is it?' he said gently. 'What do you need, Julia?'

'What do you think?' She spun round, coming toe to toe with him, so close that she had to tip her head back to look up into his face. 'What do you think I want, that I need?'

There was a dangerous flare of anger in his eyes as he answered her. *He had hoped to soft-talk me,* she thought bitterly. *He does not like that thrown back in his face.*

'To be free,' Wulfric answered. 'But you cannot be free now, Julia—you are mine.' She took two angry steps away from him, ducking out of the tent to stand at the entrance, arms folded tight across her body to stop the shaking.

Outside some of the nearer tents children were helping their mothers set up trestle tables, some carrying out stacks of pottery vessels, wooden plates, horn beakers and spoons.

'We will eat outside.' Julia began to turn, to announce

loftily that she did not care where they ate, she was not hungry, when she saw that Wulfric was speaking not to her, but to Berig, who was hefting in a box made of planks.

'*Badi,*' he said, pausing when he saw her watching. 'Bed.' Julia turned a shoulder. Why should she learn their coarse language? She was not going to be here long enough to trouble herself. 'People will stare,' he added, picking up Wulfric's reference to their meal.

'Let them. Here, help me with the trestle, it is too warm to eat inside. They will get used to the sight of her soon enough, sooner if Una can spare her any clothes.'

Julia felt something contract inside her. Change her clothes for those of a Goth? It was to lose her identity. Even now, looking around, she regretted her plain braid, so like many of the barbarian women. *I am not like them, I am Roman,* she told herself fiercely. To cease to look like a Roman was another step down the very slippery slope of accepting what Wulfric was trying to make her.

If she looked like his womenfolk, would Wulfric still look at her with that hot gaze she saw every now and again, simmering behind the cool green eyes? She must seem exotic to him, perhaps that was an attraction and homespuns would be a protection. But the heat of that look was treacherously seductive, even while it scared her.

'Come, Julia, I will show you where the things for eating are.' It was Berig, very obviously making an effort to be civil. Julia almost told him that she had no intention of eating, let alone setting a table, then turned back meekly and followed him into the tent. The sooner she became familiar with the tent and everything it held, the sooner she would know exactly what resources she had to hand to help her escape. A knife, for a start, to cut the heavy canvas of the tent side.

'Here.' The lad was lifting platters and bowls down off a makeshift shelf. 'The spoons and beakers are there, see?'

'I need a knife for eating,' she said.

'Oh.' Berig clapped a hand to his side where his eating knife hung from his belt. 'Yes, of course you do. Let's see what is in here.'

So easy. Julia took the knife with an absent air and added it to the pile of things to carry through. Too much to hope for civilised eating couches, fine linen napery and wine in glasses, of course.

Berig was carrying folding stools through, which answered at least part of that speculation. But as she began to set out the table, Julia found herself wondering at the skill of the wood turner who had produced the platters. Even the earthenware bowls were not unpleasing with their subtle glaze, thin walls and delicate scraffito decoration. She ran a thumb into the elegant bowl of the horn spoon she held and was forced to acknowledge that these people might not have the sophistication of Roman citizens, but their objects were not crude.

'Wondering where the Rhenish glass and the silver platters are, Julia?' Wulfric was watching her. Wulfric always seemed to be watching her…

'This is well enough, I suppose.'

'The Rhenish glass is in the third chest to the left of the door. I had thought ale, with Una's rich game stew, but if you have a fancy for wine tonight we can get the glass out. The silver, I am afraid, is packed a little more inaccessibly, but if you give me notice of your desire to dine off it, I am sure Berig can find something.'

A rich game stew. Her stomach roiled, distracting her from his sarcasm—although to be fair, it would probably have revolted just the same at the thought of dry bread and water.

'I would not disturb him to find such a thing for a mere slave,' she said tartly and was hard put to it not to throw a horn beaker at him when Wulfric merely grinned.

'You are determined not to show any weakness, are you not, Julia Livia?' Her formal name for the first time. 'I am well aware you feel totally disinclined to eat, let alone having to sit down out here, in full view of a good score of interested watchers, and consume game stew. But that is exactly what you are going to do. Eat, and maintain your strength.'

Julia narrowed her eyes at him. *What does he know, this big, strong, invincible man? Has he ever felt fear in his life? Ever felt his stomach turn into a roiling mass of butterflies? Ever felt small and powerless and desperate? No, of course not.*

Once she had seen a tiny shrew confronted by a hunting dog a thousand times its own size. She had thought the tiny scrap would drop dead of terror as the dog extended its nose, snuffling in curiosity. But, no, it had jumped an inch in the air and buried its sharp teeth into the nose of the dog. *Well, I am that shrew,* she told herself fiercely. *I will win.*

Berig was coming back, carrying a steaming pot, his sister at his heels with her own platter and spoon in her hands, four children round her skirts. 'Greetings,' she said to Julia, nudging the children to speak.

'Greetings,' she responded, unwilling to snub this woman because of the sins of her menfolk.

They sat down at last, platters of bread, cheese and butter on the table along with the stew, a jug of ale. It seemed a very strange way of eating, but Julia did her best. *Keep up your strength,* an inner voice nagged her.

The stew was delicious. Savoury, hot, rich. She ate with an appetite she had not thought she could ever feel again, the cold at her core melting, the spasms of shivering ebbing away. Then she looked up to find Wulfric's eyes on her. Her captor.

Julia dropped her spoon, forgot the knife she had so carefully secured, and ran for the latrine, every morsel she had eaten and drunk rising up to choke her.

She was bent double, retching miserably, when an arm came round her shoulders to support her and a damp cloth was pressed into her hand. 'Thank you, Una,' she murmured, thankful for the support. At last the misery ceased and she sagged back against the figure behind her, head spinning. A beaker appeared and she rinsed her mouth with relief. 'Thank you,' she said again, a little more strongly.

'I am sorry,' said her helper and she froze against the supporting arm. Not Una—Wulfric. 'I should have let you eat inside.'

'Let me go!' She struggled to free herself, scarlet with humiliation at the position she was in, suddenly utterly conscious of where she was.

'Of course, come on, you should rest.' For one hideous moment she thought he was going to pick her up bodily and carry her out. The thought of being carried out of a latrine in front of an interested audience of barbarian families was too much.

'Don't you dare pick me up,' she hissed, swivelling round to face Wulfric. He threw up his hands in a gesture of denial and let her get to her feet. 'Stay there,' she added, pushing back the weight of her plait and summoning all her dignity. Then she stalked out of the wicker enclosure, across the intervening space and into the tent without a glance in any direction.

Inside, away from all eyes, her determination deserted her and she clung shakily to the pole that held up the front of the structure. 'Bed,' said a voice behind her, and this time, as her knees gave way, she let him scoop her up and carry her to the curtain hung across the corner. 'There.' Wulfric laid her down on the bed and she felt her weight bear her down into the well-stuffed mattress that Berig had so reluctantly prepared. 'There's water.' He gestured at a jug. 'And here is Smoke to keep watch over you. Rest—you are of no use to me sick. Goodnight, Julia.'

He did not look back as the striped fabric fell to shield her little corner. Julia strained to hear his footfall, but only Smoke, head raised until he knew his master had left the tent, gave her a clue. The wolf circled around, found a comfortable spot and lay down at the foot of the bed. Julia could just see the tip of his tail in the light of the rush lamp that burned on the small chest set beside the bed.

She lay rubbing her sore stomach and trying to regain some balance. The knife was still on the table outside, of course, and the wolf lay in her way to the door. No escape tonight then.

Julia sat up, untied her girdle and pulled off her overtunic, leaving the long white linen undershift. She folded the fine amber cloth carefully and coiled the woven girdle, then opened the second chest. There were linen towels as fine as the one Wulfric had handed her earlier. *Stolen, no doubt, like his silver,* she told herself, laying her clothes on top, then draping her used towel on the closed box. She unlaced her sandals and washed her feet in the cool water that remained in the bowl, then set to work spreading the rugs on the bed.

It was unfamiliar work. Every morning she rose, leaving her bed rumpled for Tullia, her body slave, to make up fresh. The clothes she had discarded the night before would have been removed, of course, and a fresh selection set out for her.

On her dressing table would be her combs and mirror, her cosmetics and oils, her boxes of jewellery. All she had to do was choose. And at night, Tullia would unpin her hair and comb it out, she would cream her face and wipe away the traces of the paints and she would hold out a fresh night rail for Julia to slip into. Flowers would be set on the dressing table, clear oil burned in the lamps.

It would all be perfect. Cool, tasteful, perfect. From outside there would be nothing to hear. Slaves padded silently, all too aware that to be heard was to arouse the wrath of the mistress of the house. Her father would be in his study, or out at an important meeting, her mother would be entertaining friends, or at the theatre. The house was as tranquil, and as lonely, as the grave.

Julia arranged the bed until she had a pillow to sit up against, then climbed under a light rug. Smoke raised his head and came to stand by the bed, his tail waving slowly back and forth, tongue lolling. Smiling, Julia leaned across and scratched him behind the ears. The wolf closed his eyes, then licked her wrist before padding back to his sleeping spot.

Outside she could hear the murmur of conversation, could make out Wulfric's voice amidst a number of other men, despite the fact they were all speaking their own tongue. There was something deep and calm and dominating about his speech. She had expected the Gothic language to be harsh and guttural, instead it had a strange and almost hypnotic rhythm to it. Further away a baby cried and was hushed, dogs barked, someone came past on a horse, its feet slow and tired sounding.

Her eyes heavy, Julia looked around the space that was now hers. The hangings glowed in the lamplight, the few items had a comforting ordinariness that soothed her, and she began to drift off to sleep. Hazily there was the realisation that she was not feeling lonely, she was feeling warm and safe and at home.

Her eyes flew open. It was terrifying—her own mind was betraying her into weakness. She bit her lip, feeling the tears welling up and willed herself not to cry. To be strong and not to give in.

Chapter Four

$\sim\!\!\infty\!\!\sim$

Wulfric woke with a sudden completeness that had him reaching for the unsheathed sword that lay by his bed. Silence, except for the piping cry of the tiny owls that haunted the cypress trees. He flexed his fingers round the woven leather of the hilt grip and threw back the covers, his eyes wide on darkness, his ears straining for any sound out of place.

The sentries were quiet, the dogs silent. From the far corner of the tent he heard Berig's light snores, cut off as the boy turned on his side with a grunt. Then he heard a faint sound, repeated. A sob.

Hades, she is crying. He released the sword and lay wondering what to do. He was not used to women, not women under his own roof. No sisters, no wife, only intervals of physical release with the willing ones, for whom love was a cheerful, uncomplicated, commercial transaction.

Uncomplicated was not what he had here. What did you do with weeping women? In his experience you handed them over to the other women. Somehow he did not think either

Una, or Sichar, would thank him for waking her up at this hour to comfort a slave.

He turned over, trying to harden his heart as he would over the whimpers of a basket of hound puppies, separated from their mother for the first time. There it was again. *Damnation!* If she had been howling and shrieking, he would have stuffed his fingers in his ears and abandoned her to hysterics, but there was something about the suppressed gasps of grief that went to his heart.

With a groan he rolled out of bed, took a step, thought better of it and dragged on trousers. No point in giving her real hysterics by looming up stark naked in her bed space. As he crossed the tent, instinct steering him round obstacles in the dark, a wet nose butted him on the back of the hand. It was Smoke. The wolf took his fingers between his teeth and tugged gently.

'Yes, I know, I heard her. Let go,' Wulfric whispered, running his free hand over the animal's head. He ducked out of the tent and raked amidst the embers of the fire until he found a red-hot patch and lit a rush light from it.

Smoke led the way in the wavering light and sat down by Julia's bed, his head on one side as if puzzled. She was lying on her back, the covers thrown back, her arms above her head, sprawled in a restless sleep interrupted every few seconds by a soft, desperate sob. The wolf whimpered.

'She's dreaming,' Wulfric whispered, looking down at the slim, vulnerable body. She was beautiful, he realised, now she was not frightened or scowling. Her face was stark with a kind of misery. Her body was slender, elegant, even lax in sleep. Her calves, all that could be seen of her legs under the long tunic, were bare. He wanted to touch, to run his palm over the smooth olive skin, see the contrast between it and his own golden tan as he had when she had laid her hand on his arm in the alleyway. Was that the moment when he had decided to take her?

The sensible thing would be to leave her to work through her nightmare. She might wake in the morning with some of those fears exorcised, but to rouse her now would be to risk terrifying her—she would imagine his motives were quite other than they truly were.

Wulfric hunkered down beside the bed, lifting the little lamp to study her face, trying to push away the ignoble thoughts of what would happen if he slid into the bed beside her, lowered his mouth to hers… *Oh, yes, your motives are not so pure, are they?* he jibed at himself.

Then he saw the tears on her cheeks and something inside him seemed to twist painfully. *I have done this. She is my responsibility now.*

Cautiously he rose and bent over the bed, picked Julia up bodily and sat down, the slim figure cradled in his arms. She was no weight at all in his lap and it was easy to turn her so her head rested against his chest just over his heart. He held her to him one-handed and smoothed the other palm down over her temple and cheek.

'Shh, Julia. Shh, it is all right. You are safe.' He hardly said the words, pressing his cheek onto the smooth black silk of her hair. He could feel the wetness of her tears against the warm skin of his pectorals, the flutter of her pulse as his caressing hand reached her throat.

She breathed in a great sighing breath and lay against him, utterly relaxed in sleep, the sobs stilled. A weight settled on his knee; Smoke was resting his jaw there contentedly.

'Get off, you old fool,' Wulfric hissed. The wolf rolled an eye at him and settled himself more comfortably, as if aware his master was not going to risk pushing him away. He began to dribble gently.

Wulfric felt his eyelids begin to droop. This was foolishness. Tomorrow he had to attend Council, give his king his opinion, fight for his view against those who would oppose it, in a matter that could affect the destiny of their people for generations. Tomorrow the scouts might ride in with news that the emperor had taken the field and was marching on Rome and he could find himself preparing for battle. Tomorrow, even if everything went well, he must make plans to strike camp and lead his kin group and his allies where Alaric ordered.

And here he was, losing valuable sleep sitting up comforting a slave who did not even know he held her, while a wolf slobbered over his trousers. It felt good. Soothing Julia soothed an inner turmoil he had not even been aware he was suffering. He could feel his shoulders dropping in relaxation, he could feel his breathing slowing to the rhythm he tried to teach Berig, the swordfighter's focused semi-trance. Everything became very simple, centred on the warm, fragile body in his arms.

She shifted slightly; her hands, which had lain limply in her lap, moved restlessly, one slipping round his back, the other sliding up his chest. The innocent, unconscious, touch made his breath catch in his throat, his relaxation vanished to be supplanted by a sensual awareness that had his body hardening, his loins aching. He had to put her down, and urgently.

Smoke grumbled as his head was unceremoniously pushed to one side. Wulfric twisted on the bed and laid Julia down, drawing the blanket up over skirts that were rucked up to her knees. He backed out of the corner, picking up the rushlight as he went, as tense as though he were facing an armed opponent. 'Stay,' he breathed and Smoke lay down at the foot of the bed.

He regained his own bed, shaken. Julia was dangerous to his peace of mind, to his body's equilibrium, to his focus and control. Restless, he turned on his side and tried to get comfortable, accepting the ache in his groin as just punishment for his thoughts. *Dangerous.* Some part of his mind, the part that observed him, chided him—his conscience, he supposed—noted coolly that he did not consider taking her back with him into Rome in the morning and setting her free. *No,* he told himself as he slipped back into sleep. *She stays.*

Julia woke to a strange light, an unfamiliar room, a peculiar bed. *Where…?* She sat up, scrubbing the loose tendrils of hair back from her face, and found herself staring at a large wolf, that was watching her from the far end of the bed.

Oh, dear God, it wasn't a dream. She was in a Visigoth's tent, yesterday *had* happened, she was a captive, a slave, and she had no idea how she was going to escape. Her side of the tent must be facing east, she realised, as the strong glow of the sunrise penetrated even the heavy canvas to light her bed space.

And then the dream came back to her. Julia fell back onto the straw-filled mattress with a groan of horror and forced herself to remember her lurid night-time fantasy. Wulfric had captured her, held her against her will and yet her treacherous imagination had brought him to her bed, virtually naked. She had dreamt he had held her in his arms, caressed her face and neck, and she had felt the heat of his naked body, the sensation of silk over iron that was his skin and muscle. She had fantasised that his body had grown hard as he held her and that she had wanted to caress him in her turn, feel his mouth on hers—on every part of her…

'No!' Julia rolled over on to her side, dragging the covers over her head as though her shameful thoughts could be blanked out. It did not work. How could she be so wanton as to dream like that? To want her enemy like that? He was beautiful. There was no denying it. To depict the nude male form was considered an acceptable artistic convention; to admire the result was quite normal. But a respectable virgin did not lust after real men like that. One did not think about…

'Are you awake?' It was Berig, on the other side of the curtain, as effective an antidote to desire as any she could think of.

'Yes.'

'Well, get up, then!' He sounded irritable. 'Wulfric said I had to stay here until you were up and working with Una.'

'He is not here?' *Oh, merciful escape if he is not! To have to face him with the memories of that dream fresh in my mind…*

'He's in Rome, gone to Council. I should be there, waiting on him, not hanging around while you wake up.'

'Well, go then,' she snapped.

'I cannot.' Berig's voice became fainter, he was obviously walking away. 'I have to make sure you have breakfast and go safely to Una's.'

'I am quite capable of both.' Julia flung back the blankets and got up. 'Is there hot water?'

'Yes, my lady. In a pot on our fire if your ladyship would condescend to come and get some.' Berig sounded both angry and sarcastic.

Tugging her tunic over her head and winding the girdle round her hips, Julia scooped up her sandals and emerged into the main tent. Berig, wearing a fine linen tunic edged with heavy braid and with a silver clasp around his wrist, looked older—until she saw his expression, which was pure sulky youth.

'You are very fine,' she commented, pushing her feet into her sandals.

'I was *expecting* to see the king. I have to do my lord honour.'

'Well, go and see your precious king then and hold Wulfric's horse, or whatever you are dressed up to do.'

'*Alareiks ist thiudans thizos mikilaizos thiudos thize Gutane,*' Berig snarled at her. '*Is mikils guma ist.*'

'I understood one word of that—Alaric,' Julia said impatiently, then realised that the high colour in Berig's cheeks was genuine anger that she had spoken slightingly of his leader. 'I am sorry, I did not mean to insult your king, but he is my enemy. I give you my word, I will wash, eat and go to Una's tent—you go to Wulfric. I am not likely to escape with Smoke dogging my every step, now am I?'

Berig narrowed his eyes at her. 'Your word? Is the word of a Roman woman any better than those of the men?'

'My word is good,' Julia said steadily. *And I did not promise not to try to escape, only to go to Una's.*

'Very well.' He was out of the tent at a run. A minute later she saw him canter past, his cloak whipping in the wind behind him.

Julia went to the latrine, managing, with some difficulty, to persuade Smoke to wait outside. Still, he was as good as a bolt on the door for ensuring privacy. He hugged her side while she ladled hot water into a bowl and worked out how the suspension hook could be swung to one side so the water did not boil dry.

Washed, her clothing straight, she set her sleeping space in order, then surveyed the rest of the tent. Yesterday's platters and spoons lay unwashed in a large bucket. She pulled back the curtain that screened Berig's space and saw his bed was in disorder and a pile of dirty clothes lay on the floor. Julia prodded them with her toe, shrugged and went to investigate Wulfric's space. It was in a like state, only the pile of discarded garments was larger.

'Hmm.' Julia found bread, cheese and honey, poured hot water over the honey, dashed in a little wine and sat down inside the tent to eat. She washed up what she had used that morning and last night and replaced it on the shelves, tied a loop of leather around an eating knife and fixed it around her waist under her tunic and went out of the tent, leaving the rest of the housework exactly as she had found it.

Una was dropping clothes into a large bucket of steaming water. 'Good day, Julia.' She smiled. 'You bring…*so wasti?* I do not know the word.' She lifted a dripping garment out of the water.

'Clothes? Washing?' Una nodded. 'No, thank you. I found hot water.' It satisfied the other woman, who must have assumed she had left the laundry soaking in the tent. Julia smiled. 'I can help you?' She had no objection to assisting this friendly woman with the clear blue eyes and the swelling belly. She just had no intention of clearing up after two hulking males.

'*Thu hilpis.*' Una nodded agreement. 'You could bring more water?' She gestured to the yoke leaning against the tent wall.

'Very well.' Julia hooked on empty buckets and lifted the yoke. 'Where from?'

'The river is that way.' Una pointed. 'A very small river.'

Interested to see how far Smoke was prepared to let her go, Julia followed the direction the other woman had indicated. It led downhill and, as she went, she passed other women coming back, all carrying water. They stared, wide-eyed, at her clothing, but nodded and smiled when she greeted them. None of them showed any alarm at the wolf padding at her side— doubtless they all knew by now that Wulfric had acquired a female slave. How many of them understood her Latin, she had no idea, but *Good morning* probably sounded much the same to everyone, whatever the actual words used were.

At the bottom of the slope was the stream, its banks muddy and trampled. Someone had set stones as a makeshift hard standing and a small queue of women had built up, waiting patiently while their friends took it in turns to stand dry-shod while they dipped their buckets.

'I'll just see if there's another spot,' Julia said brightly to Smoke as she strolled off across the shoulder of the valley. She wandered along, trying to give the impression that she was interested only in the gaudy flash of a hoopoe flying past, or the spikes of wild flowers in the shade of bushes.

The first meander in the stream took them out of sight of both the watering place and any of the tents on the hill and there, straight as an arrow across the water, was a line of stepping stones, and on the opposite bank a deep grove of trees.

Now, all she had to do was to distract the wolf. There was a tree by the stones on her side. If she could just slip her girdle around Smoke's neck and then tie him to the tree… Then there was a flurry of movement in the grass in front of them, a dozen white scuts tearing frantically away. 'Look, Smoke, rabbits! Catch!'

The wolf was off from a standing start, terrifying death behind the desperate rabbits. Julia took to her heels, sliding and slipping down the slope, onto the first stepping stone. She jumped for the next, and the next. Almost across now. There was a splash to one side of her and Smoke pulled himself up out of the stream on the far bank. He trotted round to face her at the end of the line of stepping stones, head on one side, coat dripping.

Julia balanced, arms outstretched, the stone rocking treacherously under her sandaled feet. 'You are supposed to be chasing rabbits,' she said crossly. The wolf did not budge. 'Oh, very well then, let's go back and get the water for Una.'

'Well? Is there a decision? What did Alaric say? My lord?' Berig was hopping from one foot to another as Wulfric emerged from the Basilica where the king had been holding his Council. To one side a depressed-looking group of senators waited their turn for an audience with the invader. Wulfric eyed them curiously. Was one of them Julia's father? Or her betrothed? They had dispensed with their eastern silks and embroideries and had dressed in pristine white tunics, sweltering under the great weight of their togas as though to emphasise their role and status as Roman patricians. Much good would it do them.

'Lord?'

'Berig, if Alaric wished you to be privy to his councils then he would invite you.' Wulfric felt hot, irritable and sweaty. He violently disagreed with Alaric's decision for the next stage of their journey and none of this had been helped by a tendency to think about Julia at inappropriate moments. He had been on his feet for most of the day, arguing his case for them to move north west, into Gaul, into the rich, well-watered lands that lay open and inviting to a farming people. But the king, backed by his inner circle, had other ideas and nothing Alaric and his supporters could say had swayed them.

Hilderic had come to stand with him, the rest of his kin clustering close. 'They are wary of you, Alaric's men,' the older man had murmured, running a scarred hand through his beard. 'He knows there are many who would follow you and he is not well.'

'I am Alaric's man,' Wulfric had retorted, low-voiced. 'His man until death.'

'Quite,' Hilderic said with a sly smile. 'And until *his* death, of course. Look at yourself—look who stands at your back and your shoulder. Look at the gold you wear and the gold your kin have gained, following you. And then ask, who should the old men who stand at Alaric's back fear when he has gone?'

It had shaken him. It shook him still. His ambition was to lead his kin, as now he did. Beyond that, he wanted to draw into alliance with them as many strong men as he could, for their mutual protection. To be acknowledged as a leader by warriors of Hilderic's experience and standing was heady, but that was as far as his ambition had led him, despite the whispers that had sometimes come to his ears.

Now Hilderic, who spoke for most of the men in the loose alliance ranged with him, was hinting openly that he should bid for the throne when Alaric was gone. There was no harm in speculation about what would come, others would argue. Alaric's health was uncertain, his temper and judgement unsettled. One day, he would no longer lead. One would be a fool not to be ready for that day.

Wulfric realised he was standing in the middle of the courtyard, hand on sword hilt, a scowl on his face. Poor Berig was visibly quaking.

'We stay one more day. That is all I can tell you. The food is running out.'

'But—will we fight the emperor? March on Ravenna?'

'We stay one more day. When I can tell you what happens next, I will do so. Now, where are the horses?'

'Here, lord.' Subdued in his best clothes, Berig led the way to where an urchin was holding the reins. He tossed him a small coin and swung up into the saddle as Wulfric followed suit. 'You look tired,' he ventured as they rode out of the city.

'I've been sitting on my backside in a hot room with a crowd of sweaty men all day. I've been up and down like a bucket in a well, talking and arguing, and my throat is raw. My feet ache worse than if I'd been on a two-day route march and in these clothes I feel like a trussed-up chicken. Otherwise I'm fine.' He pulled irritably at the neck band of his best tunic.

'We could wrestle?' Berig suggested hopefully. 'You promised you'd show me that throw you used on Rathar.'

Wulfric shaded his eyes and looked at where they had got to. Another league into camp. When he got there, there were meetings to hold, men to brief, the whole organisation of breaking camp to set in motion. And that confounded woman to infuriate his mind and inflame his body.

'You're on. See that grove of trees? Race you.'

They rode back into camp an hour later, battered and laughing, their good tunics slung over their saddle bows, their bare chests gleaming with sweat. Berig had a split lip, an interesting bruise coming up on his right bicep and an inch of skin missing from his left knuckles. Wulfric suspected he himself would have a black eye come the morning. He certainly had a bruise over his ribs and a wrenched finger. The boy was fast, and beginning to put on weight as his muscles developed. It would be time soon to take his sword practice seriously.

'I could eat a horse,' Berig declared, sliding to the ground and wincing as his bruises were jarred.

'Two horses, but a hot bath first.' Wulfric slapped him on the back and walked with him towards the tent. 'Odd. There's nothing on the fire. Where's Julia?' He flipped back the tent flap and went in. Flies buzzed around the previous night's dirty dishes. Berig's bed was just as he'd left it and so, when he went to look, was his. He kicked at the pile of filthy clothes and strode across the tent to the curtained corner. 'Julia!'

Her bed space was immaculate, and empty.

Chapter Five

'Julia Livia!' It was a bellow now. He was hot, hungry, the warm glow of hard exercise was edging towards stiffness and he had expected comfort and soft, feminine, attention to his needs, not fly-covered dishes and heaps of grubby linen.

'She's washed up the things she used,' Berig said, prodding the dishes. 'Just hers.'

'Julia—'

The sound of Smoke's bark brought them round the corner of the tent. Julia was sitting on one of the folding stools, taking advantage of the late afternoon sun. She looked, he saw with mounting fury, beautiful, her braid thrown over one shoulder, her patrician profile smooth and calm.

There were the remains of a meal by her side and she was amusing herself by combing Smoke's thick coat. The wolf was lying on its back, paws in the air, letting her groom his stomach.

'That is my comb!' The childish complaint was out of his mouth before he could stop it. Berig gave a gasp of shocked laughter and ducked out of the way of retribution.

'Really?' she said indifferently. 'It was on the floor and

some of the teeth were broken. There's a good boy, then!' It was all too apparent that this was addressed to the wolf and not its master.

'Where is our dinner? Why isn't the washing done? Why is the tent a mess?'

'Because that is how you left it. Una gave me some food just now—I think she expected you to be eating in the city.'

'Because you told her so, I suppose?' He was so angry he was seeing red. Julia added fuel to the flames by shrugging one shoulder elegantly.

Wulfric took a deep breath. 'Smoke, get up and stop behaving like a dog. Berig, go and build up the fire, put on the biggest cauldron. Then go and buy a chicken and ask Una if she'll put it on her spit for us. Then go and get the tub off the cart and scrounge some more hot water. You can bathe at your sister's, Sichar won't be back a while yet.

'And you—' he pointed a long finger at Julia '—you make the beds and gather up the dirty clothes and wash the dishes and when you've done that you can damn well scrub my back.'

Berig left at the run, he was glad to see. As for Julia—*Halja,* he was angry enough to turn her over his knee. Smoke got to his feet and padded over to his side, tail waving apologetically. Julia just sat and stared at him defiantly.

'Move!' he roared. She jumped, got to her feet with a look of scorn and strode off to the tent. Wulfric followed, leaning against the front tent pole, watching with narrowed eyes as Julia disdainfully twitched the bedclothes back into order, kicked the dirty clothing into a pile, shovelled it into a basket and then picked up the bucket full of dirty dishes.

'You will have to move if you want me to put these in hot water.' She stood in front of him, her free hand fisted on her hip, and glared at him. If he had not been so skilled at reading an opponent, watching the eyes of a swordsman for the flicker of intent, he would have believed her unafraid. As it was, he could feel a sneaking admiration for the way she stood up to him, despite the fear flickering in the back of those big brown eyes and the betraying pulse at her temple under the fine skin.

And he was frightening, Wulfric knew it, and cultivated that reaction. To lead and to fight he had to look dangerous, and he had to follow through on it whenever necessary. He could not hide that from her, even if he wanted to—and he did not.

He was almost twice her weight and head and shoulders taller. He was half-naked, sweaty, battered and had all too obviously been fighting, and yet she did not flinch. He remembered the way she had resisted those two men in the alley—hopelessly outnumbered and outweighed, but not giving up. He had no wish to break her spirit, but he was beginning to wonder if that was what it would take to bend her to his will.

'Will you please move?' Julia repeated, trying not to let her voice shake. *Oh, but he is scary. And big. And attractive.* She was utterly horrified at herself for thinking it, but she could not deny it. Something fundamentally female was responding shamefully to the nearness of power and arrogance and sheer masculine beauty.

Wulfric moved to the side with a feline grace and she made herself walk past him and out to the fire. If his size had made him clumsy, then she knew she would not feel this erotic tug. But he moved like a panther, not like the bear he sounded like when he growled, and when he was near she could not stop watching him. Julia scooped hot water onto the greasy dishes, well aware that his eyes were following her.

What on earth would he think if he knew she had been having luridly arousing dreams about him? *Dreams so vivid I can still recall the feel of his skin under my palm, still feel the indentations around his bicep where he had removed a bracelet, still...* She gave herself a vigorous mental shake and fixed a studiedly neutral expression on her face.

A rumble presaged Berig with another youth, rolling what looked like a vast half-barrel around the side of the tent. They manhandled it through the tent flaps, then there was a thud as they rocked it flat onto the ground.

Julia went into the tent and peered into the tub. It came up higher than her waist, high enough for a big man to sit down in comfortably. 'Ugh,' she commented. 'You sit in your own dirty water?'

'In the absence of a hypocaust and bathhouse system, a strigil and a slave to oil me, yes.' Wulfric was stripping off his bracelets. He placed them on a stool and bent to unlace his boots.

'Julia, mind your back!' It was Berig and his friend again, this time laden with buckets of hot water. 'He'll want fresh towels—there.' The lad tipped his head towards the back of the tent and took out the empty buckets.

How many towels does a large wet man need? she wondered, then picked up a stack, along with the jar of soap balls. They seemed odd to wash with, but she had to admit they were effective. There was more splashing; the lads were working hard at filling the great tub.

'That should be enough,' Berig declared at length. 'I'll go and have my own bath now.' He went out, dropping the tent flap and leaving Julia alone with Wulfric.

He reached in to test the temperature, then stretched. Julia hastily put the towels down within his reach. 'No, fold one so I can rest my head on it.'

Yes, my lord, no, my lord. Fuming, Julia did as she was told and hung the result over the edge of the tub, then turned her back with a gasp as his hands went to his belt buckle. *Very definitely time to go.*

'Where are you going?'

'Out.' There had been no sound of splashing behind her, which meant that well over six foot of naked man was still standing there within reach.

'Wait. I may want more hot water.'

She stopped and stood, just inside the door, listening to the sound of Wulfric climbing into the bath, the splashing of water, his long exhalation of pleasure. 'That's *good.*' Then, 'I need another bucketful of hot water.'

Julia snatched up one of the empty buckets and ducked outside. Water was steaming in the cauldron and beside it Berig had left another bucket to top it up. Julia tried it with a fingertip. Cold, straight from the stream. It had not even been sitting around in the sun to take the chill off. With a smile she hefted it up and went back inside.

Over the rim of the tub she could see Wulfric's head, streaming wet, the long, blond hair dark and slick. He rested it on the folded towel. 'Just pour the water straight in.'

'Certainly.' The side of the tub was too high to lift the full bucket straight up. Julia pulled a stool close and stood on that, balancing the wooden container on the edge. Wulfric was lying back, his eyes closed. She let her gaze roam over the wet skin, the way the water flowed off the sculpted muscle, the shadows of the submerged part of his body.

'Where *exactly* shall I pour it?' she enquired sweetly. The green eyes flew open at her tone, but too late. Julia upended the bucket and a torrent of cold water hit him straight in the chest.

She expected spluttering, splashing and a shout of rage. What she was not prepared for was for him to rise straight up out of the water with a bellow of fury, grab her round the waist and heave her into the tub with him.

'Aagh!' She was wet to the waist, then with appalling suddenness, Wulfric sat down, dragging her with him, and ducked her under the water. She kicked and struggled, knocking against knees, tangling with legs, treading on feet, until he let her up to breathe.

'Waurms! Thaunus! Unhultha!' He gave her a shake and held her, spluttering, in front of his face. 'Serpent!'

'I am not your slave, I am not your servant, I am a free Roman citizen and I will not fetch and carry at the orders of a loutish barbarian!' Her defiance was somewhat marred by the fact that her plait had come undone and she was trying to declaim through a mass of wet hair. She twisted in his grip, tried to stand, tangled her feet in her undertunic and fell back with a splash to land painfully on her bottom. 'Oh, I can't *move!*'

Sobbing with anger and frustration Julia tugged at her skirts, then began to struggle as she felt Wulfric's hands on her girdle. It snapped as though it were a single thread and, despite her shrieks and clawing hands, he dragged tunic and undertunic together over her head and threw the sodden bundle out of the tub.

I am naked. I am naked in a tub with this naked man. I want... No! 'Let me out of here,' she demanded, her voice vibrating with feelings she did not dare express. She wrapped her arms round her breasts; they did not seem to cover very much.

Wulfric's anger appeared to have vanished altogether. He was leaning back, his arms around the rim, water dripping from his beard, an appreciative grin on his face. The water lapped around his chest. Julia tried very hard not to stare at the flat pectorals, the strong tendons of his throat. She could feel his feet, one each side of her hips as she crouched there between his legs. 'Please.'

He lifted one hand and gestured to the edge of the tub. 'Feel free.'

'Stand up? In front of you?'

'I could always stand up instead and turn my back,' he offered. She could see he was biting the inside of his cheek to keep from laughing.

'Thank you, no.' She glared at him. 'Why can't you just close your eyes?'

'Because I am enjoying myself,' he admitted simply.

Julia put her hands on the edge of the tub as though to lever herself upright, then snatched at the towel Wulfric had been cushioning his head on. He caught her wrist easily and held it. 'Now what?' he enquired, straight faced.

'This.' Her slender hold on her temper snapping she launched herself at him, striking with her free hand at his imprisoning fist. 'Let me…'

His response was never what she expected, she should have learned that by now. He made no attempt to evade her blows, simply pulling her close in against himself. Frightened, furious and excited in equal measure, she looked up into the clear green eyes so close that she could count his lashes.

'You savage! Let me go.'

For a long moment they stared at each other, then with a growl Wulfric released her hand, encircled her waist and trapped her mouth under his. It was her dream of the night before and more. Their bodies touched together, slipped apart, as her hands came up to grip his shoulders and her mouth opened under his with an instinctive, fierce response she did not know she possessed.

They were both angry. She had no idea whether she was more angry at him than herself, but there was no mistaking that Wulfric was furious with her, and utterly determined to bring her panting and pleading to his feet.

His grip on her was punishingly hard, his mouth plundered without any mercy, lips and teeth and tongue possessing and taking with a power that seemed to only increase as she refused to be cowed by it. He plunged his tongue into her open mouth, hard and hot. Innocent of a man's body she might be, but Julia knew what this invasion mimicked. Writhing against him under the water, she tangled her own tongue with his. *I will reduce him to begging for me and then I will laugh…*

He let her go as violently as he had taken her. Julia fell back against the side of the tub gasping, rubbing the back of her hand across her swollen mouth, staring at him wild-eyed.

'You are a virgin—you should behave like one,' he snapped at her, his chest heaving.

'You hypocrite! You presume to lecture me on my behaviour? You kissed me, you forced me!' Her hands were shaking. She clasped them together.

'*Forced* you? I think not, Julia.'

She could feel the shamed blood staining her cheeks, saw on Wulfric's face nothing but male arrogance and the desire to dominate. She had fought back, not with her fists but with her sensuality and he could not deal with that, she told herself, fighting for some balance.

'You are an animal,' she managed to spit out.

'I would be taking you on the floor by now if that were the case.' She gasped. He stared at her haughtily and she read his pride and the indignation that she had insulted him in the hot green look. 'Wash my back.'

'What? Now?'

'Yes, now.' He reached one long arm over the side of the tub, groped in the jar and came up with a soap ball.

'I would sooner stick a knife in it,' she retorted flatly.

'I am aware of that.' Wulfric shifted round until his broad back was towards her. His disregard for the danger she posed was an affront in itself.

Julia stared at the expanse of shoulder, the long, flexible line of his back, the strong dip to the spine, the dramatic narrowing to his hips. Below the water she could see the taut shape of his buttocks. His hair was plastered to the skin, covering his shoulder blades.

'Now,' he growled. 'The water is getting cold.'

Julia began to make lather, and then to wash her own body as fast as she could. Sharing bathwater was a dubious way to get clean in her opinion, but she was going to wring what benefit she could from this hideous situation.

'What are you doing?'

'Washing.' She ducked under the water to rinse off the suds, pushing her hair back out of her face. No rosemary hair wash, no sweet oils, just one large, sweaty barbarian's bathwater. Julia grimaced at the magnificent back in front of her.

'Then wash *me,* slave girl.'

She scooped one hand under the fall of his hair and threw it over his shoulder, then attacked his back as hard as she could. Wulfric grunted, not, she was sorry to realise, with discomfort, but with pleasure. Gritting her teeth, she scrubbed the coarse soap ball over his back, following up with her other hand, kneading the muscles as though to pummel her anger out into them. She followed the fascinating masculine lines as far as his waist. No further.

'You have stopped.' He turned his head to look at her.

Julia shifted closer, the only way to shield her naked body. Her breasts were a finger's breadth from his back.

'You can reach the rest.' She tossed the soap ball up over his shoulder. Reflexively he lunged for it and she scrambled over the edge of the tub, seized her sodden clothing and ran for her bed space.

Wulfric caught the soap one-handed, pivoting as he did so to admire the exquisite rear view of Julia vanishing behind the curtain. 'Little witch,' he murmured to himself, settling back into the rapidly cooling water. 'Little vixen.'

What had happened just now had been no part of his intentions, but with Julia Livia it seemed his prized self-control was like a reed in the wind. She could provoke him just by the way she lowered her lashes with exquisite disdain, let alone by the sight of her naked body a hand's span from his.

Wulfric lifted a foot to the rim of the tub and began to soap his leg, trying to give proper attention to the condition of his muscles and the feel of the tendon he had strained two weeks before. His physical condition was important; some chit of a girl, however aggravating, was not.

Only…he lowered that leg, satisfied with the lack of discomfort in the tendon, and raised the other. Only, she was not a girl. He had let her lack of stature compared to the women who surrounded him delude him into thinking her nearer Berig's age than his own twenty-seven summers. But she must be twenty, he supposed.

Well past marriageable age in his society. What was the matter with this senator she was supposed to be betrothed to? Had the man ice water in his veins?

He, Wulfric, was very uncomfortably aware that what was coursing around his own veins was not ice water, but hot blood. He had not meant to kiss her. He had known, without having to think about it, what the effect of taking that lush, red, angry mouth would be. His own body had predicted absolutely what her narrow frame would feel like under his hands, how the sweet curves and soft skin would feel against his own hardness, against his bruised flesh.

And he would not take what he so easily could, because his faith told him it was wrong and his honour despised the thought that he would force a woman.

Even this one who attacked him with his own weapons of sensuality and of anger. He knew what she was about, even if he doubted she could explain it to herself. She had wanted to show him that he was less than he believed himself to be, and he knew that even greater than her fear of him was her own terror of being afraid, of not living up to the standards of a patrician Roman lady.

Did she know what danger she had been in? Had she any concept of the fire she was playing with? Surely she did. Somewhere, under that angry defiance, there must be the belief that he would not force her. She had gone white around the mouth when he had flung that remark about taking her on the floor. That had shocked her deeply and yet she had the spirit to continue to taunt him, to play her dangerously provoking games with him. Somewhere there was a trust in him and in his honour. He should not care, but it seemed that he did and that the thought warmed him, deep inside where he kept the emotions that a leader could not show.

He stood up in a surge of water and reached for a towel, swathing it around his hips as Berig ducked into the tent. The boy was clean, damp and his hair was slicked back.

'Una says, do you want the salve for… Bloody hell!'

Wulfric followed his gaze to the beaten earth of the tent

floor. Trodden, swept with a stiff broom, the summer-hardened earth had made a perfectly serviceable floor. Now there was a muddy ring right around the tub, a quagmire directly in the centre of the living space.

'Your lord splashes a great deal.' Julia emerged from behind her curtain, her creased clothes clinging to her, her gaze scornfully averted from Wulfric as he stood there up to mid-thigh in cooling, dirty water. 'I was surprised to find him so clumsy.'

With a flick of her skirts she picked her way around the mud, past the gaping youth and out of the tent.

Wulfric balled the towel up in his hands. 'Empty the tub, get some straw for the floor and sort something out with that hell-cat for dinner.' He climbed grimly out of the tub onto the stool and from there to dry ground.

Berig swallowed audibly. 'What are you going to do to her?'

Wulfric stood where he was, hands on hips, and considered his tactics. He saw the shadow slide under the tent flap and raised his voice. 'Do to her? Why, nothing. Nothing at all. If she wants to eat, then she must cook. If she wants to drink, then she must fetch water, and, if she wants to sleep on a bed, then she must wash the linens.' *And if she wants to tempt and torment me with those red lips and those soft curves, those big brown eyes—then she will find I am as much a rock to her wiles as to her temper.*

Chapter Six

Julia stepped silently away from the entrance to the tent. Smoke padded round the corner and eyed her. 'We are both in disgrace,' she told him. 'You for acting like a dog, me for being me, I suppose.' Further defiance seemed pointless. She would end up hungry and thirsty, Wulfric would be no worse off than he had been before she had come into his life and Una would carry on looking after two households.

The sun was low now, the smell of food wafted from cooking pots all around, the noise levels were rising as the men returned and the children ran home after play.

It was too late to start preparing food, even if she knew how. If Wulfric told Una not to feed her, then the other woman would obey him, but surely tonight she would help.

Una came out of her tent as Julia approached, her small daughter peering round her skirts at the stranger. 'I have clothes for you,' she said before Julia could speak. 'I do not know the names in your tongue, but here.' She held out a pile of fabrics and smiled as Julia took them. 'Soon, they will be too little for me.' She gestured at her swelling figure. 'I will teach you, you can make more.'

'Thank you. Will you teach me to cook too? After tonight, Wulfric says I must cook, or not eat.'

Una smiled, a twinkle in her eyes that made Julia blush. Wulfric's voice raised in a roar would not have been stopped by canvas walls. How much had their neighbours heard? 'Help yourself.' She gestured at the fireside. 'Berig had already brought me two chickens, they will be ready soon. There is bread here, butter in the crock in the tent.'

Julia thanked her again, smiled at the shy little girl and made her way back, passing Berig laden with two buckets of dirty water as she did so. She had no intention of going into the tent while Wulfric was in goodness knows what state of disturbing undress, so she set the new clothes on a stool, poured the cool, greasy water off the dirty dishes and set to washing them.

They were draining in the bucket when Smoke lifted his head and his tail began to thump, cautiously. She turned, just as warily.

Wulfric was bare to the waist, a towel thrown over his shoulder, a bone comb in his hand. He nodded to her as casually as though they had been discussing the weather just a few moments before, tugged the wolf's ears and hooked a stool towards him with his foot.

If I tell him to put his tunic on, he will realise just how much he disturbs me, wandering about half-naked, she fumed, managing a tight smile. Berig, his friend at his heels, vanished into the tent, reappearing at length with the tub. Julia dragged out the trestles and set them up, decided she could not manage the board by herself and began to collect up the stools.

When she turned back to Wulfric, he was sectioning off a wide strand of hair. It was, now she saw it both wet and combed out, almost as long as hers. It would be a thorough-going nuisance, getting caught in chain mail, sticking to sweaty skin in battle, blowing in his eyes. All the men wore their hair long, so it must be the fashion, she supposed, but she had not thought Wulfric so bound by such trivia that he would overlook the disadvantages. Roman soldiers cropped their hair even shorter than most, which seemed eminently practical for a fighting man.

'What are you doing?'

He looked up from plaiting the bottom handspan of the section. 'Plaiting my hair.'

'I can see that.' *Why do men have to be so literal?* 'Why?'

'That is not what you asked me. Why do women have to be so indirect?' He did not wait for her to answer. 'I plait the ends, because it is the custom, and the curl takes up some of the length.'

'But why have it that long in the first place?' Obviously he had never thought about it and did not realise the advantages. He did not answer her, engrossed in the fiddly task. There had been a pair of small shears on the shelves in the tent, she recalled. She could cut it for him now, it would be easier while it was wet.

The centre of the floor was covered in straw. Julia picked her way round it, found the shears and looked at the blades. They were sharp and a few bristles of dark gold hair clung to them. He must use them to trim his beard; they would do excellently.

Julia emerged from the tent behind Wulfric's back. He had plaited half a dozen sections on each side and was reaching over his shoulder for the back hair. 'Let me.' She picked up a section and lifted it, running her fingers down it as she tried to judge where to cut. She made an experimental snip in the air with the shears to get the feel of them.

They made a sharp snapping sound. Julia raised the shears,

pulled the lock of hair tauter between her fingers and was thrown to the ground as Wulfric swung round, seized her wrists and hurled her away from him. The shears landed, points down, next to her throat.

Berig came at the run, falling to his knees beside Wulfric, who was still on the stool, his face stark white. 'Has she cut it?' the boy panted, his hands reaching for his master's hair.

'I don't know.' The words came between clenched teeth. 'Check.'

Half-winded, confused, Julia crouched where she had fallen as Berig ran his hands through the wet hair, then the comb. 'No. No, it is all right. You were in time.'

'I was not trying to attack him,' Julia gasped as both men swung round to stare at her, green and blue eyes alike in an emotion that went beyond fury. 'I was only going to cut his hair.'

'*Cut his hair!* Have you no idea what you nearly did?' Berig gasped.

'For Heaven's sake…' Julia scrambled to her feet '…you are carrying on like some lady whose curling irons have burnt off part of her hairstyle! That long hair might be the fashion, but it is hardly life and death.'

'It *is* life and death,' Berig spat. Behind him Wulfric stood up. The colour that had gone from his face a moment ago was back.

'She does not know. I do not think it was deliberate.'

'*What?* You are speaking in riddles. What does it matter if your hair is cut?'

'They call us the people of the Long-Haired Kings,' Wulfric said. He reached out and pulled her, not ungently, to sit on a stool beside him. 'No man whose hair is shorn can lead, let alone rule. His only role can be as an outcast or a priest.'

'You might as well cut off his balls,' Berig added.

'Thank you, Berig—colourful, but unnecessary.' A faint smile touched Wulfric's mouth and she saw his shoulders relax from their tautness. 'I do not know why this is, but it is sacred to our kingship.'

'But you are Christians now,' Julia protested. What she had almost done was deadly serious, she was beginning to grasp that, but she could not understand why.

'It has nothing to do with religion, it is to do with us as a people, what we are, what I am. I cannot explain it to you.'

'But you all have long hair,' she said, confused. 'You cannot all be kings.'

'We all lead according to our abilities and our stations, whether it is a family or a war band or a kingdom.'

'But it grows again,' she murmured. 'Who would have known if I had cut off a little?'

'I would have known,' Wulfric said starkly. Smoke padded across and thrust his muzzle into his master's clasped hands, sensitive to the emotion he was hiding from his human companions. Then he smiled. 'Like losing your virginity, it cannot be repaired.'

Berig guffawed, just as Una walked across, a platter with two cooked chickens in her hand. If she had noticed the scuffle, she gave no indication.

'What are you laughing at?' she asked in her accented Latin.

'Virginity.' Berig was still convulsed in adolescent sniggers.

His sister cuffed him round the ears, earning a yelp of pain. She said something sharply to both men in her own language, gave the food to Julia with a pitying look and stalked off.

'What did she say?'

'That we are both grubby little boys,' Wulfric translated. 'And that I, at least, should know better.'

'True,' Julia concurred, watching him from under her lashes. The dangerous emotion of the past few minutes had passed, leaving him apparently amused and relaxed, but she did not deceive herself. What she had almost done would have been as serious as if she had stabbed him in the back. Worse, for she could see it went to the heart of what he was as a man. And by telling her, he had handed her a weapon of awful power.

She went and picked up the shears and shivered. She could kill someone in self-defence, or to save someone else, she thought. If she had held a knife when those tradesmen had attacked her, she would have stabbed them without compunction. But she could not imagine killing someone's soul, their sense of themselves. It seemed Wulfric knew that about her, just as she knew, deep down, he would never force her, never harm her.

Julia looked up from her study of the polished metal, and met his eyes as he watched her face. Something passed between them, some flash of understanding. She had no idea of its significance, but her skin prickled as though a storm were gathering.

Her meek acceptance of domestic chores appeared to raise no comment. If Wulfric assumed she had overheard his threats, he made no reference to them. Julia cleared away dinner, shifted the soaking clothes into fresh water, threw in a soap ball and hoped Una would demonstrate the knack of getting them clean in the morning.

Wulfric strode off, saying curtly that he had men to speak to, Berig at his heels like a shadow. Smoke whined, but stayed near Julia's side while she passed an hour shaking out the clothes Una had given her and trying them on.

Two long linen shifts were not unlike her own undertunic, although both had long sleeves and neck slits. There would be no need to fasten them carefully with pins and brooches. Then there were two overtunics, one with stripes of brown and green, the other faintly chequered in natural shades of wool. Una had wrapped them up in a hooded cloak and tied them with a long girdle, which was a relief, given that Wulfric had snapped her own.

Julia pulled on a clean undertunic. It was too long, of course, Una was a head taller than she, but no doubt shortening it was another lesson for tomorrow. She tossed her own much-abused garments into the washing tub, hoping her new friend would have some magic for removing mud from fine linen—the amber tunic was a favourite.

When that was done there was nothing to occupy her. The tent was tidy, she had done all she had the skill to do. There was laughter from the direction of Una and Sichar's dwelling, someone a few rows off was singing and playing a harp, a group of women went past, giggling.

If I could speak a few words of their language, I could go and join a group at their fireside, she brooded. *Find out what would happen when they broke camp.* For that, she was certain, would provide the most confusion and her best chance of escape.

Julia folded away her new clothes and climbed into bed, blankets piled up behind her, her arms curled round her knees. Smoke decided the end of the bed had been left deliberately empty for him and climbed up, settled down with a sigh and went to sleep.

She prodded him with her toe, but he simply curled up tighter. Either she was going to have to shove him off when she wanted to sleep, or remain sitting up all night. The male inhabitants of this tent were, every one of them, profoundly provoking.

Her lips curved in a forbearing smile and Julia caught herself up sharply. After barely a day and a half she was becoming too used to this life, to the man and the youth, to Una's kind smile and Smoke's constant company. It was madness and she did not understand it. Smoke was a big, dangerous animal, and she had never had so much as a lapdog. Berig was an adolescent with all the worst characteristics of a young male and Wulfric—

Wulfric was someone of whom she should be profoundly wary. He had snatched her up, made no bones of the fact that he wanted her as a slave and he showed, even at his kindest, not the slightest inclination to let her go.

At worst he was domineering, violent and sexually powerful. She had been raised to be the wife of a powerful man, of course, but one who was civilised, suave, reserved. She was not raised to find herself attracted to a savage, to a barbarian who made her blood surge hot. She was not meant to find herself feeling alive only in the presence of a man who was an enemy of her people and a direct threat to her own liberty.

Julia shifted uncomfortably on her makeshift pillows, trying to tell herself that these ambiguous feelings were the result of her dependence on the man for everything in this alien world—and the inescapable fact that he had saved her life. She failed, which left her to grapple with the even more uncomfortable thought that it was simply his physicality that dazzled her.

But it was more than that. She was not like those women one heard about who lusted after gladiators. She did not understand Wulfric, she could not forgive him for snatching her away, but she liked him and in some perverse way, given that he was her captor, she trusted him.

'You're a fool, Julia Livia,' she said out loud, making Smoke raise his long muzzle to look at her. 'You can trust him not to let you go, and that is all. And you—' she set both feet hard against the wolf's ribs and pushed '—you can get off my bed.'

Wulfric was grinning as he swung up into the saddle and cantered out of camp at sunrise the next morning, a yawning Berig at his back. There had been no sound from Julia during the night, but, looking in on her that morning, he had found her curled up at the head of her bed, Smoke occupying the rest of the space.

It seemed that, for all their confrontations, Julia was settling down. When she learned to cook and to wash, then things would be considerably more comfortable—once he had managed to get over the state of arousal that she produced in him. It was as unexpected as it was inconvenient—she was not at all the type of woman who normally appealed to him, she made no bones of the fact that she regarded him as the enemy and that her present compliance was simply out of necessity.

Her stunningly erotic response to him in the bath-tub proved nothing, he told himself wryly. She was taunting him, hitting back by playing the same game as he was, confident that he would not take it to the logical conclusion.

'What are you frowning about?' Berig was riding alongside, so at home on his mount that he could concentrate on his master's face.

'I am wondering if I am a fool.' *A fool to have these scruples, or a fool not to try to seduce her into my bed?*

Berig just stared back, wide-eyed. In his experience Wulfric, one step removed in general magnificence from the king—an illusion he was well aware of—never suffered the slightest twinge of self-doubt.

'Come,' Wulfric said, tightening his knees and urging the ugly grey into a gallop. 'I have another long morning in Council.'

Julia too had no time to be bored that morning. Una happily demonstrated how to wash clothes, how to turn up a tunic and how to deal with a rabbit for the pot.

'Ugh.' Julia stared at the skinned carcase with repulsion and accepted the knife held out to her with reluctance. 'And you can stop sitting there dribbling,' she informed Smoke tartly. The wolf knew an easy meal when he saw one and was obviously impatient for her to get on with preparing the rabbit and give him the head.

Eventually a stew was prepared, herbs and greens collected for a salad, oils and seasonings stirred into a dressing and first lessons in breadmaking given.

By mid-day Julia was hot, weary and her back ached. The arrival back in camp of Wulfric at the head of the biggest group of men she had yet seen was a welcome distraction.

He strode up to the tent and ate the bread, cheese and ale she had set out. Around the camp, as the men spread out, taking their news with them, noise levels rose until the sound of voices filled the air like a giant swarm of bees.

'What is it? What has happened?' Julia had to tug at Wulfric's sleeve to get his attention. 'Has the emperor's army come?'

'No.' He was dismissive. 'He skulks in Ravenna with his troops around him. Not even the insult to his sister draws him out. The decision has been made—we break camp and move tomorrow.'

'Where? Where are we going?' *How will Father find me?* The panicky voice filled her head for a moment, then common sense took over. There was no way that these hundreds of people could move secretly through the Empire—her whereabouts would be no secret, but how would anyone ever find her in the midst of this anthill?

'Wait and I will tell you along with everyone else. The men have gone to call in the families, I will tell all my kin.' His face was calm, composed. Yet Julia could sense an emotion he was not revealing. She tried to read it, but all her mind could feel was anger, rigidly controlled.

And from all directions people were converging. Family groups shepherded by their menfolk, bands of young men jostling and flexing muscles, and mature warriors, swords by their sides, their faces serious, like rocks breaking the flow in the river as they stood, legs apart, arms crossed, eyes narrowed.

Dangerous men, men who followed Wulfric, men who would fight and kill Romans if they were so ordered.

Someone had pulled a wagon into a clear space on the edge of the encampment. Wulfric put down his horn cup and strode out to it. As he climbed up to stand on the planked seat the crowd fell silent, all the faces turned to him.

'Do you know?' Julia took Berig's arm. 'Do you know where we are going?'

The boy shook his head. 'No. Only the king and his Council know yet. Listen, and Wulfric will tell us now.'

Wulfric began to speak, his voice carrying across the still crowd as though he were giving orders on a battlefield. She could not understand a word he said, but his style would not have disgraced a Roman orator. There was passion, flexibility, force in his voice. She wanted to cheer without understanding why. This was a man born to lead, who had honed every skill and added them to a natural charisma. The faces round her were rapt, involved, inspired.

Then he said one phrase and there was a gasp, picked up by a hundred voices. A murmur spread round, faces showed excitement, puzzlement, fear, speculation—horror.

'Berig! What is he saying?' Julia demanded. 'I can't understand what he is saying.'

'*Hwa?* What?' Berig blinked at her as though he was in shock and struggled to find the Latin words. 'Er…we go south.'

'South? Where in the south?'

'Africa,' the boy stammered. 'Africa. The end of the world.'

Chapter Seven

'Africa? No, impossible! Why Africa?' Julia felt sick. So far away, no one would ever find her there.

All around them was turmoil. Women were wailing, men shouting questions. Wulfric's voice, raised to a roar, cut through the babble and they fell silent again as he spoke.

'Because it is rich in grain…because there is more land there…because it gives us a hold on the Empire through the grain shipments…' Concentrating on translating, Berig was more composed now. 'Because the Eastern Empire is sending four thousand men to Honorius's aid.'

'Alaric will not stand his ground and fight?' *Four thousand! It will be a bloodbath, whoever wins.*

'They are asking that now.' Berig held up a hand to silence her urgent, whispered questions. 'Wulfric says that the king declares he did not bring us here for the ravens to pick our bones, or those of the Romans, but for the land that is our due.'

'And we leave tomorrow?'

'Yes. We were always going to leave tomorrow, there is not enough food in Rome.'

Then the very first chance I have, I must escape. There will be confusion now as people pack up ready to break camp. Julia scanned the crowd and the encampment. All morning she had been up and down the path to the river; that would be the way to go, for Wulfric was sure to set Smoke on her track and her scent would be expected there. If she entered the water and waded downstream, the wolf would be confused. But for that to work, she first had to get away from Smoke.

The crowd had begun to break up, straggling back to their tents, talking urgently amongst themselves.

'You must show me how to help with the packing—' she began when a shout halted everyone in their tracks.

Wulfric had jumped down from the wagon; now he swung round to face a man who strode out of the edge of the crowd. He was a giant, half a head taller than Wulfric, built like a solid tree-trunk, his torso massive as a bear's. His hair was red, his face choleric with rage and in his hand he brandished a sword.

'Oh, Lord. It is Rathar. He has always opposed Wulfric. Traitor,' Berig began to translate, his face white. 'Coward. Alaric is wrong and all know it, you are supposed to lead, not to give in to mad schemes that will be the death of all of us. I will not follow you any longer, Wulfric, son of Athanagild, nor will my kin, for you seek some advantage for yourself in all this, you plot to take the throne yourself when this lunacy leads us all to perdition.'

Wulfric stood, hand on sword hilt while the furious giant ranted himself to a standstill. His voice when he replied was clear, steady, dismissive. *'Tho wuarda thoei thu qast, lugan, Rathar.'*

'Wulfric says Rathar lies, he says to calm down and to take back his insults and he will pay them no heed, he—'

The red-headed man gave a roar of fury and lunged with

his sword. *'Gagg du haljai!'* *Go to hell!* Berig broke into a run, back towards the tent, and Smoke vanished from Julia's side to reappear behind Wulfric, hackles raised, teeth bared.

Wulfric's sword swept from the scabbard as he side-stepped, elegant panther against the bear's onslaught. The blades crossed, the shriek of metal sickeningly loud in the total silence that had fallen. Every face was turned to the drama unfolding on the crushed circle of grass and Julia realised she was quite unguarded. Behind the nearest row of tents, out of sight, were the horse lines, she would not even have to run down to the river…

A youth broke through the crowd and held out a shield to Rathar, who snatched it as he jumped back from Wulfric's attacking thrust, just as Berig appeared behind his lord, the round shield embossed with a dragon she had seen hanging in the tent in his arms. *Thank God, they are equal again—in all but size…*

She began to work her way through the crowd, but it was not until she reached the edge that she realised what she was doing: instead of fleeing to the edge, she was now on the inner rim of the circle in plain sight of Berig and Smoke. But she could not draw back. In front of her Wulfric was fighting, not just for dominance, but for his life. She might know nothing about swordplay, but it was obvious that both men were in deadly earnest, that this would not end without bloodshed or worse.

At the edge of the ground the two young men circled too, their eyes flickering, knives in their hands, guarding their lords' backs from each other. If Wulfric was killed, what would happen to Berig?

And surely he could not win against this furious giant? The man had the advantage of weight, reach and height. Julia closed her fingers over her mouth and forced herself to watch. Wulfric was faster, she realised, gasping as he ducked low under a wild swing. He seemed no less strong than Rathar, and he was calm, ice calm. Gradually she began to see tactics in what he was doing, leading Rathar in, then moving away, trying to tire the heavier man as his own sword flashed and wove, blinding and deceiving in stroke and counterstroke.

They were sweating, both of them; Wulfric dashed his free hand across his forehead, shook back his hair, then, with his opponent's eyes momentarily distracted by the movements, lunged low, his blade ripping down one trousered leg. It was a glancing, opportunist slash and did not cut deep, but blood appeared through the cloth and Rathar gave a great bellow of rage.

He launched himself at Wulfric, cutting and stabbing, the sheer weight and fury of his charge driving his opponent back against the wagon's side, removing all Wulfric's advantage of speed and flexibility. With a grunt of triumph Rathar drew back his sword arm and thrust, straight at Wulfric's chest.

Julia had no idea how she kept her eyes open, how she kept silent, or why she did not simply collapse out of sheer terror. The great blade flashed forward, and suddenly Wulfric was not there, but on the ground, rolling under the strike, surging to his feet. He had dropped his shield, his long knife was in his left hand, his sword steady in his right hand. And down his right forearm blood spilled from a long cut, in a crimson unstoppable flood.

'*No!*' She thought she had screamed, but it was only a whisper of despair. Berig froze in his tracks, the wolf hunkered down as though to spring.

Wulfric seemed to stumble, his guard wavered and with a

roar of triumph the giant rushed him, sword outstretched. Wulfric dropped again, his weight solidly on his wounded arm, and struck upwards with his knife hand, up under Rathar's guard, up under the edge of chain mail over the solid belly to find its target.

The man went down like a felled tree, Wulfric under him, his head striking the wagon wheel. Julia saw Berig run for the shield, seize it and swing round to stand guard over the fallen men, his long, wickedly sharp knife blade holding back Rathar's follower, Smoke snarling at his side.

She found she was running, stumbling over the slippery grass, until she reached them. 'Give me the knife.' She wrenched it from Berig and held it outthrust towards his opponent. 'Get him out of there, we have to stop the bleeding.'

Rathar's man reached for her and Smoke snarled. 'Do you want your throat torn out?' Julia demanded. 'For I swear I will set him on you if you do not back away.'

Then Una was at her side, her husband at her heels to take the knife from Julia, and between them the two women and the boy rolled the body of Rathar off Wulfric.

Ice-green eyes stared up into hers. 'Why did you not go when you had the chance?' Then the keen gaze faltered, blurred and his lids closed.

'Idiot man,' Una snapped, on her knees at Julia's side. 'He needs to ask?' She took Julia's hands and fastened them around the savage wound on Wulfric's forearm. 'Here, hold tight, we must stop the bleeding.'

'His head—'

'Is like oak,' the other woman countered. 'But a hard head is no good without blood.' She wrenched off her girdle and tied it around Wulfric's upper arm. 'See? This stops the blood, but we must not have it tight too long or the arm will die.'

She's teaching me, Julia realised, trying to ignore the nausea rising inside her, trying to focus on what she was doing, determined not to faint as her hands slipped in the blood.

Men came with a hurdle and rolled Wulfric onto it. Julia followed them back to the tent, listening to Una counting, watching her loosening the girdle, then retightening it.

I can go now, they will not notice. The camp was in turmoil, keening cries rising from the site of the fight as Rathar's womenfolk gathered round the body, men loyal to Wulfric clustering in knots to debate what had happened. Berig was kneeling at his lord's side, Smoke crouched on the other, growling softly. *He is alive, there is nothing I can do. I will go…*

But her feet would not take her. Instead, inexplicably, they carried her into the tent to Una's side. 'What can I do?'

'Get water, and towels.' Una looked up at her brother and spoke in her own language. 'I have sent him for needles and linen thread, that arm must be stitched.'

'You will do it?' Of course Una would, she could do all these things that left Julia feeling clumsy and helpless and ashamed of her pampered, heedless existence.

'Julia will do it.' Both women stared at Wulfric. He was pale under his tan and there were lines of pain around his eyes, but he was smiling. 'Julia Livia Rufa can sew a fine stitch, I am certain. It is not good for you in your condition, Una, to sit hunched up over my battered body.'

'I…I have never sewn up a wound,' Julia protested. *Why isn't he unconscious?* 'A skinned rabbit turned me sick to the stomach.'

'I am not a rabbit.'

'No.' He was certainly not that. Julia kept her gaze fixed well away from Wulfric's arm. 'I do not know how.'

'Yesterday you did not know how to gut that rabbit, or to knead bread or to wash clothes. Do you now?' Incredibly, it was Una who asked.

'Yes! But…but this is different!'

'How else will you learn except by doing it?'

'But why, when you will do it better?'

'Because you are his woman,' Una said, getting to her feet with a grunt and rubbing the small of her back.

'I am not!'

'I saved your life. I own you. That makes you my woman,' Wulfric said. 'And if you are not, why did you not run just now?' There were more than questions in that green gaze, there were assumptions and demands and something that pulled her…

'Because I was stupid,' Julia said furiously. 'I should have gone.'

'Too late now.' Incredibly, despite the fact that his arm was laid open to the bone—she risked one, nauseated glance—and that he had sustained a blow to the head that would have killed most men, Wulfric appeared quite able to carry on a conversation in his most provoking manner.

Berig came in at a run and thrust a small roll of cloth into his sister's hands. 'No.' She nodded towards Julia. 'She will do it.'

'Her! I am his man, I will do it if you will not!'

'I have no wish to look like a badly darned pair of hose,' Wulfric said drily. 'Julia will do it.'

It seemed there was no escape. While Una ordered Berig about, Julia pulled up a stool and sat by the side of Wulfric's bed. 'I will hurt you.'

'It will hurt whoever does it. Not to have it sewn up will be worse,' he pointed out, holding his arm out to her. 'I would do it myself if it was my left arm.'

'Oh.' Berig pushed a towel into her lap and Una handed her a needle with a long brown thread hanging from it. 'What do I do?'

'Make lots of small stitches all along, tie each one off. I will tell you where.'

'Una…Berig…' They had gone, fading back into the shadows of the tent, leaving her alone to cope.

Wulfric put his left hand on the wound, drawing the edges together nearest his elbow. 'Start there.'

It must hurt dreadfully. She tried to blank it from her mind, tried not to think about the living flesh she was driving her needle through as she made knot after knot, Wulfric's voice calm in her ears as she learned to get the tension just right, the spacing just so. Under her hands she felt the flesh flinch as she pushed in the needle, but he kept his arm as steady as when he had held the sword and his breathing never faltered.

After the first few stitches her hands steadied and her entire focus was on the next finger's breadth of the wound, on the precise depth, on the right tension. She kept going, the blood roaring in her ears, until she heard him say, 'It is done,' and realised that the whole thing was over.

'No, you cannot faint yet, Julia.' Wulfric's voice was as matter of fact as though she had been sewing braid on his tunic. 'Wash away the blood and bandage it tightly.'

Una had left the things for her. Julia did as he instructed and finally sat back, her hands red to the wrists. She looked down at them, holding them away from her body as though they did not belong to her.

'Now wash your hands,' Wulfric said patiently.

'Yes…yes, of course.' Julia set the water to one side and stood up, reaching for a blanket. 'Lie down now, you must rest.'

'No.' Wulfric swung his legs over the side of the bed. 'I need to be seen, and I need to go and speak to Rathar's kin.'

'You are in no fit state!' Julia pressed her hands to his shoulders and tried to push him down. He might be wounded and weakened by a blow to the head, but he was still as solid as a rock against what strength she could muster. 'And surely it is not safe to go to them just when you have killed him?'

'It was a fair fight, he challenged me before witnesses. There is no cause for judgement. I will see what his woman needs, and the children, and give them blood money, although it is not due in such a case.'

Wulfric stood up and lifted her chin in his left hand as he had once before and stared into her eyes. 'I am glad.'

'What about?'

'Because it seems you chose to be here.'

'I told you, I was too foolish to run when I had the chance. Why should I choose to stay with a man who kidnapped me, who forces me to work for him, who makes me…who makes me…?' To her horror her voice wobbled.

'Makes you what, Julia?' His hand was no longer on her face, but round her shoulders, pulling her in to him.

'Who makes me sew up his disgusting wounds,' she snapped, fighting the urge to simply lean on him and be held. He was hurt, but it was she who hardly had the strength to stand. 'I never want to see the insides of anybody again as long as I live. I could see *bone*.'

That provoked a snort of amusement. 'We would have difficulty standing up without it. Sit down, Julia, you have had a shock. Rest.' Wulfric pressed her down on the spot she had been urging him to take and walked to the entrance. For a moment she saw him hesitate, his left hand resting on the pole, the first sign of weakness she had ever seen from him, and then he squared his shoulders and was gone. A shout greeted his appearance, voices were raised, then ebbed slowly as the speakers followed him away.

Following a man who has killed three men in front of me in the three days I have known him. Julia stared at her hands, half expecting to see blood on them again. *And I stayed with him when I could have run.* Without a conscious decision she lay back on the heaped blankets. *But two of those men were murderers and rapists, and Rathar attacked him. What else should he have done?*

Julia curled up, the shivering that had afflicted her before returning. She pulled one of the blankets over her shoulders and found she was inhaling the scent she had come to associate, quite unconsciously, with Wulfric. The tang of the soap balls, leather, male musk. *I am in his bed. I should move…in a minute, when I feel better. This feels safe… In a minute I can creep down to the river and escape.* Her lids drooped and closed.

'She is still asleep,' Berig grumbled, staring at Julia who lay huddled under the covers on Wulfric's bed.

'Hush. She has had a shock,' Wulfric murmured. His head was pounding, he felt light-headed in a way that he knew from experience was due to blood loss and would only be cured by resting, and his arm ached with a sickening relentlessness that made it hard to focus.

For the past long hours he had sat with his own followers, discussing, planning, explaining Alaric's decision, justifying as best he could a plan he secretly deeply disagreed with, but must support out of loyalty.

Now the moon was high and he had sent them, still debating, to their beds. It would be a long, hard, physical day tomorrow. And that woman was in his bed. *Infuriating,* she had called him. The pot calling the kettle black with a vengeance.

But why had she stayed? Not through lack of courage to take a risk, not through lack of intelligence to see the chances. He shook his head, the echo of Una's words in his head. He had been almost unconscious, so perhaps he had misheard Una's response to his question, *Why did you not go?*

Idiot man, Una had said, as though there was some blindingly obvious truth in front of him. A woman's thing, obviously, something a mere man could not expect to understand.

'I'll wake her up, send her back to her own bed.' Berig stretched out his hand. 'She is cold.'

'I told you, shock. How much fighting and bloodshed do you think a well-bred Roman maiden sees up close?' And he had forced her to sew up that wound. Why? It had seemed right at the time; now he was unclear about his motives and vaguely guilty. Was he testing her courage, testing why she had stayed and not fled him? Or was it simply that he wanted to feel her hands on him again?

'Leave her,' he said abruptly, drawing another blanket over the slender body that seemed so small in his bed. Smoke climbed up and stretched out beside her, appearing to approve of the bigger bed that gave him more room.

'Do you want my bed?' Berig said. 'I can sleep on the floor.'

'You snore, brat.' Wulfric slapped his shoulder lightly. 'I need the width of the tent between us if I'm to sleep. I'll take hers.'

It took a while to get comfortable in the smaller bed. It was his arm aching that made it so difficult to settle. It was nothing to do with the soft feminine scent that crept into his nostrils from the covers, nothing to do with the sight of the pitifully small number of female gewgaws that Una had lent Julia and which stood on the chest: a comb, a girdle, a small jar of some oil.

Tomorrow, on their way south, he could take her into the city, leave her at the Basilica. It had been declared a place of sanctuary; she would be safe there until she could send word to her family. And he knew, as he thought it, that he would do no such thing. She was his now, and his she would stay. But what she was to him, he found he had no idea.

Wulfric curled his left hand around his sword hilt and tried to make himself relax. It felt strange, wrong-handed, unsettling. But perhaps that was just this strange mood, he had practised fighting using either hand often enough.

A gentle, bubbling snore from the far side of the tent made him smile. Nothing, it seemed, disturbed Berig's sleep. The boy had done well that day. Wulfric had been aware of him on the edge of his vision, circling, watching his back, standing up to Rathar's man who was older, taller and more experienced.

He would let the boy use his own second sword now; it was time he learned to handle the heavier blade. Planning sword exercises for Berig was soothing. Wulfric's hand relaxed on the hilt, and he slept.

'Oh!' The exclamation was soft, but it woke him, the weapon already in his hand. It was Julia in her shift, with Smoke by her side. She was flushed, tousled, and had obviously just pulled off her tunic as she had stumbled across the tent to her bed space. 'I am sorry, I thought you were still out.'

Wulfric laid the sword beside the bed. 'Are you warm now? You were cold before.'

She chafed her hands up and down her arms. 'I was, I should have brought a blanket.' Her eyes were heavy and blurred with sleep.

He moved across the bed, flipping back the cover. 'Here, get in.'

Julia did as he told her, slipping in on his left side. It caught him by surprise, he had not expected her to obey, then he saw she was almost asleep on her feet, far too tired to take in what was happening. He pulled the blanket back, curled his good arm around her and lay still while she shuffled herself into a comfortable position, tucked in against him.

'Julia—' But she was already asleep again, her head heavy on his arm, the curves of her bottom snuggled against his hip. Wulfric drew in a deep breath, thankful he had left on his linen drawers. He had acted on impulse just now and the consequence was to find himself in bed with almost overwhelming temptation. On the other hand, attempting to seduce a well-bred Roman virgin with one arm virtually useless was hardly likely to end in satisfaction for anyone.

He grinned at himself, set his mind to ignore the discomfort her closeness was causing, and closed his eyes against the soft darkness of her hair. *At least you've admitted it,* his conscience murmured. *You want her.*

Chapter Eight

Julia began to drift up out of sleep into a warm, semi-waking doze. She was snug, comfortable, and there was a safe, strong body pressed against her back. Warm breath tickled her temple, stirring the hair. 'Smoke! Stop it,' she grumbled. Something moist touched her ear. 'Bad wolf! I want to sleep.'

The throaty chuckle brought her fully awake with a gasp. Wolves did not chuckle. Wolves, she realised belatedly, were not large enough to stretch along the full length of her body, nor did they have hands to hold her while their mouth teased over her cheek and neck.

'What are you doing?' Her voice was muffled by her own hair.

'Trying to kiss you.' Wulfric's voice was husky and amused.

'Don't—' It was half-hearted; the sensations the gentle brush of his mouth were creating were playing havoc with her shyness and her good sense. She tried again. 'You should not.'

'I am not moving my wounded arm.' The words buzzed, his lips had found the soft skin behind her ear and were nuzzling it. His moustache and beard added an extra layer of sensation to the skilful touch. Julia wriggled and froze as she realised just how hard, and how aroused, the long male body she was spooned into had become.

'Never mind your arm! That is not what I meant and you know it,' she tried to scold. It did not sound very convincing. 'You promised me you would not… Aah!' The fall of his hair brushing her cheek felt as though a million feathers were brushing the skin, every touch seemed to find a nerve.

'I promised I would not ravish you. Do I appear to be ravishing you?'

'Seducing, then.' He was certainly doing that. Why should the nip of his teeth on her earlobe have her stifling a moan? He took the flesh gently into his mouth and she gasped as he suckled it.

Reluctantly he released her ear. 'I never said anything about seduction.'

'I am a virgin,' she protested, as much to remind herself as to shame him.

'I am not.' Wulfric's left hand began to stroke over her breast, the heat of his skin burning through the thin shift. To her mortification the nipple hardened instantly under his palm.

'I can tell,' she said shakily.

'Good.' She could feel his smile against her skin. He turned her within his arm until she lay on her back and he could raise himself on his left elbow and look down at her. 'Just what do you expect me to do when I wake up to find a woman in my bed? My woman?' He bent and began to lick thoughtfully along her exposed collarbone. 'You taste… good.'

'It is my bed,' she protested faintly, fighting the instinct to reach up and pull the weight of his body down over hers. The scent of him, male, musky, aroused, filled her nostrils, over-whelmed her senses.

'I was here when you got into it,' he pointed out. 'And you were in mine first. Where was I to go?'

'Stop teas—' His mouth silenced her, sliding with sleepy sensuality from side to side while his tongue worried at the join of her lips. He wanted her to open her mouth, let him invade it as he had in that hot, furious encounter in the bath-tub. Well, she would not. Not this time. Julia pressed her lips together and tried to ignore her body's urgent message that it wanted her to open to him, to have him touch her everywhere, to move his weight over her and take her.

Oh, but it was hard to resist, so hard when she wanted to yield more than anything. Anything—except that tiny flame of pride and resistance and the fear that if she once gave way to him she would go down like dried grass before a fire.

Julia reached up, wove her fingers into the mass of hair that fell around their faces, and tugged. She wanted to stroke it instead, to feel it sweep over her naked body, to fist her hands into it and drag Wulfric's lips to her breasts, but she persisted until he freed her mouth.

Amused, sensual green eyes looked down into hers. She tried to project anger and rejection, but knew all she could manage was a sort of helpless yearning.

'You want me to stop?'

'Yes!' He rolled on his back and Julia suppressed a shiver at the sudden sense of loss. 'Besides anything else,' she hissed, 'Berig is asleep just the other side of the tent.'

'I was kissing you very quietly,' Wulfric pointed out. 'Just kissing.'

'That was all you were going to do?' she asked, suspicious.

'Of course.' Wulfric sat up, giving Julia a magnificent

view of his naked torso. She suppressed a gulp. This close, and without her vision being clouded with anger and fear as it had been in the tub, she could see the superb muscle definition, the marks of old wounds, newer scars, fresh bruises. She gripped her hands together to stop herself reaching out and touching him.

He swung his legs out of bed and she instinctively put up her hands to cover her eyes. When she peered out between cautiously spread fingers she saw he was at least decently clad from the waist down and dropped them before he saw her reaction.

'Why?'

'Why what?' Wulfric bent to pick up the sword in his right hand and she saw the beads of sweat start out on his brow as the wounded muscles tightened.

'Why were you kissing me? And don't do that! You will burst the stitches, or make it bleed or something.'

He shifted the weapon to his other hand. 'I was kissing you because you are mine,' he said with the arrogance that never failed to take her breath away. 'And one day you will not want me to stop—we just have to find that day. And you are right, it is too soon to use that arm.' He lifted the edge of the curtain and looked back at her as she sat, bolt upright and rosy with desire, anger and shame. 'Time to get up, Julia Livia, we have a long day today.'

She was still in turmoil when she joined Una outside to make the porridge that the other woman declared they would all need to give them energy.

'What is the matter? The milk, please—yes, that is enough.'

'That man is the most infuriating, arrogant, high-handed—' It was easier to rant about Wulfric than to wonder if she was not in part to blame for what had just happened.

'His arm hurts?' Una stirred the pot and added a handful of dried berries and nuts. Around them the camp was like a disturbed ants' nest. People, many still rubbing the sleep from their eyes, were moving carts, untying tent ropes, herding protesting animals.

'Yes, although he will not say so.' Julia took the goat's halter rope and tied it up away from the food. She had a sinking feeling that milking it was next on Una's list of useful skills she must learn.

'He is in a temper?'

'Oh, no, it isn't that—' Julia realised where this was going and shut her mouth with a snap.

'Oh, ho!' Una grinned. 'So he is wanting to—what is the word?' Her brief gesture was shockingly explicit.

'Make love?' Julia mumbled. 'Have sex? Yes.'

'Do you not want it? Wulfric is a very attractive man,' Una added with all the impartiality of a happily married woman.

'Yes, I do, and yes, he is, and, no, I am not going to give in to him,' Julia said emphatically.

'Another man would force you.' Una stirred the porridge. 'You are his to do what he wants with.'

'If he were that sort of man, then I would not want him, so all I would have to worry about is where to find the knife to kill him with.' Julia banged the water bucket down in front of the goat, splashing it and making it back away with a wild roll of its strange yellow eyes.

Una gave a gasp of laughter, then her face became expressionless. Julia turned to see what she was looking at and found herself almost face to face with a tall woman of about her own age. Golden plaits clasped with gold knots lay on either breast. Her clothes were edged with fine needlework and bracelets clasped her arms.

She looked down her long nose at Julia, then turned her wide blue eyes on Una. 'Una.' Julia could not follow the rest of the exchange, but it seemed to be a patronising enquiry about Una's health delivered in a manner that showed no real concern whatsoever.

Julia untied the goat and led it firmly—and quite unnecessarily—through the gap between the two women. The stranger drew back her skirts with a glare, and a further question.

'This is Julia, of Wulfric's house,' Una replied in Latin.

'A new slave? Is she any good?' The woman switched languages with ease.

'At cooking?' Una pursed her lips. 'No.' There was such a wealth of meaning in her expression that Julia felt herself go scarlet. 'That is not why Wulfric took her.'

The other woman swept Julia with a furious look and turned on her heel.

'Una! How could you! She thinks that I'm his…his…'

'She thinks you are where *she* wants to be, in his bed. That is Sunilda, daughter of Hilderic. Her father wants Wulfric as a son. Sunilda just wants Wulfric.'

'To marry? Would he? She does not seem very pleasant.'

'Oh, yes, he would marry her. He would have already, I suspect, if he had not so many other things to think about. She would bring the allegiance of many men to his side and she is strong, fit to be a leader's wife. And not displeasing to the eye.'

'But you do not like her?'

The way Una broke an egg was sufficient answer. 'She thinks I am below her. She speaks to me only because Berig serves Wulfric.'

'She is my enemy now you have said those things to her.' Julia led the bewildered goat back and tied it up.

'And you are hers, that is more important. You are fore-warned. Do you want her as a mistress?'

'No!' *And I do not want her as Wulfric's wife either.* 'Does he love her?'

'He hardly knows her. And it is his duty to marry well for his kin and his allies. Love is not—oh, I do not know the words. Love is not in the stew pot.'

'But you are trying to tell me I can stop the marriage—that I should stop it?'

'Sometimes it is necessary to see a long way forward. Not everything is what it seems at this moment.' Una was looking into the porridge pot like an oracle reading the entrails of a pagan sacrifice. She raised her head and held Julia's questioning gaze. 'You will not leave now. You will not run away.'

'I will!' The promise was startled out of Julia before she had the wit to keep quiet. 'How would you like to find yourself a slave of Rome? Wouldn't you try to escape?'

'Not having heard what you Romans do to runaways, no,' Una said drily. 'You do not like being Wulfric's, but if you run away he will not hurt you, only bring you back.' She reached for the bowls and began to ladle porridge. 'Call the men, it is ready. Have you seen a slave being mistreated while you have been amongst us?'

'I have seen no slaves.' Julia took the bowls and began to set them out. Berig had already loaded their trestles onto a cart, so they were sharing Una's table.

'That is because you cannot tell the difference by looking. Slaves belong to families, are part of families. Everyone has duties.'

Wulfric had been furious with her because she did not know the little slave girl's name, Julia remembered. It had seemed strange then; now she began to understand. Once you were in a barbarian household, however you got there, everyone had a responsibility towards you, just as you had duties to them. She had felt lonely all the time at home. Here, she had never felt that sense of distance, the chill of her parents' house. She had told herself that marriage to Antonius Justus would give her a sense of belonging, of being valued for who she was, not as a gaming piece on the board where family and civic status was decided. Now she wondered.

'Where are they?' Una fisted her hands on her hips and looked around. 'Berig! Come and eat!' She nudged Julia, gently. 'Sit down, do not wait on the men or it will be cold. What do you think about?'

'The man I am supposed to marry.' Julia picked up a horn spoon and attacked the porridge, suddenly ravenous.

'Ah! And what is he like?'

'He is a senator. Thirty years old. A prosperous man with influence with the emperor.'

'You are not hot for him?'

'Una!'

The older woman grinned and nodded her head to where Wulfric was striding towards them, Berig at his heels. 'He is not—' Defeated, she waved her hands towards Wulfric in one of her graphic gestures. It conjured up height, power and, although Julia had no idea how she conveyed it, sex.

'No,' she agreed ruefully. 'He is not.'

'What are you women talking about?' Wulfric enquired as they both burst into giggles.

'*Gumans,*' Una said. *Men*. Julia knew that word, she realised. Gradually things were sinking in. 'And how you are never on time when you are wanted.' She gestured at the cooling bowls of porridge. 'Eat, it is the last hot food you will get all day.'

They ate, and then they packed. Julia folded textiles into chests, nested cooking and eating utensils together in boxes of straw, lugged everything to the front of the tent for Berig to drag out.

It seemed Wulfric had not been joking when he had teased her about Rhenish glassware and chests of silver. As the tent emptied and the two ox carts outside became even more laden, the men carried out locked chests with great care and loaded them in the centre of the front cart.

'Where is all the gold?' Julia asked, half jesting as she paused for a rest, rubbing the back of her forearm across her damp face.

'Where I can find it,' Wulfric said, his eyes narrowing as he looked at her. He was hefting a bundle of spears one-handed, his wounded arm thrust into a belt as a makeshift sling. 'Why? Are you thinking of departing with a bag of it?'

Julia pursed her lips and shrugged, aiming for maximum insolence. She had no intention of taking anything, but she did plan to slip from the back of the cart as close to the city as possible. There would be throngs of people and animals; it would be easy to get lost in the crowd, in a confusion of scents that even Smoke would have difficulty interpreting.

The wolf was standing outside the tent, his tail waving slowly back and forth as he eyed the oxen through slitted green eyes. Julia had never seen him so much as lift a lip towards the goats and chickens that were everywhere in the camp: perhaps he regarded oxen as outside the prohibition on killing livestock.

'Fool of a wolf.' His master grinned at him. 'They are too big, even for you. Go and guard.' For a moment Julia feared Wulfric meant to guard her, but the wolf sprang up into the front cart and lay along the wide box seat that formed the perch for the driver.

Ah, so that is where the gold is. Not that it was any concern of hers. All she needed to concentrate on was getting away while she still had some peace of mind left. But she was beginning to fear that peace of mind was not what she truly craved and that what she wanted was to throw pride and duty and all the years of her upbringing to the winds to be with this man.

Wulfric was leaning against the cart, laughing at something Una's husband had said to him. His head was thrown back so she could see the tendons of his throat, the hard, strapping muscle of his neck. His stance shouted of power and arrogance and confidence, but his eyes were full of humour and, as she watched, he stooped quickly to scoop up a toddler who was intent on making his escape from his mother.

Children trust him, she thought, recalling the small boy he had lifted onto his horse that first day. *Berig would die for him, hundreds of men will follow him to the ends of the earth.* She saw the flickering sideways looks that virtually every woman who passed gave him and the broad smile of the young mother who came to take her child from his arms. *And the women all want him. And he wants me…as a slave to warm his bed, and cook his food and stitch his clothes or his wounds. He will protect me and give me pleasure—and* that *woman will marry him.*

'What are you thinking about, Julia?' He had turned from the cart and was watching her, the laughter still in his eyes, and her heart contracted.

'I was thinking it was time to be going,' she said steadily.

'Aye.' He looked up at the sky. 'The sun is climbing. Another hour and we must be gone.'

Chapter Nine

The carts were loaded at last, the tents were strapped over them to protect the contents, and the oxen were turned to the south. All around small boys were herding goats and sheep, the older ones mustering the spare horses while mounted guards rode out on the flanks. Somewhere up at the head of the column was the king, his household and the emperor's captive sister, Galla Placidia. What was she thinking now? She did not even have the distraction of loading wagons and chasing errant goats.

Julia reached up to climb into the back of the second of Wulfric's wagons, then gasped as he caught her round the waist and steered her to the front of the first. 'Up you go.' His hand in the small of her back moved to give her a firm boost under one buttock as she scrambled up onto the high seat of the front one. 'Here, take the reins.'

'I cannot drive,' she protested, trying to ignore the sensation that his fingers had branded their impression on her behind.

'Of course you can, there is nothing to it. Just follow the cart in front. Berig is right behind you, driving the other.'

And he was, of course, right behind her where he could not fail to notice if she left the cart. And, as the driver, her absence would be noticed by everyone around them. Wulfric put the reins into her hands. 'Here, you need do nothing unless they begin to veer off the road.' She snatched them and shuffled the heavy leather between her fingers.

'You…' Julia bit her lip to catch back the angry words. He had guessed what her plan would be and had acted, without fuss, to check her. What could she say?

It was clear Wulfric could read her thoughts quite easily. 'Know your opponent, Julia Livia. It always pays to imagine what you would do yourself if you found yourself in their shoes,' he added, with what seemed to her to be typical male smugness.

'Really?' she retorted. 'Your imagination runs to being the female sex slave of a barbarian kidnapper, does it?' She did not want to leave him, but she knew she must. The fact that he was frustrating her every effort to do what, in the long run, would be better for both of them made her furious with him. Did he really want her around when he brought home the imperious Sunilda?

She expected to shock him perhaps, or to anger him. What she did not expect was for him to burst out laughing. *'Sex slave?'* He grinned up at her as she sat fulminating on the high seat. 'You cannot begin to imagine the ideas that *that* conjures up.'

'Oh! You oaf!' Julia reached for the long iron-tipped goad that was the equivalent of a whip for the oxen, but Wulfric had already vaulted into the saddle of the grey horse and was riding off, audibly chuckling.

Ideas? What on earth could he mean? The problem was, the more she thought about it, the more arousing it became, even with her very limited experience of sensual matters.

Lurid fantasies of chains—light, and of a precious metal,

naturally—of skimpy silken garments, of Wulfric stretched out on a couch, watching her from under hooded lids as she prepared to oil his naked body, all chased their way through her imagination. She was vaguely aware of her breath coming shorter, very acutely aware of the weight of her breasts, of her nipples peaking hard against the linen undershift, of the heat pooling in her…

There was a lurch. Julia woke from her erotic trance with a start and grabbed the reins as the oxen, not waiting for her, began to plod along behind the cart in front.

Oh, my goodness, is Wulfric thinking about things like that too? Probably not, probably nothing so naïve. Probably he is imagining things so shocking I would faint if he told me…perhaps he would show me… Julia gave herself a sharp and painful pinch on the wrist. *Stop it! This is wrong, so wrong. You do not belong here, you should not want him, let alone think about him like this.*

But it seemed that her only hope of escape now was the force of four thousand sent by the Eastern Empire, and, if they came, then many of these people, people she was already beginning to like and admire, would die. Honorius had promised them land, she thought, as they moved at the speed of a creeping tide across the wide grassy plain. No one denied that on either side. Why then did he not give it to them?

She racked her brains to recall the conversations she had dismissed as boring and irrelevant only weeks before. Her father and Antonius Justus had seemed to feel that to break these promises was justifiable because they were not in Rome's interests any longer and both she and her mother had nodded at this sage and eminently sensible male opinion.

Now she seethed with indignation at the perfidy of such a course. One of the oxen stumbled, bringing her attention back to what she was supposed to be doing. 'Oh, get up, you clumsy beast,' she berated it irritably, then heard herself.

It seemed she did nothing but lose her temper these days—at Wulfric, at the emperor, at the oxen. Or was it simply that she felt everything more intensely since she had seen the big man stride out of the drifting smoke to turn her life upside down? She felt anger and injustice and fear and passion and deeply conflicting loyalties, all with a fierceness she had never experienced before. *When I get home,* she thought, sitting up straighter and making herself pay attention to her surroundings, *when I get—where has it gone?*

She craned round, desperate, and realised that as she had brooded they had passed out of sight of the city, out of sight of the walls, and were now following the Via Latina south. Familiar road under the wagon wheels, familiar tombs set along it under the shade of the pines, familiar milestones marking the slowly increasing distance between her and everything else that was familiar.

The vague certainty that sooner or later she would be rescued faded and was gone. Julia stared unseeing between the horns of the oxen. She could not deceive herself any longer: she was entirely in the power of a man who was as alien as the stars to her. And all he wanted from her was obedience, sex and food.

Sex slave! Wulfric kept chuckling to himself as he wove in and out of the wagons, checking who was where, making sure everyone had sound beasts, then riding out to the flanks. Trouble was coming—they were moving too slowly for it not to catch them sooner or later. He did not think it would come yet, but they could not afford to let their guard drop. That was just a fact of life, one they had all lived with for years.

He spent an hour checking, forcing himself to concentrate on every detail while his mind wanted to wander off and play with the lurid images conjured up by Julia's outburst. They simply would not go away and were uncomfortably distracting, if enjoyable.

He found his way back to Berig's wagon, hitched his horse on behind and climbed up to sit beside him. 'Water?'

'Just behind me. I'll have some as well.' They sat in companionable silence, handing the flask back and forth. Berig was watching the passing scene with interest and an alertness that Wulfric knew he should be sharing, instead of gazing at Julia's head and shoulders that were all that was visible of her over the heaped contents of the wagon.

Sex slave indeed... She was just so desirable, and so innocently unaware of how provocative she was. Julia appeared to expect the worst of his motives—which was understandable, considering the circumstances in which he had found her, and the fact that he had snatched her away. But she also appeared to have realised that he was not going to force her.

What she did not realise was that her own untutored body was on his side. Her reactions to his caresses spoke of a deeply passionate nature that the chilly standards of a Roman household had repressed. She certainly did not appear to be pining for her senator.

Wulfric's lip curled as he imagined a pompous, middle-aged, toga-clad type. He would exercise religiously at the gymnasium to keep his body trim for the inevitable marble statue, of course, but he would expect his wife to be as disciplined as himself in dress, deportment and manner. What would he make of the Julia who launched a furious sensual assault on her tormentor in a bath-tub, or who gritted her teeth and sewed up a savage wound despite her churning stomach or who sat in the sunshine rubbing a wolf's stomach while she combed his coat?

'Wulfric?' Berig appeared to have been talking for several minutes. Wulfric jerked himself back from his daydream. 'You said we were going south to get to Africa—where? Is it a long journey?'

'To a city called Neapolis, forty-five leagues or so, so eleven or twelve days, unless we are held up.' Berig's eyes narrowed and Wulfric could see he knew what *held up* meant: a battle. 'There we should find ships.'

'Ships? Is there a river, then?'

'There is a sea. Did you not realise? Africa is the other side of the *Mare Tyrrenhum*.'

Berig shook his head, eyes wide. He had never seen the sea, could hardly imagine it. Wulfric had seen it once, but had never been on it, and he was not at all certain he wanted to start now. Still, if that was the only way to get to the land full of wheat, then that was what they must do.

'Does Julia know?'

'I expect so.'

'She did not seem very worried.' Berig sounded resentful that a woman was not afraid of this mysterious force that made him quake inwardly.

'I don't think she was still expecting to be with us when we got there,' Wulfric said wryly, his eyes returning to the dark head in front.

It took twelve days to reach Capua, just north of Neapolis, and by the time they got there Julia was beginning to feel she had lived no other life than this. Up at sunrise, loading their overnight things onto the wagons after a simple breakfast, the slow lumbering progress along the valley of the River Trerus, a noon meal of bread and cheese snatched as they moved and then the evening camp.

It was curiously enjoyable. She had given up all plans for escape while they moved, for her place on the wagon had effectively chained her in full view as Wulfric had intended. Instead, the very absence of freedom was relaxing. There was nothing she could do, so she could watch the unfolding scenery, spend minutes gazing up at a wheeling eagle, or look for fish jumping in the river.

People began to move from wagon to wagon, sitting for a while at each to gossip. Una joined her now and again, bringing friends, patiently trying to teach her some words and phrases in Gothic.

Berig she saw only in camp, Wulfric hardly at all except as an ever-present beacon in the mass of travellers. Tall on the grey horse, he seemed tireless, riding the boundaries of the group, chivvying stragglers, talking to the outriders, vanishing now and again over the bordering hills and returning to gather the men around him.

He was using both hands on the reins again, she noticed, wishing he would let her dress the wound again, check that there was no infection. In the evenings he would join them, help Berig pull the tent out from the wagon on to poles to make a shelter, return for the evening meal and then ride out again. Julia supposed he slept, but she did not know where or when, for he was dressed and ready by the time she was sleepily heating water in the morning.

After six days she cornered Berig. 'Why is Wulfric ignoring me?'

He squinted at her against the rising sunlight. 'He isn't, he's busy. Why, is there something you want to know?'

'No, not exactly. It's just…' *Just what? I expect him to be trying to seduce me, to be stopping by for long, friendly chats? You are a besotted fool, Julia Livia.*

Berig shrugged, mumbling through a mouthful of bacon. 'Don't know what you're fussing about, then.' He shifted, looking vaguely embarrassed. 'Did you know we've got to go in boats, across the sea?'

'Yes, of course. Didn't you?' She put down the knife she was cutting bread with and regarded him with some amusement. Berig was considerably less cocksure all of a sudden.

'Er, no. Have you ever been on the sea?' She nodded. Coastal voyages for short distances only, but she was not going to admit that. 'What is it like?'

'Huge, wet water as far as you can see to the horizon and beyond. And waves. Great big ones.' She plunged her hand into the water bucket to demonstrate. 'The ship goes up and down and side to side and you have to learn to balance.'

Berig was going faintly green just thinking about it and she stopped teasing him, conscious that, for all her nonchalance, she was not looking forward to being out of sight of land either. All the more reason to escape before it came to it.

Five days later she was brooding on that exchange when the lead wagons began to pull up. All around her people were reining in, men jumping down, pulling weapons from under their covers, mounting up.

'What is it?' Julia stood up and turned round, calling down to Berig, who was leading his team up alongside hers.

'We go to take Capua. Here.' He thrust the reins into her hands. 'You'll have to make camp by yourself. And get the medical kit out.'

'I…why? When will you be back?'

Berig was already swinging up onto his horse, Wulfric's shield in his hand, a long knife hanging at his belt.

'When we've taken it, of course.' And then he was gone, leaving her staring after him. Wulfric? Where was he? He had gone without saying goodbye and he might never come back. *But why should he bother? I'm not anything important to him, I'm just a slave he doesn't even talk to any more.*

Julia sat down with a bump. For the first time since he had taken her the tears filled her eyes and fell unchecked. When Una found her she was crouched on the seat, head in hands, a huddle of damp misery, two lots of reins tangled around her feet and the oxen, heads down, cropping grass amidst the organised chaos of making camp.

'Julia! What is it?' Una climbed up awkwardly, sat down next to her and gathered her in her arms. The warm, maternal affection made it worse. Julia sobbed harder. 'He is coming back. He always comes back.' Una patted her back.

'He didn't say goodbye.' Julia emerged, scrubbing her hand across her wet face, awkwardly aware that she was making an exhibition of herself. 'He has hardly spoken to me for days.' It was embarrassing that Una had known unerringly what she was crying about.

'Tsk.' Una clicked her tongue. 'You have to get used to that. He is a warrior, he has other things to think about at the moment. Now come, jump down and wash your face and we will help each other.'

The men returned by nightfall the next day, captured pack ponies and wagons behind them. The women fell on their menfolk to check for wounds and then on the food in the carts; the guards who had been left behind gathered noisily around their comrades, demanding details and receiving their share of the plunder.

But there was no sign of either Wulfric or Berig; the crowd was too dense to get through and her pitiful few words of Gothic vanished entirely in the effort of making herself understood.

Then, just when she thought she would collapse with tension and uncertainty, Wulfric strolled out of the crowd, leading his horse and followed by Berig. Neither of them appeared to have so much as a scratch on them, both were filthy with sweat, dust and soot and, to Julia's wrathful eye, both seemed to be indecently pleased with themselves.

'At last!' she stormed the moment they were within earshot. 'Everyone has been back an hour and now you condescend to put in an appearance. I suppose you want hot water and food? Well, there isn't any. I assumed you were both dead and wouldn't be needing it.'

She flung down the dead chicken she had half plucked and mangled in her distracted state and fled round the back of the wagon.   Behind her she heard Berig's voice raised in mystified indignation. 'What's the matter with her? You'd think we had lost!'

Wulfric answered, 'There is a great deal you must learn about women, Berig, not least that the more worried they are about you, the louder they shout at you and the harder they beat you when they know you are safe.'

He was coming around the back of the wagon now, and there was nothing, short of fleeing through the camp making a spectacle of herself, that she could do about it.

'Are you going to beat me?' he enquired. Julia kept her back turned and shrugged.

'You aren't worth it. I wasn't worried, just annoyed that I did not know what was going on. And…and your stupid arm probably hasn't healed and you wouldn't be able to fight properly and you'd get yourself killed and then what would happen to me…but that aside, why should I be upset?'

Wulfric did not answer her, simply put his hands on her shoulders, cupping the narrow bones with the hard framework of his fingers, and turned her against his chest.

'I don't know why you had to go and attack the town anyway, can't we simply go round it?' He smelled just as bad as he looked, he was probably making her tunic filthy and her face was pressed against decidedly uncomfortable chain mail. She wrapped her arms round as much of his torso as she could manage and clung harder.

'We needed the food and we had to make sure there was no garrison there that could swing round and attack from the rear,' he explained patiently.

'There was no gold, I suppose?' Julia said, attempting to maintain her anger. She could feel bare skin against her forehead as she snuggled closer. A pulse beat steadily. Hers was going wild with what had to be relief and reaction.

'Some, my disapproving Roman.'

Julia pulled away from his chest, tipping her head back to look up into his face. From this angle his lashes were long, shuttering his expression, making him seem more serious than his jesting tone implied.

'Was anyone hurt?' She bit her lip. 'Tell me truthfully, and about your arm.'

'We lost five men. Perhaps twenty are wounded, not very badly. And you may inspect my arm if you wish.'

'Who has been looking after it?' Julia demanded as Wulfric leaned back against the wagon, pushed up his sleeve and began to unknot the bandage. It was not the original one, she was glad to see, but it was filthy and stained.

'Berig. It is not very nice to look at while it heals.' He began to unwind the bandage.

'It was not very *nice* when you made me stitch it. Let me.' She had to soak off the cloth in the end, horrified at how the wound looked. 'Where are the stitches?' Running to find fresh linen rags, she began to swab it clean.

'I cut them out once it started healing, otherwise they pull.' He put a finger under her chin and tipped up her face. 'Are you crying?'

'No. My eyes are watering with the smoke. Oh, yes, all right, I am trying *not* to cry, if you must know. I don't like people I…'

'People you what, Julia?'

Oh, Lord! I love him. Why did I not realise that before?

'I don't like people I know being hurt.' She jerked her head away and bent over the wound again. 'There, that's better. Just keep it still and I'll get some of Una's salve.'

Julia hurried off, thankful for the excuse. She had nearly told Wulfric she loved him, almost blurted it out before she had known it herself. He would be kind about it, of course, she knew him well enough now to know that. But she had not the slightest doubt that he would use the knowledge ruthlessly to seduce her. He already regarded her as his property—she had almost handed him the lock and key to the door.

And her head was spinning with what she had found out about herself, what it would mean. *Nothing but trouble, nothing but pain. Oh, but I love you…*

Chapter Ten

As Wulfric had seemed to distance himself from her on the journey south, now Julia tried to keep her distance from him. The violence of her anxiety when she knew he was fighting had shaken her into acknowledging her feelings, but she had not realised love would be like this, that it would make her berate him like a fishwife out of sheer relief that he was safe or that it could tangle her tongue and drive a chariot and horses through her wits. And she had no idea how to hide how she felt from him.

Una had guessed, but she did not tease Julia when the men were near enough to hear. Julia wished she could confide in her, but she hardly knew herself just what it was she feared or what she might expect, or hope for, in her future.

She was more prepared when the men rode out to take Nola, and they were gone for a shorter time. Wulfric sent Berig back directly to the wagon to tell her they were safe, although she disguised her relief by telling him he had only been so thoughtful because he wanted her to begin cooking the evening meal.

So another town had fallen, filling the larders, and making the axles of the treasure wagons creak. Satisfied he had covered their rear, Alaric the King swung his followers towards Neapolis and its great bay.

'There is smoke coming out of that big mountain,' Berig observed as they sat waiting while the tactics for the siege were discussed. He was showing very little interest in the sea and Julia guessed he was trying not to think about it, or what it would be like on one of the ships that bobbed on its surface like so many toys.

'It is called a volcano. Its roots go down to Hades and sometimes the Devil sends up molten fire and ash and it covers the land. At least, that is what I have been told.' Looking around at the fertile slopes covered in vines and olives and little tilted fields, it was difficult to believe.

'Often?' Berig looked alarmed.

'Not for three hundred years,' Julia reassured him. 'Anyway, we will not be here long, will we?'

She had meant it would not be long before Alaric had subdued Neapolis and forced the surrender of the ships that clustered in the bay, enough to ship even his great army of Goths across the sea. But the city held out stubbornly behind its thick walls. Supplied by sea, it could not be starved into submission, and two weeks later Julia found she was still looking out over the same wide, beautiful azure bay—from the shore.

Wulfric climbed back to the level ground where the encampment lay. Behind him the besiegers were breaking camp, following Alaric's order to abandon the attempt on the city. He rolled his shoulders, glad of the chance to move again after two hours of tense Council.

The king had decided to press on south to Rhegium. His

brother-in-law Athaulf counselled turning back. Wulfric, opposed from the beginning to the march south, had been torn. They had gone too far, beyond the point of no return. To have come south in the first place had been an error, to go back would be to march into the teeth of an army. Today he had thrown his weight behind the king and was in no very sanguine mood as a result.

'We pack and move tomorrow,' he threw at Berig as he strode up to the wagon and pulled a flask of wine from the back. It was good stuff, too good to be gulped down like water, but it answered his need. 'Where is Julia?'

'I don't know. I haven't seen her since early.' Berig peered about as though she might be hiding behind a wagon. Smoke lay in the shade, his tail stirring the dust in greeting. 'Perhaps she's with Una.'

'Then go and check.' Wulfric hunkered down alongside the wolf and resisted the temptation to scratch his healing wound, which was itching like the devil as the new skin grew. He scratched Smoke's ears instead. 'Where is she?' The wolf whined and got to its feet as Berig ran back.

'Una hasn't seen her all day,' he panted. 'And I haven't seen her since we broke our fast.'

'And it is now mid-afternoon.' Wulfric got to his feet, his heart suddenly erratic. 'Are there any horses missing?'

'There's been no cry put up, the horse lines are all quiet.'

'Then she's on foot.' With perhaps six hours' start. She was light on her feet, toughened by weeks on the road, she could have covered two leagues by now, or have gone to ground in one of the numerous villas and farms that scattered across the fertile slopes.

I could let her go, back to her own people. He gripped the side of the wagon and dropped his head as he wrestled with the thought. *Or she could be hurt, a twisted ankle or worse. Or she could have fallen into the hands of some man—not every Roman in the area is going to treat her like a senator's daughter, especially not dressed from head to foot like a barbarian woman.*

'Smoke! Find Julia, go seek.' The wolf lowered his nose to the ground and began to circle. 'Berig, stand still, let him work. When he picks up the trail I will follow. You pack up. If we aren't back when it is time to leave, get one of the other lads to drive the second wagon and go with everyone else, we will catch you up.'

'If you don't find her?' Berig's face betrayed an anxiety he had never allowed himself to show about Julia before. 'She is only a girl, I don't think she's ever been out in the countryside all by herself before.'

'I will find her.' Wulfric whistled and the big grey walked out from under the shade of an umbrella pine. He unhooked the shield from the pommel and handed it to Berig. 'Give me a short spear. There are wild boar out there.'

Smoke stopped, raised his head and then began to head up the slope. Wulfric mounted and urged the horse after him.

'Good luck!' Berig called, and he raised his spear hand in acknowledgement, forcing his mind into calm as he followed the grey shadow into the scrub. Julia needed him, whether she realised it yet or not, and he was going to find her.

The wolf trotted on steadily, climbing all the time, zigzagging across the slope along the line of a goat track. She did not seem to be heading for the nearest dwellings, which was sensible, but he would have expected her to head south to the angle of the bay where residences clustered thickly. Surely she did not intend to climb the mountain?

He had heard the stories about it, seen the smoke. The

Mouth of Hell, they called it. By now all the demons of hell could have dragged her into it. If she hadn't been raped by some passing peasant, or had fallen into one of the gullies that cut the slope, or... Damnation, he had never been this scared for anyone or about anything. What in Hades was wrong with him now? His nerves seemed to have seeped out of his boots.

Ahead, Smoke gave the sharp bark that was a sign of greeting, his tail began to wag and he bounded forward onto a wide, flat area of short grass that cut the side of the mountain like a terrace. Perhaps it was an old abandoned one, Wulfric thought, craning to see what had excited the wolf and to secure his surroundings, all at the same time.

And there Julia was, demure on a rock, swinging her feet and admiring the view. There was a ridiculous straw sun hat on her head that she must have plucked from a scarecrow as she passed; a rumpled cloth and a flask spoke of a comfortable noon meal, and she was safe. Quite safe.

'Hello!' she called, bending to pull Smoke's ears as the wolf fawned round her feet.

Wulfric threw a leg over the pommel and slid to the ground, slamming the spear point down into the earth as he did so. It was insufficient release for his feelings. He stalked across to the rock, took Julia by the upper arms and hauled her to her feet.

'What the devil do you think you are doing?' He found he was shaking her and made himself stop; she was having trouble answering him with her head jerking back and forth.

'I went for a walk to admire the view. I was bored sitting down there listening to Berig grumbling and having nothing better to do than mend your tunics.' She twisted in his grip. 'Let me go, you oaf—and stop shouting at me!'

'I am not shouting. I am asking you a reasonable question.'

He lowered his voice to a mere bellow and gave her another shake. 'I thought you were lost, or that you had fallen down a ravine or that some peasant had raped you or—'

'Or that I had run away?'

'Yes, or that.' They fell silent, glaring at each other.

'You are angry,' Julia observed at last, watching him from under her lashes.

'Of course I am angry. I was worried about you.'

'I thought only women got angry when they were worried. I thought that men simply took well-planned, decisive action and remained cool and in control.' The minx was taunting him.

'Well, this time I got angry.' *And let her make of that what she will; I have no idea what it means.*

'You are very impressive when you are angry,' she said thoughtfully, deploying those lashes to lethal effect. *Has she the slightest idea what she is doing? I doubt it.* The tip of her tongue came out and just touched the swell of her bottom lip as she pondered.

'Indeed?' Something inside him was building to a dangerous pressure.

'But, naturally, I am not scared of you.'

'You are not? I think that might be somewhat rash of you, Julia Livia.'

'Why?'

'Because I might do this.' He pulled and lifted and in a heart's beat she was in his arms, her feet dangling, her face on a level with his. 'And then this,' he growled, and kissed her. If she had struggled, he would have dropped her, the reasonable voice in the back of his mind told him, and he hoped he believed it. But she did not struggle, or kick. Julia opened her mouth under his, tasting of wine and honey and sweet femininity, and kissed him back with an untutored passion that made the blood roar in his veins.

Her hat fell off. He wanted to run his hands into her hair, but holding her as he was, he could not do anything else. With a snarl of frustration he set her on her feet.

'Ta...take that mail shirt off first,' she stammered, sounding as breathless and disorientated as he felt. He was supposed to be in control of the situation. When the time came he had intended to seduce her slowly, skilfully, until she begged for him. And then, he had planned, he would initiate her into the act of love. And now what was happening? He was as hot and desperate as the most callow youth.

Wulfric unbuckled his sword belt, throwing it to the ground, then bent and dragged the mail tunic over his head, letting it and the linen shirt fall at his feet. The warm breeze ran over his damp skin like a caress as he straightened up and looked at her.

'Are you scared of me yet? Because if you are, say so. Now.'

Julia was looking at him, eyes wide, lips just parted. He thought he had never seen anything more lovely than this slender girl standing knee-deep in wild grasses, her gaze fixed on his face blazing innocence and trust and desire. For him.

'No, I am not scared.' She heard her own lips say the words and marvelled at herself. Of course she was scared. Scared of the sheer size of him, scared that she did not know what to do, scared that she might not please him, terrified that she would let slip that she loved him.

Wulfric stood there in the sunlight, flexing his shoulders now the weight of mail was gone. His upper body was naked except for the bandage on his forearm and the gold bands that strapped wrists and biceps, the heavy gold at his throat. Golden in the light, he looked like a pagan statue against the green of the pines, each muscle defined, the sheen of sweat like the sculptor's gloss on metal.

'Undo your hair.'

Julia lifted her hands and began to free the heavy plaits, watching the way the breeze stirred his long hair on his shoulders, the prickle of his beard still a pleasure-pain on her lips. She shook out her hair and waited, her breath hitching in her throat.

'Julia.' He took a long step forward until he was close in front of her. The heat came off his body like the sun. He ran his fingers through the loosened tresses, combing out the weight, the fine hairs snagging on the roughness of his palms. She reached up and stroked the curling ends of his hair as it lay on his shoulders. It should have made him seem less masculine, but somehow the thick length of it spoke of virility and life. She could understand the potent symbolism of kingship it carried.

He untied her girdle, let it drop, and she kicked her feet free of her sandals, feeling the grass smooth under her soles, every part of her vibrant and alive as she curled her toes in it, seeking sensation.

Wulfric followed suit, dragging his boots off, hurling them aside. Smoke leapt to catch one, making them both laugh, and the apprehension left her like a cloud lifting.

Wulfric came and lifted her chin gently so he could study her face. The clear green eyes that so often seemed cold or jewel-hard were gentle and clear. 'Certain?' he asked quietly.

'Certain.' She nodded.

His thumb pushed at the corner of her mouth as it had once before and this time she let her lips curl up. 'I want to kiss your smile.' His lips, when they met hers, curved in an echo and this time she parted for him, gasping at the heat of his breath in her mouth, fascinated by the taste of him. His beard pricked and tickled, but his moustache was softer against her lips, sending an additional *frisson* of sensation to add to the layers of touch and scent and taste that were assaulting her.

His hands curved round her head, cradling it, angling it gently as he explored her mouth. She was conscious of the sheer size of his hands and of the long fingers as they cupped her skull, conscious that here was a man strong and skilled enough to snap her neck like a corn stem and yet he was touching her with a gentleness that stole her breath and chased away her fear.

Cautiously Julia let her own tongue touch, darting it away with a gasp the first time, then coming back to join his. She had had no idea that kissing could be so complex, so all-involving. It seemed an end in itself, a source of pleasure, of communication, almost of speech. She freed her hands from where they had been crushed against Wulfric's chest and let them stray round his sides, running over the hard muscle, fascinated by the feel of masculine skin under her palms, enjoying the way his body tensed at her touch.

Innocently she had expected that she would simply be a passive recipient of his lovemaking, that he would take his pleasure from her body and she would simply have to allow it. But her instincts, now she was in his arms, were telling her something quite different. They were telling her to make love to him, to take her own pleasure, not just from what he was doing to her, but from her own exploration of his body.

He was so big that reaching round him was futile. She had been tempted for days by the deep valley where his spine curved so elegantly between the muscles of his back, but that would have to wait until they were lying down, she thought hazily. What she could achieve now was to let her hands slide down to where his waist narrowed and the tantalising arrow of hair vanished into the band of his trousers.

Coordination was difficult while Wulfric seemed intent on driving every coherent thought from her head with his kisses. Clumsily she slid her flattened hands beneath the waistband on either side and used her fingertips to stroke as much of the narrow hips as she could reach.

It was enough to bring his head up on a gasp of indrawn air. 'Julia!'

'Yes? Should I not have done that?'

'Ah…' It took him a moment to compose himself. Julia wondered if she was doing something very wrong, or perhaps, very right. 'I think we are wearing far too many garments,' he managed at last.

'Four, I should imagine,' she said earnestly, trying to follow his thoughts. She had not used a breast band since she had begun wearing barbarian dress, which left tunic, under-tunic, his trousers, and, possibly, linen drawers beneath.

'I wasn't counting.' Wulfric caught her tunic and slid it up and over her head. There was a tension, an urgency, in his voice that Julia had not heard before. *I am having this effect on him!*

Her hands, apparently quite capable of carrying on deci-sively while her mind was turning to a sort of sensual mush, were working at the fastenings of Wulfric's trousers, freeing them, and, with quite scandalous boldness, pushing them down over his hips, taking his drawers with them. Until they caught on something.

Wulfric hastily released her and untangled the cloth from the startling evidence of exactly what an effect she was having upon him. 'Oh!' Wide-eyed, Julia took a step back, staring. 'Oh…' *No, that was not physically possible.*

'Do not worry about it.' Wulfric pulled her back against him, still faintly exclaiming. *Surely not…that's easy for him to say!* The panicky thoughts were drowned in a fresh on-slaught of kisses, not so gentle now. They were demanding, forceful, and reduced her to trembling need, even as she curled her arms around his neck to pull his head closer. The hot, hard pressure against her belly reminded her of what she had just seen, but somehow it was less frightening, more exciting.

With a growl Wulfric took the neck of her shift in both hands and tore it open without lifting his mouth from hers. It hung from her arms as his hands found her breasts, bringing gasps of delight against his lips as he stroked and fondled.

She was moaning now against his mouth, arching into his body, desperate for some sort of release from the new, terri-fying intensity of the feelings that were possessing her body. She wrenched her mouth from his to plead. 'Wulfric, please, please…I feel so…'

He bore her to the ground, twisting to cushion her body with his, then rolling her onto her back on the hot, springing grass. His hands were everywhere, stroking, teasing, bringing her quivering flesh into an agony of arousal.

He shifted, his weight over her, nudging her legs apart with his knee. He lifted his mouth and with the release from that sensual onslaught her fears flooded back. 'You are so… Will it hurt?'

'No,' he said firmly, looking down into her eyes. His hand slid between her thighs, into the tangle of hair, into the hot core of her and Julia gasped, her head falling back, her eyes closed. His fingers moved as though they knew her body already, teasing, caressing, touching part of her that had her gasping and arching towards him. Somehow his fingers felt slick, then she realised she was wet, hot, quivering with shameless need for him.

She felt him shift, then without warning he surged against her, filling her, driving into the heart of her with a thrust that filled her with exultation, then a shock of pain that had her eyes flying wide with shocked betrayal. 'You promised!'

'I did not promise, and I lied so that you would not be tense. It was better that way.' He was stroking gently in and out of her, the rhythm stretching yet soothing. The pain did not return, even the residual soreness began to vanish as Wulfric's fingers caressed her temples, brushed lightly where heat and passion stuck the fine hairs to the skin.

The sensation of being utterly filled, utterly possessed, was overwhelming, but Julia realised she was no longer apprehensive. She let herself move with the rhythm Wulfric was setting and stared up in wide-eyed wonder at the elemental strength of his set jaw and rigid muscles. His eyes were closed. She had somehow assumed this would be an easy, a simple, thing for a man, yet he seemed as intent and intense as she.

Even as she thought it he opened his eyes and smiled at her as his fingers brushed again into the tight heat of her body, squeezing between their joining. The spiralling, tight, sensation that had been building became intense, she gasped, panting, reaching for what she did not know, and then as he thrust deep and slow the world spun, fractured, disintegrated into nothing but pleasure and darkness.

Chapter Eleven

It was dark and hot and she was lying crushed under a weight that pinned the whole length of her body. Strangely there was no pain, only, as her senses began to return to her, some strange twinges and aches and a warm glow of pleasure and a certainty that her entire body had experienced some force beyond her understanding.

'Julia?' Wulfric's voice rumbled very close to her ear.

'Wha…what happened? Did the volcano explode?' It was far too difficult to open her eyes.

He gave a snort of laughter and she realised that the weight was his naked body stretched out over hers. 'I *think* I am flattered by that. No, we made love.'

'Oh. Yes.' Her hands were out by her sides. Cautiously she raised them and found she could curl them around his shoulders. He began to nuzzle gently at the angle of her neck and Julia gave a little whimper and clung tighter. 'Are we doing it again?'

His mouth left her skin and his weight shifted, pressing down deliciously on her pelvis. 'I want to.' *Yes, that much was becoming very evident!* 'But—'

'But I did not please you?' Her eyes flew open and she saw immediately that she was wrong—Wulfric looked very pleased indeed. Partly with himself—she was sure there was more than a little smug masculine delight at having reduced her to this state—but mainly, she could see by the tenderness in his expression, with her.

'Oh, yes. Yes, very much. But Berig is going to be worried about us; we thought we had lost you.' His hips began to rock gently against hers and she felt her body arch up to meet his.

Lost you—not *that I had escaped*, Julia realised. There was a difference, although she was not certain what it meant. 'Have we got to go back at once?' she murmured, experimentally running her hands down his flanks and then gripping his buttocks, her fingers digging into the curving hardness.

'Yes, we must, and if you do that—' his head fell forwards, the sweep of golden hair curtaining her face '—it will be midnight before I have the will to stop making love to you.'

Julia raised her head and kissed the sinfully tempting mouth just above hers and pulled his hips as hard as she could against hers. With a growl Wulfric deepened the kiss, his knee pushing her legs apart. It was frightening to make him lose control, but the wickedly feminine delight at being able to do so was far stronger.

'Oh, yes… Urgh!' A hot, wet tongue swiped across her ear and cheek—and from Wulfric's reaction, across his as well.

He rolled off her into a crouch, then sat down with a thump when he saw the culprit. 'Smoke! *Bad* wolf!'

'He was getting bored.' Julia gurgled with laughter, sitting up to pull Smoke's ears. 'Poor old thing.'

'What about me?' Wulfric grumbled, his expression as he turned to look at her belying his tone.

'Not so old,' Julia murmured provocatively. 'Unless, of course, you were glad of the interruption?'

'You—' He leaned to take her shoulder, then rocked back on his heels. 'If I touch you again now, it will be dark before we get back.'

Julia watched him from under lowered lids as he got to his feet as lithely as he had when he was fighting. The movement of his muscles fascinated her as he walked about the meadow, quite unselfconsciously naked, retrieving items of clothing and finding the boot Smoke had made off with. He was beautiful. It was a ridiculous adjective to apply to someone so overwhelmingly masculine, but the combination of proportion and height and colouring could be described no other way.

She sat up, curving her arms around her knees, and stared, quite openly, schooling her face from the wide smile she wanted to give way to into an expression of calm.

'What are you looking at?' Wulfric demanded, one foot into his trouser leg, the other just lifted. Even in that position, a difficult one to maintain with any dignity, his balance was perfect.

You. Just you. 'Nothing, nothing at all.' *I love him so much. I cannot let him see how vulnerable he makes me. And now nothing can ever be the same again.* She shivered, eyes wide, then dropped her head onto her crossed arms, suddenly frightened by what they had just done.

'Get dressed,' he said abruptly, turning to whistle to his horse.

Julia felt a cold knot in her stomach. Had she overstepped the mark in some way? She was so ignorant of men, and of the act of love and what to expect in its aftermath, of how to behave. With uncharacteristic meekness she pulled on her clothes, tied her girdle and waited.

* * *

Hades, she is regretting it already, all the light has gone out of her. She was looking at me with all the joy gone, and then she shuddered and could not meet my eyes. I don't know what to say to her now. Those great brown eyes... Wulfric studied Julia's expressionless face, her downcast lashes, as he rode back to her. *I was clumsy, I hurt her, she's so small.* Even as he thought it, his groin tightened at the memory of how tight she had been, how her body had felt, yielding to his, caressing his within herself.

I meant to make it as easy as I could, and I misjudged it. I gave her some pleasure, but... She puts a brave face on it, teases me...I want more. I want her trust, I want...what? Deep down she must hate me for taking her away, taking her just now.

'Here, take my hand, put your foot on mine.' He leaned down, grasped her wrist and pulled her up easily, turning her so she ended up sitting sideways behind him. After a moment's hesitation slim arms encircled his waist and her body pressed against his back.

What to talk about? *How* to talk to her? All his sexual en-counters before now had been uncomplicated, friendly. You had fun, took and gave pleasure, then lay there afterwards idly talking, drinking perhaps. When you were rested you parted as casually as you had come together. He knew he had learned to be skilful at lovemaking. He enjoyed giving pleasure, enjoyed the softness and inner strength of women, their moods, their laughter—but this one he could not fathom.

'It won't take long to get back down,' Wulfric tossed back over his shoulder. She had probably had more than enough of him and wanted to go and find Una for some feminine company and reassurance. He sat up straighter so that only her clasping arms touched his body.

He was feeling guilty, a thoroughly unfamiliar state. He could recall losing his virginity, a clumsy, fumbling, wonderful experience. It would not be the same for a woman, although he knew he had given her some pleasure, that she had clung to him, kissed him back with fervour. At the time she seemed to enjoy it, while she was in his arms, had wanted more—and now, afterwards, she was regretting it. It was as though he had picked a lily and its tender leaves and petals were wilting, bruised, in his big hands.

They rode in silence until they emerged into the camp ground. 'We move south tomorrow,' he said curtly. 'To Rhegium. With any luck Berig will have packed away everything we do not need tonight.'

He expected questions, but got none. 'Here, let me…' But as he reined in and twisted to help her down Julia slid off the big horse and stood on the trampled earth as though uncertain where to go now. *She does not know where she belongs any more,* he thought with a twist of his heart.

'Julia.'

'Yes?' She looked up, the wide brown eyes shuttered and wary.

'Why did you let me?'

There was a long silence. She did not pretend not to understand him. Then she said the one thing he least expected, her voice cool. 'Because I am yours.' Julia turned on her heel and walked steadily towards the wagon.

Berig was sitting, back against a wheel, rubbing oil into the wooden back of Wulfric's shield. He looked up at the sound of Julia's approach and his face split into a grin. 'Hey! I thought we had lost you. Where did you go?'

'Just for a walk up the mountain. The view over the bay

is lovely from up there, and there is a breeze.' She kept her voice light and cheerful. 'What shall we have for dinner?'

'Fish. I have cleaned it and skewered it and Una brought some green stuff and bread. She is worried about you.' He bent his head over the shield again and added, 'She said to go and see her when you get back. I'll cook the fish if you like.'

'Why, thank you, Berig.' Julia was surprised, and it must have shown in her voice. The youth wriggled uncomfortably and muttered something. 'What?' Julia knelt down next to him.

'I just said, I was worried about you. I know I haven't been very friendly sometimes. Sorry.' He wriggled his shoulders awkwardly. 'You're good for him.'

'Who? For Wulfric?' She could feel the blush hectic on her cheeks. 'How?'

'Don't know.' Berig appeared to be out of his emotional depth. 'You just are.'

Julia did not know what to say. Her feelings were in enough of a turmoil as it was, without trying to fathom out what Berig meant about Wulfric, or why he was apparently prepared to like her now.

'Thank you,' she managed at last. 'I don't blame you for being suspicious of me at first. I didn't much like being here with you both either.'

'You do now?'

'I…I really don't know.' It was days since she had thought of escape, but it was not apathetic resignation or fear that was keeping her here. It was, she realised, a sense of belonging. That, and the fact that, against all sense and prudence, she was in love with Wulfric. 'I'll go and see Una.'

The need for feminine company was pressing. And that was another change. Before, Julia had always kept her thoughts to herself. If she had lost her virginity in Rome, she would not have dreamt of confiding in a friend, let alone her mother. Now she just wanted Una's calm good sense.

'He found you!' Una was playing with her youngest daughter, but she shooed the little girl off to play with her brother when she saw Julia's face. 'Child, are you all right?'

'Yes. Yes, I am perfectly all right.' She sat down on the stool Una pushed towards her and stared at her own clasped hands. 'I think.'

'He made love to you?' The other woman pulled a stool close and put her arm around Julia's shoulders.

'Umm.'

'Do you want to ask me anything?'

Julia shook her head. 'I…it was…I enjoyed it.'

'Well, good! I should hope so, with a man like that!' Una laughed and hugged her. 'And better after the first time, I promise.' Julia stole a sideways look and saw a flicker of anxiety cross Una's face. 'When he—' She flapped her hands in her usual irritation at not knowing the Latin. 'When he finished, did he finish inside you or outside you?'

'Una!' Julia could feel her face reddening. 'What does it matter?'

'It matters if you do not want a baby.'

'Oh.' Naïvely she had not thought of that, even with the constant reminder of Una's burgeoning figure. 'Inside.'

'Ah.' Una took a deep breath. 'Well, not to worry. And if there is one, Wulfric will look after you both.'

'Yes,' Julia said flatly. 'I am sure he will.' She had not been able to think beyond the next day about what the future held for Wulfric and herself. A baby was impossible to imagine.

'You love him, don't you?'

Julia was so preoccupied that she answered without

thinking. 'Yes. Oh, yes, so much. Una—you will not say anything? Please do not.' She caught the other woman's hands in hers imploringly.

'No, I will not. But he will surely know—I do not understand why he has not guessed already. I could see it when he was wounded, even if you could not!'

'I am his slave,' Julia said flatly. 'He owns me, he does as he wishes with me. Now he is kind to me, and he seems to like me. He seemed to like having sex with me. Soon he will need to make a good marriage—to Sunilda probably. I do not want to be the slave girl he—' She struggled to find a repeatable word. 'The slave girl he *uses* when he wants a change from his wife. I do not want to bring up children who have no father and a slave for a mother.'

'He does not have to marry a Visigoth,' Una said slowly.

'What?' Julia stared at her. 'Marry me? Is that what you are saying? You know that is not what he needs. Berig says Wulfric is king-worthy, that when Alaric dies he is a contender to succeed him. For that he needs the right wife who will bring him alliances, does he not? How many spears will I bring to his side?'

'They say that Alaric's brother-in-law Athaulf will marry Galla Placidia. His own wife is long dead.'

'She is the emperor's sister. There is a slight difference,' Julia pointed out drily. 'That would strengthen Athaulf's position, would it not?'

'Yes. With those who think, like Alaric, that we should be some kind of new Romans.'

'What does Wulfric think?'

'Ask him. You may not be married to him, Julia, but you are his woman now. Talk to him.'

Julia nodded and got to her feet, pressing down on Una's

shoulder to stop her rising too. Una caught her wrist. 'When are your courses due?'

'In a day or two.'

'If they do not start, then come and speak to me and we will talk to Wulfric about more than politics.'

Her courses came and Wulfric made no move to so much as touch her hand. Julia wondered if Una had said anything to him, and then became convinced of it when either he or Berig carried the water, lifted the cooking pots and lugged the firewood. She spent a day being embarrassed, then decided that the benefits outweighed the discomfiture and let them do all the manual work.

And the cramps she had suffered before had vanished, she realised with delight. Whether it was simply that she was fitter than she had ever been, or whether it was a welcome outcome of losing her virginity, she had no idea, but she felt well. If she had not been in such a state about Wulfric, she would have been unconditionally happier too.

At the end of the week they were nearing Rhegium. The journey had been slower the further south they went. It was hotter despite the fact they were into October, the road worse, the landscape raw and difficult. There was an edginess about the way the men scanned the horizon constantly, the numbers of outriders patrolling the hills, the way the women kept the children closer.

Julia realised that Wulfric was remaining as distant as a man who ate and slept every night next to the same wagon as her could be. Was it simply the same tension that gripped them all, the sense that the closer they came to the very tip of Italy, with their backs to the sea, the more vulnerable they all were?

Or had Una told him she was in love with him, and he was avoiding her because of that? Or did he fear she would expect him to make love to her again and he did not want to? *Talk to him,* Una had said. Well, she would if she could, for she had a head full of questions, but no chance to ask them.

But he had time to talk to Sunilda, she noticed, watching them through eyes narrowed by sunglare and suspicion as they stood in the shade of a grove of olives encircling a wellhead.

The boys were raising water to tip into the long troughs for the livestock and the stop would last for over an hour. Sunilda had sauntered up, hips swinging in a predatory prowl that had Julia hissing with dislike. Instantly she had taken her water jug and gone back to the wagon, leaving them alone.

They made a handsome pair, she thought miserably. They were both tall, both golden haired, both so obviously with shared understandings and backgrounds. Sunilda was flirting, Julia decided, watching the way she gazed intently into Wulfric's eyes as he was speaking, the way the full red lips parted in little exclamations at what he said. The tall woman raised one elegantly long hand to touch her hair, allowing the sleeve of her tunic to fall back baring her arm, and thin gold bangles chased themselves down, chiming like bells.

Wulfric seemed intent, watching her. He smiled and she immediately laughed, a sycophantic tinkle of amusement that grated on Julia's raw nerves. Sunilda turned to go, then glanced back over her shoulder, deploying her long lashes in a demure look that sat oddly with her almost physical self-assurance.

'Makes you want to throw up, doesn't it?' Berig observed.

'Yes,' Julia agreed fervently, then caught herself up. 'What *do* you mean, Berig?'

'You know. She's all over him, expects to marry him.

She'll be a pain in the bum when she does,' he added gloomily. 'Bossy cat.'

Julia gasped back a crow of laughter. She really should not encourage him to be rude about the daughter of a powerful ally of his master. With masculine predictability, Wulfric was watching the retreating view of swaying hips with interest.

'She is very attractive,' she said, trying to be fair.

'Huh! He's just bewitched by her tit—um, I mean…' Berig subsided, blushing.

'Well, they are very handsome tits,' Julia said, straight-faced, reducing him to whoops of adolescent laughter.

The silly joke lifted her spirits a fraction, making her feel as young and careless as the boy. Then she looked back at Wulfric and felt her stomach contract with longing. She and Berig might scoff at Sunilda, but the blonde woman was the one who would win, and make both their lives miserable.

'I am going for a walk,' she said to Berig. 'I'll take Smoke, so don't worry.'

The big wolf trotted at her side as she followed an old track along the river bank. After a ten-minute strolling walk it widened out and bent to cross the river by an ancient arched bridge, scarcely wide enough for one laden mule. Julia walked up and leaned on the parapet, staring down into the crystal-clear water beneath her. It was the colour of Wulfric's eyes, just there at the edge of the shadow, she thought. Fish flickered over the pebbles, weed rippled in the current and a little further down an egret rose in a flash of white, circled and landed on a branch over the water. Peace.

Smoke's head turned, the long muzzle lowered, then he gave a gruff bark of welcome and his tail began to wave. Wulfric.

Julia started to straighten up as he strode up the roughly

laid slabs to her side. 'I told Berig where I was going,' she started, defensively.

'I know. I wanted some peace too.' He came to stand behind her. Julia lowered her forearms back onto the parapet.

'There are fish, but they look too small to eat.'

Wulfric moved closer, the hem of his tunic brushing against her, then he was leaning over, his hands braced either side of her elbows, her body trapped between his and the stone of the bridge. 'Show me.'

'There, see in the shadow.' She swallowed, wondering why he had not stood beside her.

'I see.' He bent his head and she felt his hair swing down to brush along the sensitive skin of her neck and shoulder at the edge of her tunic. His hands moved to clasp her hips and he pulled her back against him in one smooth motion.

Julia gasped. He was obviously aroused. She wriggled. He growled. She stood still. He began to bite gently up the column of her neck while one hand freed her. Then her tunic was being pushed up and she felt the friction of his trousers against the backs of her thighs, her buttocks—and then hot flesh pressing against her.

'Wulfric!' She tried to turn, but he held her, bending her forward, holding her still. 'Sunilda—'

'Sunilda is not here.'

What did that mean? That if she was, he would be caressing *her* body?

His hand slid intimately between them, then between her thighs. Julia tightened her muscles, but his knee pushed her legs apart. His fingers slid into the core of her with deadly accuracy. 'You are wet for me. Tell me to stop and I will.'

'Yes! No…' But how? He braced himself over her and slid into her heat with a gasp of pleasure that forced an echo from her own lips. Trapped, penetrated, filled with shocked delight, Julia gazed down helplessly into the water below and saw her own reflection, Wulfric's behind her. It was shockingly arousing.

He began to stroke slowly in and out, his clever, wickedly knowing fingers teasing and tormenting her as she moaned shamefully, arching back against him.

'Come for me, Julia.' His breathing was hoarse in her ears, the spiralling tension was gathering faster, harder, more intensely than before. Almost sobbing, she surrendered entirely to the demands of their bodies and felt the world splinter as he pulled free from her and convulsed against her back with a guttural cry.

Below her, the water seemed to spin into a whirlpool, sucking their reflections down into the depths.

Chapter Twelve

It seemed Wulfric must have picked her up and carried her, for Julia came to her senses sitting on his lap. He was leaning back against the trunk of an old chestnut tree.

'Mmm.' She rubbed her head shamelessly against his shoulder, revelling in the scent of him, the musk of their lovemaking, the aroma of crushed herbs where his boot heels had torn them.

'What is this nonsense about Sunilda?'

Julia had never felt any link of sensibility with her mother, but in that moment she found herself rolling her eyes in exactly the same way Vibia Octavia did when confronted by one of her husband's more obtusely masculine statements.

The mood shattered; she scrambled off his legs and sat facing him on the sheep-cropped grass. 'Nonsense? You flirt with her and then you make love to me and wonder why I question it?'

'I was not flirting.' Wulfric narrowed his eyes and stared at her. 'We were merely talking.'

Julia snorted inelegantly. 'She wanders up, swinging those

hips, pouting those lips, patting her hair and stands there gazing at you as if you are the most wonderful thing in Creation, and you have your tongue hanging out.'

'My tongue was *not* hanging out,' he retorted with dignity, ruining the effect by crowing, 'You are jealous!'

Wulfric obviously considered that flattering. Despite the quivering ribbons of desire that still teased her body, Julia glared at him. *Oh, but he was beautiful,* her treacherous heart sighed. *Like a big, lean, elegant hunting cat coiled there in the shade, waiting to erupt into lethal action.*

'I have no right to be jealous, I am just a slave,' she stated flatly. 'But I have a right to resent it when you flirt with a woman under my nose and then saunter after me to take what you want because you cannot decently have it with her.'

Until she said it, she had not realised that was what she had been thinking. Now her stomach cramped with distaste. Who had he been seeing in his mind as he thrust himself into her? Her dark head or Sunilda's blonde?

Wulfric moved so fast she did not have time to recoil or to be afraid. One moment he had been lounging against the tree trunk, the next he was on one knee before her, his hands clasping her shoulders.

'You are not—you have never been—*just a slave,*' he said flatly, the very lack of emotion in his voice lending the words weight. 'And I would never use you like that, to slake my lust for another woman. That demeans us both.' A slash of angry colour showed on his cheekbones as she nodded agreement with his words. 'You truly believe I would treat you like that?'

'How should I know?' Julia asked, staring into the hot green eyes, unable to read his mood. 'I have never been with another man, I have never been a slave before. How should I know what to believe, what to expect from you, Wulfric?'

'Do you not know me?' His questioning look was as puzzled as hers had been as he sank back to sit on his heels, his hands still cupping her shoulders. 'You see me every day. Do you not know me at all?'

I see him every day. I see him leading, fighting, laughing. I see him heaving water and sharpening his sword. I see him teaching Berig and watching over Una when her man is not there. I see him playing with small children and disciplining unruly warriors. And what I see is what he is: a brave, honourable, tireless man carrying the burden of his own destiny and that of his kin. His public face is his private face as well.

Julia realised several minutes had passed as they had sat there, frozen like statues. 'You are not a Roman,' she said slowly, then shook her head to silence him as he opened his mouth to agree with the obvious. 'Do you understand how Roman men are expected to behave?'

'Like any man of honour.'

'They are expected to show a public face, a face of civic responsibility and virtue. Whatever they are in the privacy of their own homes, once they are on the public stage of the street or the Forum or the Basilica, then they are different. That face is all important in delivering their civic duty, and that duty is to Rome.'

She was working it out as she went along. It was never something you spoke of, although doubtless fathers spelled it out to their sons. It was simply the way things were. 'It does not matter what a man is behind his closed doors—he can beat his wife, fornicate with his slaves, create elaborate schemes to make himself rich at the expense of his neighbours—so long as his public face is correct. And it is the same with the Empire. The public face is what matters, what goes on behind the scenes—' She shrugged. 'The ends justify the means, I suppose.

'But for you, and for your people, I do not think there is that separation—you are the same at your own hearth and in the king's Council, making love or making war.' Julia put up her hands and caught his, pulling them down so she could cradle them in her lap. 'I am only just realising that. Forgive me.'

The big hands lay still within her clasp. 'No, forgive me. I think we should begin again. I thought your people treacherous, yet they are acting within their concept of honour. You thought me two-faced, capable of taking and using you on a whim?'

'For a Roman to criticise another person for taking and keeping slaves would, indeed, be a hypocrisy. I thought you took what you wanted, when you wanted, because you were strong enough to do it, to gratify your desires. And I expected you to treat me no better, and perhaps, no worse than your horse, because I do not expect my monetary value is as much. Although…' she risked a small smile '…it is a very ugly horse.'

'Very,' he agreed, an answering smile tugging at the corner of his mouth.

'Now, I do not know what I am to you. You must marry and do so for advantage. Sunilda is an obvious choice, Una has explained it to me. You must forgive me, though, if I do not want her for a mistress.'

'And that is why you would object to me marrying her? She would become your mistress?'

'I have come to enjoy the way we live now,' Julia said slowly. 'I am a slave and yet this seems like freedom. I like the people in my life now, I feel well and fit, I am involved in something momentous. But this is not for ever. Sooner or later your people will settle in their new land and build villas and start to farm and then what will I be? I will tell you—I will be at Sunilda's beck and call, no better than that poor child who was killed when you saved me. You must excuse me if that prospect fills me with dread.'

'That will never happen.'

'Why? Because you will never marry? I do not think so. Because you will let me go?' The shake of the golden head was instant. 'No, you will not release what you have captured, will you?'

Wulfric's gaze was lowered, apparently studying his strong, scarred hands captured in the fragile cage of her fingers. 'The world is changing. I do not know what the future holds, what I must do for the best. All I know now is that my king leads me, and all my kin, south to Africa. He wants to make us new Romans, Romans with Visigoth honour. I want that too, I want for my children the good things of this Empire and the good things of their heritage.

'I do not know whether this is the best way to achieve that. I say to you, and only to you, that I argued against this course. I wanted us to go north and west into Gaul, into lands with wide rivers and good pasture, where there are four seasons in a year and the sun does not flay the skin from a man's back. I was overruled and so I will obey my king.'

The big hands twisted in hers, the long fingers slid between her own and Julia found herself looking down, not at a capture, but a joining. 'When we get where we are going, then I must do what I must, whatever that is. Until then, I will not marry, you have my oath upon it.' Her eyes flew up to meet his. Wulfric was smiling. 'Trust me.'

'I trust you.' Julia hesitated, then whispered, 'And if there is a child?'

'Una has already flayed me for carelessness, and I try to heed her.' He looked towards the bridge with a grimace. 'I am being careful, but if there is, never fear that I would not acknowledge it.'

Wulfric got to his feet, their hands still clasped, pulling her with him. 'Never fear…' The sound of a horn, a long drawn-out note, echoed round the valley. 'We are moving. Come.'

Come. Follow me. No, walk with *me.* Wulfric kept hold of her hand and they went together back up the track and towards the well-head and the sound of hundreds of people and animals beginning to move. How long would this closeness last? How long could it? Julia gave his hand a squeeze as they reached the last turn in the track and then pulled free, running on ahead to help Berig, Smoke at her heels.

They reached Rhegium at last, with no fighting along the way, and no resistance as they entered the port city through its open gates. Either word had not reached the people of the vast army bearing down upon it, or, more likely, as Wulfric observed, the local population had decided that an easy surrender was better than to undergo the fate of Nola and Capua.

It seemed strange to Julia to be within the walls of a town again, and a Roman one at that. She should have felt at home, passing familiar-seeming blocks of houses, temples that had been converted into churches with façades that echoed every other temple façade in the Empire. There were little markets at street corners, the stalls empty as their owners had snatched up their wares and fled to hide before the torrent of Goths reached them. There were public fountains, inscriptions and statues, but she found herself staring round wide-eyed at them, just as Una was.

They moved through the town like a tidal wave, sweeping aside the inhabitants as they passed. Then they were through, out of the sea gates, out into the harbour and staring across

at the straits that separated them from the island of Sicilia.
The prospect of the sea voyage was real now to everyone, and
there were wails of horror as well as excited babbling rising
above the lowing of the oxen, unsettled by the salty sea
breezes.

Berig came spurring back, weaving through the mass of
wagons and flocks of livestock. 'We are to turn south,' he
called to each driver as he passed. 'Out of the city, down to
the plain beyond. There is water, pasture, room to camp.'

'Where is Wulfric?' Julia leaned out and caught his arm
as Berig reined in beside her wagon.

'With the king.' Berig's excited expression turned to one of
faint worry. 'Alaric is not well, they say he has pains in his chest.'

'Poor man,' she said, prodding the oxen with the goad to
make them turn in the direction Berig indicated. 'Will that
delay us, if he is not well?' She hardly knew what she wanted,
or what was best for all of them. To go, or not to go? But they
could not stay here, trapped in the toe of Italy until the troops
of the Empire reached them. And she wanted Wulfric, here,
now. How long he would be hers she did not know, but every
second was precious, and the seconds were running out, as
through a sand clock in her mind.

'Don't know.' Berig circled his horse, craning to see who
had still not got the message. 'He will be with us tonight.' He
was not referring to the king.

Wulfric rode into camp late, long after most people had
retired to their lean-to tents or under the shelter of their
wagons. The guards patrolled the perimeter, solitary souls sat
by their dying fires. Berig was snoring, he could hear the
familiar sound wafting on the hot, still air even before he saw
the wagon. Smoke's tail begin to wave.

Berig had told him approximately where they were camped, the wolf had guided him home. *Home.* He had never realised that before—that was what this wagon and its tent were. He had given up calling anywhere home years ago, clinging instead to the vision of a villa somewhere in Gaul, shady court-yards, lush fields, a vision that Alaric's orders to go south had dashed to fragments. It had become an impossible dream and yet now one slender girl with brown eyes and the courage of a warrior had given him a home wherever she was.

A drift of savoury smells assailed his nostrils as he slid off the back of his horse and stood, his forehead resting against the saddle for a long moment, too weary to unharness the animal.

Christus, but he was tired. It seemed as though he had been travelling for his entire life, and in the wrong direction at that. The grey turned its head and butted him impatiently. Wulfric squared his shoulders and straightened up as a slim shadow slipped under his arm and took the reins.

'Go and sit by the fire. There is food in the pot, and warm water by the hearth.' She pushed him, a kitten pushing a mastiff, he thought with an exhausted flash of humour. 'Move, you big lump, how can I get the saddle off with you leaning on it like that?'

'Yes, *domina,*' he murmured, straightening up and walking towards the glow of the fire.

He folded up when he got there, not onto a stool, but cross-legged on the ground, his back against a wheel. There was the water, a towel draped across a stool where he could reach it. There was the pot of stew, the platter of bread, bowls set ready. He washed his hands, splashed his face and towelled himself dry, then just sat there, eyes closed, too bone weary to eat.

Somewhere on the other side of the wagon he could hear

Julia talking to the horse. It was obviously not cooperating, he thought, listening to her scolding.

Eventually he heard the light footsteps, knew exactly when she had seen him by the way they turned from a walk into a tiptoe. 'I'm awake,' he said, eyes still shut.

'Eat something, then,' she ordered, in much the same tone she had used to the horse. There was the scrape of a ladle in the big cooking pot, the splash of wine into a beaker. Then, 'What did you call me just now?'

'*Domina.* You are the lady of the household, are you not?'

She gave an amused snort. 'Of course, look at me, mistress of two ox wagons, two makeshift tents and a cooking pot.'

Wulfric reached up a hand, judging her whereabouts by sound, and snagged her wrist. 'Mistress of me.' He tugged. 'Come and sit down.'

'I will when you open your eyes and eat. You need your strength.' He did as he was told, smiling sleepily up into her vivid face, animated by concern and lit by the firelight.

'Very well.' He picked up the spoon. 'Now sit.'

For once obedient, Julia curled up next to him and began to nibble on a piece of crust. 'Berig says Alaric is sick.'

'Yes. Heart strain, I think, made worse by a fever.'

'And you are tired because you have to help and support him?"

'We all do, those in Council.' He spooned up the stew and found he was hungry after all. 'This is good.'

'Of course.' He hid his smile. Julia was taking pride in her cooking, but she would deny it vehemently if challenged, saying that if she did not cook then they would have to rely on Berig and that was too grim to contemplate. 'Not all of you bear the same strain,' she persisted. 'There are those who have most followers, you have most influence, most to do. You and Athaulf.'

'And Willa.' The dark horse. The tall, taciturn man who seemed to share Wulfric's concerns about their current course and who gave every indication of thinking more than he talked. There were times, when he was as tired as he was now, when Wulfric seriously considered forming an understanding with Willa now and not risking waiting. Athaulf lacked his brother-in-law's charisma, and perhaps his wisdom, for all that he seemed the likely next king. Loyalty to Alaric kept Wulfric from considering too seriously challenging Athaulf, but after him…

'Wake up!' He jerked awake before the bowl could slip from his fingers. Doggedly he finished the food, drained the wine and contemplated getting to his feet and trudging round to the other side of the wagon where he and Berig were sleeping under a width of stretched canvas from the big tent.

'Wulfric, there is a bed right behind you.' Julia nudged him.

'Yours.' They had constructed her a lean-to with rather more privacy than their own.

'Oh, go on, for goodness' sake. It is hardly as though we had not lain together in the same bed before.'

But not very often, Wulfric realised. Just the once, in fact. Since the bridge they had found places in the countryside to make love, creeping away like young lovers to tryst and coming back quietly so as not to wake Berig.

Not that Berig would be in the slightest doubt what was going on—his cheeky grin was evidence of that. Still, the desire to preserve Julia's modesty and an innate instinct for privacy made him discreet. But now Berig was snoring, deep in the sort of adolescent slumber that would take a Hun attack to rouse him from. And it was not as though Wulfric was going to do anything but sleep.

Julia's bedding smelled of her: sweet, spicy, female. Wulfric stripped off his clothes and lay down, not bothering with a blanket in the warm night air, breathed deeply—and realised he could not sleep. Something, something on top of all the responsibilities that he knew how to cope with, was keeping him awake.

'What is it? What is wrong?' Julia whispered, sliding into the tent. 'Did I keep you awake clearing up?'

'No. And nothing is wrong,' he lied. It was her, of course. The lady of his household. Only, once they had landed in Africa, once they began to settle and establish *real* households, what would become of her? He needed to marry, to raise children, to take his place in their new society. A Roman mistress could have no place in that. She was already wary of Sunilda, the obvious candidate for a wife; he could not imagine the pair of them co-existing peacefully for one moment.

'Then what are you thinking about?' She had curled up against his naked flank, her own bare skin soft against his side. *Sunilda.* Not the most tactful things to reply, however honest. *I must leave Julia here when we sail. Leave her with the most senior magistrate and sail away, out of her life.* He let his hand drift down her shoulder, over the swell of the side of her breast to the sweet curve and dip of her waist and hip. He would leave nothing with her but a memory; he had been careful ever since the bridge to withdraw and not risk making her with child.

His head fell back on the pillow. It seemed he had made a decision, he was certain it was the right one, and he felt as though someone was twisting a red-hot knife in his guts. 'Thinking about what to take on the voyage,' he said eventually, as she kept her head tipped up interrogatively. He could feel her candid eyes on him.

'You think too much,' she chided, slipping down towards his feet. 'You need to relax.'

The sudden fall of her hair across his belly as she knelt up beside him was anything but relaxing. The moist heat of her mouth as she took him between her lips had him rearing up on his elbows. 'Julia!' She had never done such a thing before, he had not even contemplated asking her, and here she was, when he was utterly exhausted—or perhaps not; his body was responding with enthusiasm.

Julia freed him and raised her head. 'Lie back, let me make love to you.'

'But you—'

'This is what I want, let me be selfish.'

'But Berig's just the other side of the wagon.'

'Then be quiet,' she said with a provocative chuckle and bent to trace the hardening length of him with her tongue.

With a moan of surrender Wulfric dropped back, his hands fisted into the bedding as Julia explored with hands, lips, teeth and tongue in wanton abandon.

It became a battle of will to be silent under her onslaught. When he reached for her she slapped his hands away and went back to torturing him with a skill that seemed to grow with every stifled moan and aching shudder of his body.

And then when he could stand it no more and his body began to arch into ecstasy, she took him hard in her hand, slid up the length of his body and kissed him full on the mouth, swallowing his cry. As he stilled at last she wrapped her arms around him and held him tightly and the last thing he knew as he slid into sleep was the touch of her lips on his temple.

Chapter Thirteen

Julia woke and lay, eyes closed, knowing she had a wicked smile on her lips. She had wanted to make love to Wulfric as she had last night for days, ever since she had recalled the erotic graffito of the act she had once seen scrawled on a wall. At the time it had seemed distastefully improbable. Now, as she learned to explore every inch of a magnificent male body, it was deliciously arousing.

But she had guessed he would not let her touch him like that, so the opportunity when he was tired and his guard was down had been irresistible. Still smiling, she rolled over and opened her eyes. Wulfric had gone. Julia sighed. He was going to be difficult about this, she could tell. He'd be gone all day and then when he came back she was going to receive a lecture about behaving in a wanton manner. He was very protective, which normally made her feel exceedingly feminine, but, as he initiated her deeper into the arts of love-making, she did want to be more adventurous herself.

Smoke came and poked her with his wet nose, grumbling in the low growl that meant he wanted her to get up and find him something to eat. 'Go and hunt, you lazy wolf,' she scolded back, pushing him to one side so she could get up. He padded behind her as she ducked out of her tent.

Berig had gone too. The men had left the devastation that they appeared to find necessary as a consequence of breaking their fast, but when that was cleared away there seemed little to do. Julia strolled off to see if Una wanted any help.

She found her friend rubbing her swelling stomach and grimacing in discomfort. 'What's the matter?' Julia felt anxious. She had had nothing to do with pregnant women, let alone with childbirth, and had a horror of finding herself the only one with Una when some crisis arrived. You boiled water and found lots of towels, that was the limit of her knowledge. 'Is it the baby?'

'He's fine.' Una was convinced it was a boy, on the grounds that the bump was all at the front. This seemed as logical as anything else about the process to Julia, so she accepted it. 'It's me. My skin is so dry it itches, I'm hot and sweaty and washing out of a bucket doesn't help, and I'm far too clumsy to get into Wulfric's big tub, even if we could unload it.'

'What you need is a proper Roman bath,' Julia said. 'Me too. I miss that more than anything. A relaxing time in the warm, a cool plunge, a good sweat and an oiling, being able to scrape oneself all over with a strigil—bliss.'

'It sounds wonderful.' Una scratched her arm absently. 'What a pity we haven't got one.'

'Yes,' Julia agreed, then, 'But we have! Rhegium is certain to have public baths, probably more than one.'

'But we can't…'

'Why not? There has been no fighting, people are coming and going into the town. The local people are not thrilled to have us here, but they aren't hostile.'

'*Us?*' Una raised an eyebrow. 'Have you become one of *us* now, Julia?'

Julia found herself smiling back, suddenly certain. 'Yes, I have. But, if it will make you feel better, I will change into my tunic and dress my hair in the Roman style and that will make things easier. Do say you'll come—now I've thought of it, I can't bear not to, and Wulfric won't want me going by myself.'

Una bit her lip in doubt, then grinned. 'Come on, then. Rigunth will look after the children.'

Feeling more than a little strange in her stained amber linen, with the weight of her hair plaited and knotted on her head, Julia purchased two flasks of oil and two strigils from a stall outside the baths.

The stallholders had begun cautiously to return when they realised this vast band of invaders was not going to sack and pillage and instead was prepared to pay for supplies. It was good policy, she realised. If Alaric wanted cooperation in assembling a fleet, then he needed the local people to at least tolerate them.

'We will be provided with towels inside,' she explained, leading the way through the entrance portico. 'I hope they either have a women's bath suite or we have arrived at the right time. Some people don't mind mixed bathing, but I certainly do.'

They were in luck. The baths were big enough for two wings and Julia rapidly skirted the palestra where a group of men in skimpy tunics were throwing a heavy ball to each other and led Una into the women's baths.

'This is the apodyterium where we change. See, you put your things here.' Una stripped rather nervously, clutching her towel around her unwieldy body as best she could. Julia took her clothes and folded them into a niche alongside hers, tipped the attendant to keep an eye on them and led her wide-eyed companion through into the tepidarium.

'Here we are, now sit down, relax and warm up a little. Then we rub oil all over ourselves.'

There were several other women already there. They took no notice of the friends, continuing their laughing exchange of gossip, and Una began to relax. When Julia began to oil her back for her, she positively purred. 'Oh, this is good. Let me do yours.'

When they strolled out two hours later, glowing and with skin as soft as a prolonged soaking in best olive oil could make it, Julia felt too relaxed to scuttle modestly through the palestra to avoid any exercising men. But two masculine figures walking round the corner of the colonnade straight into their path brought her up short, automatically ducking her head. Then she realised that, while one of the men in front of her had bare legs below a Roman tunic, the view of the other was all too familiar.

Oatmeal-weave trousers were tucked into soft ankle boots. Julia's eyes rose past the hem of a tunic trimmed with rich red braid that she had tacked back only days before. His hair wet on his shoulders and a strigil in his hand, Wulfric stared at her with as much surprise as she was showing at seeing him.

'Julia!'

'Ah,' said the Roman jovially, 'what a coincidence, this will be the la—'

'These are two of the ladies from our camp, yes,' Wulfric intervened smoothly. Not smoothly enough to cover up his companion's use of the singular. Whoever this man was, Wulfric had been telling him about her. Julia felt the blood draining from her face. Why? What possible reason could Wulfric have for telling a respectable citizen that he had a captured Roman woman in his household?

'Good morning,' she said assertively, abandoning years of training in modest good behaviour. 'I am Julia Livia. To whom do I have the honour of speaking, sir?'

'I…er…I am Decius Marcus Cilo, Lady.'

'I can see you are an important citizen of Rhegium,' she persisted with shocking brazenness. 'Are you the governor, sir?'

'Oh, no, my dear.' Flattered and taken aback by this frontal assault by an apparently well-bred young woman, Decius Marcus beamed indulgently. 'I am the chief magistrate.'

'Goodness.' Julia batted long brown lashes. Her stomach was knotting with a terrifying sense of betrayal, even as she fought for poise. It was becoming very clear to her: Wulfric was going to leave her behind. While she and Una had been relaxing in the women's baths, Wulfric had been in the men's side, calmly arranging to dispose of her to this official. Somehow she kept talking. 'How terrifying. I do hope none of us has done anything wrong.'

'Not at all. We have just been agreeing how a, um…knotty problem might be suitably resolved.'

'I am sure you have succeeded admirably.' Julia smiled at him sweetly. The taste of Wulfric's treachery was sharp on her tongue, like metal when one inadvertently bit into it. She forced herself to look at him. His face was unreadable, but she could see his shoulders were braced, his hand, which was resting with apparent casualness at the buckle of his belt, was clenched. His lids were half-lowered over the clear green eyes, shielding all emotion. Perhaps he did not feel any, beyond relief that he had found a solution to the embarrassment she appeared to present.

My love. The man I thought cared for me. The man who is arranging my disposal neatly and conveniently. They'll send me back to Rome between them, back to a cold sterile house where I will be in disgrace until my father can marry me off to some complacent, well-bred idiot. And Wulfric can marry Sunilda.

The tears were pressing at the back of her eyes. With all the strength and courage she had learned these past weeks Julia smiled at the magistrate. 'Goodbye, sir. I do not believe we will meet again.' *There.* His eyes flickered, and he looked uncomfortable, betraying the truth of what he and Wulfric had been plotting. 'Come, Una, let us be getting back to the camp. We must be ready to welcome our menfolk home.'

Una held her tongue until they were out of earshot. 'What was that all about?' she demanded the moment they turned the corner. 'I know you now—and you may have sounded very polite, but I can tell you are furious.'

'That *bastard* means to leave me with the magistrate,' Julia stormed, all her hard-earned control vanishing the moment she was out of Wulfric's sight. 'I hate him.' The effect was spoiled by a racking sob she could not suppress. 'When you all sail, I'll be here, a disgraced woman to be packed off home to my father to deal with. And Wulfric will marry that blonde harridan.' She dashed the back of her hand over her eyes. 'I refuse to cry over him. He is two-faced and treacherous.'

'Oh, my dear.' Una pulled her into the shelter of a shaded fountain. 'Are you certain?'

'Yes,' Julia said shortly.

'What will you do?' Una put her arm around her shoulders while Julia dabbed at her eyes with the hem of her overtunic. 'If you go with him to Africa and he marries Sunilda, what would become of you?'

'I could marry Berig,' Julia said darkly, then laughed abruptly at Una's face. 'I am joking.' She fiddled with the end of her girdle while she thought. 'I do not know what I am going to do. I suppose I always thought some sort of miracle would happen and Sunilda would disappear.' Julia straightened her shoulders. 'That was foolish, there would be other Sunildas.'

'You could pray,' Una said seriously. 'It is Sunday tomorrow. We could go to church.'

'Pray for what? That Wulfric decides I am more important to him than his ambition to lead, perhaps more important than the chance of becoming king? He told me he would do nothing about the marriage while we were in Italy, that is all I can hope for. I was a fool to expect anything, but I did at least believe he would discuss things with me.'

'What will you say to him?'

'I have no idea.' Julia stared blankly at the carved lion's head from which water was spurting. 'I have no idea at all.'

They walked back by way of the sea front. 'So many ships.' Una shaded her eyes with her hand and gazed around. The wide harbour was crowded with vessels. 'Alaric laid out his gold well as we came down the coast. So many have gathered already; surely there are almost enough here now.'

'Yes.' Julia started to count, then gave up. 'A few days to provision—and then you will be gone. Will you be glad?'

'To leave you, no. To go to Africa? I do not know. Sichar does not say so, he is too loyal, but I think it is only Wulfric's leadership that convinces him it is right, and I am not certain that in his heart Wulfric truly believes.'

'Then why do they do it?' Julia demanded, suddenly furious with every bone-headed man in the world.

'Because they have given their oath and their fealty unto death. Wulfric will argue with Alaric until a decision is reached, then he will walk through fire for him, right or wrong.'

Back in camp Julia persuaded Una to leave her and go back to her children. Then she vented her temper on their tent site, cleaning and sweeping, shaking out clothes and chopping vegetables in a whirlwind of activity. But it could not stop the thoughts circling wildly in her head, the constant treadmill of pointless, unanswerable questions.

When the men finally came home she was waiting. 'Berig, please go and see your sister, I want to talk to Wulfric.' The youth blinked at her tone, the total lack of greeting, but turned his horse's head and rode away without a word. The rapid glance he threw Wulfric was not lost on Julia: Berig had known something was wrong already.

'You do not order my men, any of them, ever,' Wulfric said flatly, swinging down from his horse. He obviously believed attack was the best form of defence.

'I order whom I please,' she retorted. 'You have forfeited my respect and with it any obedience I might show you.'

'I am not going to discuss it.' Leaving her staring after him, he led the big grey off to the horse lines.

Julia waited while he took his time coming back. 'Discuss what?'

'Whatever it is that has put you in this mood.' He walked over to the water bucket and began to wash.

'I did not heat water—after all, we have both had a bath today, have we not?'

Wulfric towelled his face briskly. *His beard needs*

clipping, Julia thought. *It is becoming difficult to read his expression.* 'I do not discuss my business with you.'

'I am not interested in *your* business, it is when you discuss mine that— Come back here! How dare you turn your back on me when I am speaking to you!'

He spun on his heel, the violence of the movement bringing him close in front of her. It was as much as Julia could do not to flinch back. 'I do as I please at my own hearth.'

'And no slave dare answer back, no doubt.'

'You are not a slave, you know that. How could you not, from that first night when you cried in my arms…?'

'What?'

'You cried in your sleep, I went to you. Do you think I treat every slave like that?'

'I thought it was a dream.' She shook her head, forcing away the image of him cradling her so gently. 'You saved me from rape and probably worse, but you took me away by force. *Mine,* you said. You took me from everything I knew, from my home, and now you plot to uproot me again, this time to throw me back. Could you not even discuss it with me?'

Wulfric stared down at her, the rays of the sunset colouring his face so that he looked like a gilded pagan idol. Every emotion was contained; he was showing her the face he showed an opponent, without a flicker of weakness for her to read.

'I do what is best for the people in my care.'

'And this is best? I have tried so hard to become what you wanted. I have learned to cook, to clean, to sew. I have tended you when you were wounded, I have done my best with your language.'

One eyebrow rose slightly.

'*Ik mag qithan managa waurda in razdai Gutiskai,*' she snapped. 'I know many words, and I do my best to pronounce them, to make sentences. I am *trying*.

'You took my virginity—and do not think I do not blame myself as much as you for that. I wanted you, fool that I am. Now I am inconvenient, so you pack me off to a man who will despise me, for he knows all too well what I have been to you.'

'He can hardly begin to guess,' Wulfric said softly, his eyes on her face.

'Oh, yes, he can! You send me back to be the disgraced daughter of a respectable household and all the warmth I have ever known, all the people I love, will be lost to me.' Her eyes were stinging with tears, but she fought them back. When his face changed, it was blurred, but she did not miss the way his brows drew together, the indrawn breath.

'Love?'

'Una is the best friend I ever had. I love her like a sister, I love her children, I want to hold her new baby in my arms. Berig is the younger brother I never had. And you would send me away from them.

'But why should you not? Look at this unseemly display of emotion! I give you nothing you cannot get elsewhere. Another domestic drudge will be easy enough to find and there are whores enough, I am certain, to warm your bed until you marry Sunilda. Doubtless she is too prudent to anticipate the ceremony.'

'Do not liken yourself to a whore!' He was angry now—the mask had slipped. He took her by the upper arms and shook her.

Julia stared at the passionate, sensual mouth, now set in a

hard line. 'No money exchanged hands, to be sure. And I was willing enough to learn. The man who is so anxious to please my father that he will marry soiled goods will enjoy the benefits of your tuition.'

Wulfric snarled, jerking her towards him. 'Will you hit me, then?' she jeered, too angry to be afraid.

'Never.' Then he brought his head down and kissed her with all the violence locked in his big, hard body. His tongue thrust into her mouth, filling it, plundering the heat with a crude rhythm that spoke of what he wanted to do to her, what he was holding himself back from with every vestige of self-restraint he had left.

Julia struggled, reached up and knotted her fists in his hair and pulled, her puny strength as nothing as she felt him set his neck muscles and resist her. Then he let her go as suddenly as he had taken her and she staggered back.

'You plotted to deceive me,' she gasped, dragging the back of her hand across her swollen mouth. 'When would you have told me? Or would you just have delivered me, trussed like a parcel, to the magistrate's door?'

'I would have told you the day we sailed,' he admitted finally. 'I did not want to upset you.'

'Upset me?' She knew her voice had risen wildly. She struggled for control. 'You wanted to prevent this confrontation, you wanted to deceive me for as long as possible. You have no honour. None.'

'*What did you say?*' Wulfric had gone white under the golden tan. The sun was almost down now, the last red flare of the sunset turning him into a creature, not of gold but of flame, something terrifying from the pits of hell. His hand was on the hilt of his long knife. This was the face his enemies saw just before they died. The face of a barbarian in a killing rage.

Chapter Fourteen

They stared at each other, the words hanging in the air between them. They could not be unsaid. They could not be ignored. *No honour.* If any man had said that to him, they would be dead by now. But this was a woman, the woman who had burrowed under his skin, into his heart, against all reason, all sense.

He had hurt her, he could see, as much as she had just hurt him. And, from the stricken look in those wide brown eyes, she was bitterly regretting what she had said, whereas he at least knew he was doing the right thing. It was like searing a suppurating wound with a red-hot knife—agony, but the right thing. Something to be done and to be endured.

'Do you mean that?' He realised he had spoken in his own tongue and said it again in Latin.

'No. No, I do not mean it. I am sorry for it.' Julia closed her eyes for a moment. He knew just how the tender skin of her lids felt under his lips, against the sweep of his tongue-tip. He forced himself to stand still and hear her out.

'You have hurt me beyond reason, beyond my ability to restrain my tongue. I trusted you and you have failed to live up to that, but it is my fault, for we had no agreement. I believe you have acted as you see best. You must forgive me if I hate you for it.' Wulfric flinched inwardly as she shook her head in frustration, searching for the words to express how she felt. 'You are an honourable man, I acknowledge it; I hope never to be in the power of another.'

She turned and walked towards her shelter. 'Julia—' Wulfric took one long step, then stopped as she threw up her hand.

'Your dinner is in the pot. If you touch me now, I swear I will take that knife and I will hurt…one of us.' She raised the flap and vanished inside.

The long, aching sigh knifed his ribs. Wulfric welcomed the pain. It was physical, he could deal with it. Not like the pain in his heart, in his mind, in—he was very much afraid—his soul.

He stood there, staring into the red heart of the fire, aware that what was blurring his vision was not the heat, but unshed tears. When had he last wept?

The night he had left his family and gone to join Alaric's household, that was when. Ten years old, skinny as a rail, all hands and feet he had yet to grow into, as terrified as a puppy thrown to wolves. He had sobbed his heart out, his face buried in his blankets for fear someone would hear, and the next morning Alaric—the *king,* by all that was wonderful— had stopped and looked down at him and had laid a hand fleetingly on his shoulder. 'My smallest warrior,' he had said, and Wulfric had never wept again.

Looking back, especially since his experience with Berig, he guessed the king had heard him in the night. But Julia had been stronger than he had; she had not given way to her fears until sleep had overwhelmed her.

Her words slashed at his nerves like white-hot knives. He

had hurt her beyond reason, she said, yet even carrying that hurt like a wound, she had the grace to take back her accusation about his honour. He expected women of his own kind to have honour, to understand it. He had not expected that from a Roman woman.

'My lord?' It was Berig, hovering anxiously just at the edge of the fire's reflected glow. It had become dark while he stood there.

'Come, eat, if it has not burned. Julia has…gone to bed.'

The boy did not come closer. 'Una told me what you have done.'

'And you think me wrong?' It was unfair, but he had to hit out at someone.

'No, my lord. If you decide, then it must be right,' Berig said loyally, misery in his eyes.

'Come. You can tell me what you think. I will not be angry.'

'I…I like Julia. I do not want you to send her away.'

'She loves you like a younger brother. She said so.' Wulfric reached for a bowl and began to ladle meat from the pot. 'Here, eat.'

'Does she?' The boy's face lit up. 'She is very brave, isn't she?'

'Very.' Wulfric realised he had reduced the bread to crumbs in his hands. 'She is going to need to be, to go back to her own people.'

'You will send her back, then?' Even with his brow wrinkled with anxiety, Berig was capable of spooning food into his mouth. Wulfric wondered if he would ever feel like eating again. 'Won't they be unkind to her because she has been your lover?'

So much for discretion. The pain made him speak harshly.

'Yes, they will. Which do you think she will prefer? That, or for Sunilda to be her mistress?'

Berig's eyes dropped to his bowl and he did not speak until he had chewed for a while. 'It is not easy, knowing what is the honourable thing to do, is it? I thought it would be easy when I was a man, that I would know. But this isn't.'

Out of the mouths of babes. 'Then learn from it,' Wulfric said. 'We sail in six days.'

Wulfric woke in the night, thinking someone was moving in the tent, then heard the sound of weeping and knew Julia was crying in her sleep again. Julia would not consciously give way, not while she knew he was near. Wulfric lay there, staring up into the darkness, fighting the urge to get up and take her in his arms.

He gave in, rolling quietly out of bed so as not to wake Berig, and crept round to Julia's side. He raised the flap and at the slight noise the pale oval of a face tipped up towards him. It was Berig, hunkered down beside her, her hand in his. She had stopped crying and was lying peacefully asleep.

'Go away,' the boy hissed, his face contorted with tears Wulfric knew he would rather have died than have seen.

He nodded abruptly and let the tent flap drop. Berig was growing up. His heart contracted. Jealousy? Of a boy? He made himself stand up straight and walk out to the horse lines. He would walk the perimeter—there was going to be no sleep tonight.

Julia woke to find Berig asleep across the entrance to her tent and Smoke with his head on her feet.

'Berig?' He scrambled up, knuckling his eyes and looking uncomfortable. 'What on earth are you both doing in my tent?'

He looked away. 'We were keeping you company. You were…upset in the night.'

'Oh. Thank you,' she said softly, reaching out to touch his shoulder. 'That was very gallant of you. Where is Wulfric?' There, she had said his name, it wasn't as hard as she had feared.

'Gone into Rhegium. At least, that's what he said he was going to do last night. We are helping with the provisioning of the ships.'

'Then you must hurry and break your fast and go and join him.' He nodded and lifted the tent flap. 'Will he be angry with you for staying with me?'

'Don't know.' Berig frowned. 'Don't care.'

'He is doing what he believes is the right thing,' Julia said. She had no wish to see Berig become disillusioned with his lord. That would be a despicable revenge.

'He made you cry.'

'In my sleep? Is that why you came here?' He nodded and was gone, Smoke padding behind him.

Julia washed, dressed and gave them both food, then sat on a stool in the sun, her hands clasped round her knees and tried to think what to do. To go back would be to enter a world of disapproval and disgrace. Her father would still want her to marry Antonius Justus, but she doubted he'd accept her now. A young widow was one thing, a woman who had lost her virginity to a Visigoth was doubtless quite another. And if he did take her, there would be the daily unspoken thought that she was married on sufferance, and, if something went wrong, then he would doubtless throw her history in her face.

Or she could try and make a living here, in Rhegium. But that would be difficult, given that the chief magistrate knew who she was. He had everything to gain by letting a powerful senator know the whereabouts of his missing daughter.

And what could she do? She had no craft skills, no money to start a business. She eyed the wagon and the driver's box seat. If she was correct, that contained part of a fortune in gold. Gold stolen from Rome—surely she had as much right to it as Wulfric?

But he would argue that they were collecting on the emperor's unfulfilled promises. And whose ever it truly was, taking it would feel uncommonly like stealing. Or taking it in recompense for the loss of her freedom and virginity. Which was an uncomfortable thought.

'Are you ready?' It was Una, Sichar, her husband at her side and the children, pink-faced from a good scrubbing, clustered round. 'We are going to church, had you forgotten?'

'Yes,' Julia admitted, getting to her feet. 'I had.' She was respectably enough dressed, she decided, joining the others.

Little Ulf, Una's middle son, slipped his hand in hers and grinned up at her. A front tooth was missing and he had freckles, gold-brown hair that stuck up despite his mother's best efforts with comb and water and his father's blue eyes.

What would Wulfric's child look like? she wondered, feeling the knife twist in her breast as she thought it. *What would our son look like?* Could she seduce Wulfric before he left her, do it so well he lost control and was no longer careful? Would once be enough?

And what sort of life would a half-Goth bastard have in Rome in a respectable household? Perhaps if she was in bad enough disgrace her parents would give her money and let her vanish off to Ravenna or Neapolis and she could set up a small business.

'Did you have a chance to speak to Wulfric last night

about that matter?' Una asked, her voice light and casual so that Sichar and the children thought nothing of it. 'Berig thought you might have.'

'Yes. I spoke to him.' It was an effort to match her tone. 'He is determined upon that solution. I do not think I will change his mind.'

'Change Wulfric's mind?' Overhearing, Sichar, a man of few words, snorted. 'He thinks long and hard, that one. Then when he decides, that is it. Bull-headed.'

'Pig-headed, more like,' Julia muttered. She wondered if there was a time when a woman was most fertile. Would Una suspect if she asked her? And was it fair to try to bring a child into the world without a father? Not, she decided, if she could arrange it so there was no suspicion and no stigma. But what if she could not? The fantasy of a tall, green-eyed son helping her in a flourishing caupóna, where her newly acquired cooking skills drew in crowds of customers, faded, to be replaced by the memory of her father's face when he was in a rage, and she shivered. It was an impossible, selfish dream.

'Here we are.' Una stopped in front of the steps of what was obviously a new church, not a converted temple. The front was rich with inlaid stone, the doorway jammed with an orderly stream of well-dressed citizens and the smoke of incense and candles floated out to perfume the air. 'St Agnes.'

They filed in, the women pulling shawls over their hair, the children hushed by the high arched roof and the crowd. Sichar found Una a place on a stone bench running along the edge of the wall and the rest of them stood around her.

Julia did not expect to be able to concentrate, but to her surprise the atmosphere, the rhythms of the service, the smells and the pools of light slanting down from the high windows, soothed her.

After a while she began to glance round discreetly, keeping her gaze shielded behind lowered lashes. The sight of respectable Roman families seemed as alien as her first glimpses of Goths in their encampment had. She sighed, then a flash of gold caught her eye.

Wulfric was down on one knee, his right arm resting on his thigh, his golden head bent in contemplation or prayer. The light from above caught him, the dust motes swirling in the shaft of sun. It sparked off the armlets on his powerful biceps, off the metal fitments of his scabbard. His hair flowed down his back like a living thing.

She could not take her eyes from him. He was absolutely still, kneeling on the hard stone in the humble pose of devotion. Yet for all the still hands, the vulnerable neck, the closed eyes—she could see his lashes lying on his cheek—this was no priest. No one, even seeing him now, could mistake him for anything but a hard man, a warrior.

And yet he had been gentle with her, always. Julia felt the love building in her heart until she thought it would burst, that she would cry out, that she would run to him. But she stayed still, her lips closed, her eyes fixed on him.

She saw Wulfric's lashes lift, and then his head. The relaxed right hand closed and his head began to turn towards where she was standing and her breath caught. He had felt her gaze, felt her love, she knew it.

And then, in a flutter of rich blue skirts, a figure moved to his side, blocking Julia's view momentarily, and a tall figure stood elegant, hands clasped, eyes modestly lowered, a pure white veil lying like a swan's wing on her gilt hair. Sunilda.

Wulfric stood. Julia could see him lower his head and speak softly to the other woman, whose cheeks coloured. She felt pain in her hands and looked down, opening them. Four white crescents marked each palm. With a murmur of apology to Una, Julia eased her way back through the congregation and out of the church. This was not the place to indulge in jealous thoughts, or to feel the peace of worship rent by dislike. They looked magnificent together. Appropriate. Meant. And she had to accept it.

Berig was lounging in the shade, holding the horses. 'Why aren't you in church?' she scolded mildly, perching next to him on the low wall.

'Why aren't you? Sunilda, I suppose.' He grimaced, obviously not expecting an answer, then looked up at the clear sky. 'There's going to be a storm.'

'Surely not. There isn't a cloud.' She shaded her eyes and squinted up. 'And it is hot.'

'Hotter than yesterday,' Berig agreed. 'Can't you feel it? The tingling under your skin? The pressure on your temples? Storm coming.'

'I thought that was just the way I was feeling. But you are right, it is oppressive.'

'And look at Smoke.' The wolf, uncomfortable in the heat, was pacing back and forth, his slanting green eyes narrowed, his tail low.

'I'd better go back and start digging drainage channels round the wagons. We're in a good position—up the slope, but not on steep ground. We won't get flooded, but if there's a cloudburst we could have a sheet of water sweeping down through the tents if I don't make a channel.'

'Do you do this very often?' Julia blinked at his brisk efficiency.

'Not now we're in Italy. But where we come from, it rains a lot.' He grinned and swung up on his horse, tossing the grey's reins to Julia. 'Tell Wulfric what I'm doing. I don't need any help.'

He cantered off, leaving Julia sitting on the wall, regarding the ugly grey horse with some concern. What was she supposed to do now? Sit here like a stable boy in the full view of passers-by and the congregation until Wulfric came out of church? She could just hitch the animal to the nearest tree. No one was likely to steal it with Smoke on guard, but Wulfric might be angry with Berig for leaving it.

She was still dithering when the worshippers began to file out. Julia hopped down, smoothed her clothes as best she could and tried to hide behind the horse.

'Goodness, has that boy of yours started wearing skirts?' Sunilda, of course. Like Wulfric, she seemed to speak Latin interchangeably with Gothic, especially in public.

'No.' At the sound of Wulfric's voice, Julia ducked under the grey's neck, unwilling to be discovered skulking. ' Julia! Where is Berig?'

'He has gone back to camp. He thinks there is going to be a thunderstorm and he wanted to dig drainage channels.' She thrust the reins into his hands. 'Good day, Sunilda.'

The wide blue eyes shot pure poison at her, but the other woman smiled sweetly. 'How novel, Wulfric, a female slave to look after your horse.' She did not return Julia's greeting.

Julia flushed, biting her lip to catch back the retort. She *was* a slave, even if Wulfric did not treat her as one.

'Julia is not a slave,' Wulfric said flatly, making both women jump.

'Oh, really? Then what *exactly* is she?'

Hades, he has walked right into that one, Julia thought with a flash of grim humour. *What is he going to say? That I am his lover?* She caught Wulfric's eye and saw an answering wry look in them. It was back, that bond of understanding between them, and suddenly she could have laughed out loud.

'Julia Livia is a guest,' he replied calmly. Sunilda's jaw dropped. 'A guest who comes and goes as she pleases, and is kind enough to look after Berig and me at the present.'

'Indeed? You have many Roman guests, do you?'

'No.' Wulfric maintained his calm. That seemed to be infuriating Sunilda almost more than anything else. 'Julia is doing wonders for Berig's Latin vocabulary.'

With an undignified snort Sunilda spun on her heel and stalked off, her immaculate veil flapping behind her.

'You've upset her,' Julia observed.

'She has a temper. We value women of spirit.' Wulfric was still frowning after the retreating figure.

'Does she have her own battleaxe?'

'I am not even going to answer that.' He turned back and regarded Julia seriously. 'Are you all right?'

'No, if you want the honest truth. But I'll live. Nothing I am going to say is going to change your mind, is it?'

'There is no good answer to this mess,' he said slowly, his eyes sliding over her with a look that was a caress of regret. 'I believe I have decided on the least bad one.'

'Perhaps you have.' Julia gave a little shiver. 'Is Berig right about the storm?'

Wulfric turned on his heel and stared south. 'Yes. See.'

Far away, a distant smudge at the horizon, a thin dark line marked the division between sea and sky, when for days there had been nothing to show where one blue ran into the other, like a fresco painter's colours in his water pot. 'That is why it is so hot, the storm is coming from Africa.

'Go back to the camp, prepare for the evening meal, but

put everything that would be damaged by water into chests. Take the tents down. Berig will move enough of the heavy stuff out and put it under the wagons to make room inside for us, then we will stretch the canvas over the top and tie it down.'

'Is it going to be bad?' That seemed a lot of work, just for a thunderstorm.

'I do not know, I have never been this far south. But I will go down to the harbour and tell them to stop loading and concentrate on making all secure. Julia—' He stopped, frowning down at her. 'I am sorry about Sunilda.'

There was no gracious answer to that, so she simply said what she thought. 'So am I.'

Chapter Fifteen

Word spread as the darkness on the horizon grew more and more obvious. Men returned from the harbour, and the camp began to resemble a disturbed ant heap as the wagons were turned into shelters and the bulky and less vulnerable loads were pitched out onto the ground.

Families who had pitched camp near the bottom of the slight incline were moving up towards the top; there had already been three collisions and one cart overturned despite the orderly way everyone was working.

Berig, who had finished digging his run-off channels, leaned on his mattock and took a breather while Julia stopped packing clothes and textiles into chests and came and sat on the end of the wagon.

'Are they deep and wide enough?' she asked. 'Wulfric seemed worried.'

'Wulfric is never worried.'

That is what you think! 'Concerned, then.' And about more than the storm. She should accept his decision and try harder to pretend all was well; he had more important things to think about than her broken heart. Not that he realised it was broken, thank Heavens.

'I could go round again. Make them wider and deeper. There's a lot of water in those clouds.' He frowned at the approaching storm. They could see the cloud masses now, as tiny as a painted landscape on a villa wall, in black stark contrast with the untroubled blue above and below them.

'Help me get the really heavy stuff off first,' Julia suggested. 'Then I can sort out the wagon while you dig some more out.' She stood up, measuring space and looking at what needed moving. 'We can make a bigger space in this one and all get in it, then we can use all the canvas in one place.'

They worked a little longer, then sat, panting slightly, on a chest to drink. 'The air is completely still,' Berig said uneasily, sucking a blister, his grubby brown hand clasped round a horn beaker.

'And the birds have stopped singing.'

'Don't blame them,' he said with a lopsided grin. 'I don't feel like much like singing either. Wish we could fly away too.'

'Where is Wulfric?' Julia wondered out loud. She had been trying not to think about him, but the words slipped out.

'With Alaric, I expect, and the fleet. I'll look after you.' Berig squared his shoulders.

'Yes, of course, I know you will. We'll be fine.' She smiled at him, reassuring herself as much as him.

Even so, three hours later, she saw Berig heave a great sigh of relief as Wulfric came back into the camp at a canter. He jumped Berig's deepened side ditch and reined in. 'Good work. Where are they setting up the horse lines?'

'Up there.' Berig pointed uphill. 'There's a hollow on the far side of the ridge, Sichar's organising it. I've taken my horse and the oxen up already.' He took the reins Wulfric tossed to him and vaulted up into the saddle the moment Wulfric slid down.

'Time to eat, I think.' Wulfric nodded towards the sea. Julia had been concentrating on cooking and had not looked for some time. Now she gasped at the sight of the boiling mass of black cloud with lightning flickering along its base.

'Yes, that would be sensible, I am sure it will rain very heavily soon,' she said, trying to match his matter-of-fact tone. He was standing on the driver's seat of the wagon, scanning the camp. 'Is everyone else ready?'

'I don't think any have trenches as deep as Berig has dug, but it's too late to do anything about that now. Just be grateful we haven't got any chickens to share the space with us.'

'You think it will be too bad for them to be out?' Julia was startled. 'I thought people would just put the chickens and goats under the wagons.' As she spoke the still air moved, trailing hot fingers across her face. A banner flapped, then cracked with sudden force, making her jump. Swirls of dust began to rise from the parched earth and Smoke growled deep in his throat.

'I think it will be rough, yes. Here comes Berig, let's start. I want everything packed away and secure.'

Wulfric kicked the last of the blocks under the wheels of the front wagon, then checked the lashings over the canvas covering the rear one. Why he should feel so uneasy about this storm he had no idea, but he had never seen one come in over the sea before and the boiling black mass with its lances of fire thrown at the waves sent a primitive shiver down his spine. Almost he could imagine the pagan gods of his fore-fathers riding in it on great black stallions, seeking retribution on their overcivilised descendants who had abandoned the old ways to follow a new faith.

With one last sweeping glance around the darkening camp, he slid under the canvas and began lacing the gap closed from the inside. The space was hardly big enough for one large man, a growing boy, a slender young woman and a wolf. They would certainly be snug through whatever the storm brought.

'Smoke is trying to sit on my lap,' Julia complained in the gloom.

'He wants to hide and he is used to sleeping by your bed,' Wulfric said, grabbing the wolf by the scruff and hauling him to the end of the space. 'Lie there or go outside.' With a grumble Smoke lay down.

'Now he's pushing his wet nose into my ankle,' Julia complained, half-laughing.

Wulfric felt around in the half-light. Julia had spread a layer of blankets on the floor of the wagon and rolled more at the sides and head of the space. 'We will be better lying down,' he decided. 'If we touch the canvas when it is soaked, we will create a leak. Julia, lie in the middle, between us.'

For some reason the image of wagons sliding in a torrent of mud, crashing into the side of theirs, crushing her slender bones, would not leave him, despite the gentle slope they were on. The superstitious dread that had gripped him as he watched the clouds was focusing on Julia and the threat to her. A guilty conscience, he had no doubt, and one that prolonged reflection in church that morning had done nothing to soothe.

He saw the questioning tilt of her head, but she did as she

was told, wriggling down. Berig turned on his side, propped up on his elbow, and faced her. 'Is this like Roman dining couches? How do you eat lying down?'

'Perfectly easily, although you can't eat fast.' Julia began to talk to Berig, telling him about dinner parties at her parents' home, making him laugh with exotic recipes. Wulfric smiled, easing himself into the space between her back and the side of the wagon. While she was teasing Berig about larks' tongues in honey and potted dormice, neither of them would be listening to the gathering wind and the constant grumbles of thunder.

The first blast hit the solid wagon like a blow from a mailed fist. The light vanished as though a lamp had been blown out and the rain lashed down on them.

He felt, rather than heard, Julia's gasp as she recoiled instinctively, the movement flattening her body back against his. Wulfric put out an arm and gathered her to him, finding as he did so that his embrace encompassed a shivering Berig as well. 'It's all right, it sounds worse than it is, the rain drums on the canvas,' he said, trying to be matter of fact.

Berig, radiating embarrassment, disentangled himself and turned over, leaving a hand's span of room between his back and Julia's front. Wulfric, with no inhibitions about close contact with the lithe softness pressed against him, pressed his face against the warmth of her hair and closed his eyes. Staring wildly into the darkness was not going to help.

The violence of the storm seemed to increase at the speed of stampeding horses. He could hardly believe that the solid, low wagon on its four wheels could rock, but it seemed to be quaking under the ferocious onslaught of the wind.

The thunder was overhead now. Wulfric pulled Julia over and pillowed her against his chest, pressing one cheek against his body, cupping his free hand over her exposed ear. She burrowed closer, endearingly trusting, despite the huge rift that had opened up between them. He had to fight to keep from kissing her forehead, which was all he could have reached with his lips.

There was a blinding flash that lit their canvas shelter like noon, gone as soon as it had come and followed by an enormous crack as the lightning struck close by. Berig rolled over and flung an arm across Julia as though his skinny body could protect her against fire from Heaven, and the three of them clung in a tangle of bodies as the lightning came again and again. It was like being under attack by an army of spear-throwing giants, and through it the rain and wind never eased.

Outside he could hear crashes, the thin wailing of a baby, a woman's scream in one of the brief intervals between thunder and lightning, but there was nothing he could do for them, nothing he could do but try to keep these two safe as the world went mad around them.

Slowly the thunder began to move away. The blasts of lightning, still coming with terrifying frequency, lit their shelter less vividly, but the rain did not stop, nor did the wind, and the air grew colder as though all the heat of the sun had been stripped away by the storm. Wulfric dragged blankets over them as Julia began to shiver.

Every inch of her body was pressed hard against his, but he could feel no stirring of desire, only of an intense possessive protectiveness. *Mine.* It was going to tear his heart out to leave her behind. For a while, when she had first guessed what he was planning, he had thought her distress was that she was leaving him. *The people I love, will be lost to me,* she had said, and his heart had stirred. But she had lost no time in making it quite clear that meant Una and her family and Berig, and not him.

Love, the word that had never been uttered between them. Wulfric lay in the darkness, eyes open, staring sightless at the sheltering canvas roof a hand's span above his face. He loved his kin, his tribe, his king, his family, his God. But a woman? In his position a man married prudently and, if he was fortunate, found himself tied to a woman for whom he could feel a growing affection.

What he was feeling for Julia was not a tepid affection. It was certainly not prudent. *Do I love her? Am I in love with her?* He pressed his cheek against the crown of her head, conscious that she had drifted off to sleep, despite the racket outside. Beyond her, Berig's slow breathing showed he had managed to sleep too.

Thinking of harm coming to Julia gripped him with a fear he had never felt for himself, yet he had taught himself to ignore fear and danger. The knowledge of how badly he had hurt her seared his conscience, yet he was a man who knew full well that not to do the right thing because of a personal consideration was wrong. He was a leader, leaders made hard choices.

And none of that helped. This must be love. 'I love you,' he murmured against her hair. *God.* It was weakening to feel this, to feel it for a woman he should not love, a woman he must send away for her own good as well as his. But how did you stop loving? How did you plight your troth to another woman, knowing your heart was already given?

It was only a matter of days now. He only had to stay strong, go through with his resolve and he could sail away, leaving her safe with the magistrate. In a month she would be back in the bosom of her family, and even if it proved to be a chilly haven, it was the best place for her.

I must not let her guess how I feel. His eyelids were

growing heavy. Wulfric gave up thinking and simply let his mind drift as sleep pulled him under.

Julia woke to stuffy gloom and comparative silence. Berig was, inevitably, snoring, Wulfric's deep breaths were stirring the hair over her ear, his lax arm was heavy on her ribcage. Outside she could discern a murmur of voices, but the wind and the rain had ceased.

She stirred and the man holding her was instantly awake. 'It's stopped. Berig!'

'Wha…?' Berig sat up with a start, his head bouncing against the taut canvas. 'Ouch!' A drip began. 'Ugh!' He rolled to one side and scrabbled at the cord lashings until he could poke his head out. 'Oh, my God…'

'Don't blaspheme,' Wulfric said automatically, rolling over onto his elbows in an effort to get at the lashings. He thrust himself out of the gap and Julia saw his feet disappear, just as Smoke shot through the hole after him.

'Don't bother about me,' Julia grumbled, finding herself alone. 'I can manage.' She wriggled out, disorientated. The camp had been transformed from an orderly mobile town into muddy chaos. The ground was littered with sodden debris, people stood around their wagons, attempting to right chests and barrels that had been scattered and broken; others, trying to walk, were slipping and sliding on muddy ground or tripping over hastily dug drains.

Trapped in the half-filled trench at the back of their wagons was a chicken coop, its inhabitants limp, soaked and dead. A bedraggled kid stood, head low with exhaustion, hardly able to bleat. Berig jumped down and picked it up and Julia threw him a piece of blanket to dry it with. The ground steamed like the slopes of the volcano as the morning sun hit it.

Wulfric was standing high on the piled baggage in their second wagon, calling to people who waved back as they saw him. 'It isn't as bad as it looks,' he said. 'I can't see anything overturned or smashed. People prepared well.' Then he turned, his narrowed eyes scanning the wide field until he was facing the sea and Julia saw him stop as though struck.

'What is it?'

'The fleet.' He was staring out across the wide bay as though unable to believe what he was seeing.

She scrambled up beside him and looked out over tossing grey waves, foaming white horses and an angry sea devoid of any vessel whatsoever. The fleet had gone.

'There's nothing,' she said, the shock making her stupid. 'Where have they gone?'

'To Hell,' Wulfric said flatly.

Julia sat down with a thump on the soaked wood of the driver's seat. 'Those poor men. So many, I cannot believe it. Perhaps some were saved. Some must have been able to swim, surely?'

'In that?' Wulfric jumped down. 'But you are right, some may have survived. I must go and help with the search for them.'

'I will come too. They are Romans, local fishermen, traders. My people.' She saw his mouth thin, then he shrugged.

'If you wish. It will not be pleasant. We will find more corpses than survivors, I would guess.'

'What does how *pleasant* it is matter?' Julia retorted angrily. 'All they are—were—are ordinary people trying to make a living. They saw an opportunity to earn honest money by hiring out their boats and now they have lost everything, even their lives.'

'I am just trying to protect you. Shelter you.'

'I am not a child. I am not even a respectable Roman virgin any more, am I?' Why she wanted to hit out at him, she did not know, not after her resolution to accept calmly what he had decided. Then the realisation of what this meant to the Visigoth clans gathered across these muddy acres came to her.

'What are you going to do? Not one ship is left. How can you leave these shores now?'

Wulfric turned to look at her, the breeze taking his hair back from his face so that every fine lineament was exposed to her. She could see the sculpture of the underlying bones, the tension of the muscles and tendons. He was tired, bone weary with this endless journeying, this search for a homeland and now, just when it had been within his grasp, fate and the force of nature had snatched it away.

'We cannot. We are trapped here.'

Chapter Sixteen

Their search for survivors and repairable ships became, inevitably, an exercise in collecting up a pitifully small number of bodies amidst a wasteland of wreckage.

Wulfric left the Council chamber at last, after an afternoon of ruthlessly practical analysis had left none of them with any illusions. They could stay here, trapped in the toe of Italy, until the Roman army found them or they could turn back, retrace their steps up the long road north and meet their fate somewhere where they could at least choose their ground.

'We will not get as far as Rome,' Alaric said. He had sat on the carved throne that travelled with him everywhere, had been brought by his great-grandfather out of the forests to the north and east, his gnarled swordsman's fingers caressing the worn animal heads that snarled from the ends of the arms.

'He is dying.' The soft words by his ear had Wulfric glancing sideways to meet Willa's steady gaze. 'See how blue his lips are, how bloodshot his eyes. His heart is failing and a fever is on him. He hopes to die in battle, but I doubt he will have that grace.'

'We must try.' Both men looked across to the speaker.

Athaulf, the king's brother-in-law, stood, one foot on the dais, his head thrust forward to try to ram home his argument. 'We go now, move fast, take them by surprise before the news of what we are doing reaches them. We do not stop, not for Rome, not for Ravenna, not for the army of the Eastern Empire, but press on for Gaul.'

'How? Over the Alps like Hannibal?' The king was having trouble maintaining the level of his voice.

'No, my lord, by the coast.' Wulfric stepped forward and found Willa still by his side.

'Aye,' the other man said. 'Narrow, but safer. The high passes will be closed by the time we reach them.'

'You three are in league to gainsay me?' Alaric leaned back in his chair, studying them. *He knows he is dying. He is amusing himself, speculating about who will succeed him,* Wulfric realised as the faded blue eyes rested on his face for a moment.

'No, lord,' he said steadily. 'We agree on how we can bring our people to a good land, as you wish.'

'Hah! And who will lead?'

'You, lord.'

'You are a diplomat, Wulfric, son of Athanagild, son of Thorismund. I taught you well. Will you be so diplomatic when I am gone and the three of you sharpen your swords and eye each other across the fires?'

'When you are gone, lord, we will mourn, and then the people will decide.' It was Willa, smoothly taking the pressure off Wulfric. 'But that is a matter for far in the future. Now we must act.'

Alaric turned to Athaulf, beckoning him, and his kinsman went to kneel beside the throne, head bent to hear the king's words.

'The crown will go to him, if we do not take care,' Willa

murmured. 'Alaric will name him. Besides, he has Galla Placidia in the palm of his hand. While he holds her, even this dishonourable emperor will not strike hard.'

'You would oppose Athaulf?'

'Wouldn't you?' Willa's mouth curled in a humourless smile. 'And then it will be you and I. A pity. I like you, we think alike. I would not enjoy killing you.'

'You are welcome to try, my friend.' Wulfric kept his gaze on the two men on the dais. 'But I would be sorry not to have you at my side—we work well together. I may yet choose to support Athaulf.'

'You have no ambition?'

'Not for a killing spree that would leave our people vulnerable to the Romans, no. But if you choose to attack me, I will defend myself, be in no doubt.'

'And if I go for the throne?'

'I will let you know my decision if, and when, that happens,' Wulfric countered. 'But if I decide not to support you, I give you fair warning, you get to that chair through me.'

Willa had responded with an inclination of his head and had said no more. Wulfric respected the man, respected his ambition, although it was not his own way to speak of such things so openly. There would be no shame in following such a king, the decision was whether to accept him, or to oppose him on his own behalf or Athaulf's.

'Why would a man want to be king?' he asked Berig whimsically as they rode back to camp.

'Why? For honour and glory and fame, of course. To bring renown on the names of his ancestors and eminence upon his descendants. To lead our people, which is a great thing.' The boy frowned and stared at him. 'Is that a trick question?'

'No.' Wulfric shook his head. 'No, I just wanted to be reminded.' What should he do? What were the voices in his heart saying and were they speaking out of duty, or ambition or habit? He dug his heels into the grey's side and urged it into a canter.

'When do we leave?' Berig asked breathlessly, as he brought his own horse alongside.

'Have you been listening at doors, boy?'

'No. Any fool can see we cannot stay here.'

'We leave tomorrow, as fast and direct as we can, up the west coast.'

'Towards Rome?'

'Yes, towards Rome.'

'And then what?'

'I don't know.' *It all depends who is king.*

'I don't know.'

Julia stared at Wulfric. Behind her Berig was packing the wagon, cursing under his breath as he slipped on the muddy ground. All around the camp was in turmoil as people packed their battered and waterlogged possessions.

'You don't know? But we are going back to Rome—you are sure at least of that?'

'We go towards it. We may not reach it,' he said reluctantly. 'At least, not without a battle.'

'Well, then, you had better take me with you, hadn't you? Who else is going to sew up your sword cuts?' Her skin crawled with fear she would not let show on her face. She had watched all the men at sword practice, could see for herself their courage and skill. She had seen Wulfric fight one man, showing both those qualities and more. But this was the Roman army they would be facing, the greatest army the world had ever known.

'I shall stick to my plan and leave you with the magistrate's family. You will be safer there.' As they talked, Wulfric was systematically pulling weapons out of the oiled wrappings in which they had been stored, checking them, testing edges with his thumb, then re-stowing them where they would come easily to hand.

'I don't—'

'You will do as you are told.' He slammed a sword back into its sheath and turned to her, angry and implacable. 'You will do as I say, if it means I have to truss you up like a hog roast and deliver you to the magistrate's doorstep like that. You will not argue with me, you will not try to seduce me away from doing what is right, and, if you dare to weep at me—'

'I am not!'

'Your lower lip is quivering.' Wulfric turned back to the weapons. Julia stared at the power of his bare forearms, at the raw scar of the sword cut she had stitched. She thought of those arms holding her with tenderness, of those big, calloused hands, which now were sweeping a knife blade over a whetstone, and the wickedly erotic way they brought delight to every tender crevice, of the feel of his lips, now set straight and implacable, as they grazed over the skin of her temples. Of the gentleness in those fierce green eyes when he made love to her.

'Please.' She laid one hand on his arm, felt the muscles tighten involuntarily under her palm, but his hand with the knife did not falter. She let her fingertips drift up and began to play with the embossed gold work on the broad gilt-and-garnet band that clasped his bicep.

'No.'

She ducked suddenly under his arm, up into the space

made by the side of the wagon, his arms and his body. 'Please? Must I beg you not to leave me here? Don't you want me any more?'

With a snarl he slammed the knife into the wood behind her, dropped the whetstone and snatched her into his arms. 'Yes, I do, and what in Hades has that got to do with anything?' His mouth crushed down on hers and his tongue plunged into her mouth with an angry force that made her sway. Then she fastened her hands in his hair and clung on, matching him with her intensity, refusing to let him cow her with the savagery of his passion.

Her body burned with wanting him, she ached, yearning against his mouth, uncaring that they were in the open, in the middle of the camp, surrounded by people.

Wulfric released her and she stood there, panting, as he glared at her, green eyes burning. 'That is why I will not take you with me. That is passion beyond sense and you cloud my mind and my judgement. When I am not touching you I know what is right to do about you, and I am damned well going to do it.' He jerked the knife out of the wood, as easily as if it had been in sand and not stuck two inches deep into oak. 'Go. I have too much to think about to be worried by women.'

Aroused, furious and humiliated, Julia swept round the back of the wagon and bumped into Berig, who was red in the face and obviously wishing he could sink into the mud and hide. 'Men!' she hissed at him.

'I didn't do anything,' he protested as she stalked past him. 'Julia—'

Of all the idiotic things to do! she railed at herself. *You know he desires you, you don't have to prove it, you've just handed him the perfect reason for leaving you behind. If you*

*were quiet and unobtrusive, he might have been well clear
of the town before he remembered you and—*

'Julia?' It was Una, distractedly trying to keep two small
boys out of the worst of the mud while she helped Sichar pack
their wagon. 'Honestly, look at these two! Could you have a
rummage in that chest and find some more trousers for them?
I've got mud on my hands, they are covered in it…'

Glad of the distraction, Julia did as she was asked, helping
Una get the two children into clean clothes and perching
them up on the wagon.

'Oh, look, those are Berig's.' Una pointed to a pair of
trousers and a tunic at the bottom of the chest. 'I had forgotten them. Could you take them to him?'

The plan formed in her head in the seconds it took to lift the
garments out and fold them neatly. 'Yes, of course. Una,
Wulfric is adamant I've got to go to the magistrate's house
tomorrow.'

'Oh, no!' Her friend ran and put her arms around her, heedless
of the big puddle she splashed through. 'But we're going north,
towards Rome. Why can't he take you back himself?'

Julia dropped her voice, one eye on the boys. 'He says it
isn't safe. Una, I can't thank you enough for everything
you've done for me. You've been like a sister—I can't speak
about it, I get too upset.' Her voice broke, even though she
thought—prayed—this farewell was false. She had thought
she knew what she wanted to say to her friend—now it was
all too much. What if she never saw her again? 'I love you.
Goodbye.' She bundled Berig's clothes close to her chest and
ran.

The next morning Wulfric borrowed Una's eldest son
Gunthar to drive the wagon that had been Julia's respon-

sibility. She stood by the side, awkward in her stained Roman clothes, gathering her courage to deceive him.

'You can sit up beside Berig and we will detour into the town and take you to the magistrate's house.' Wulfric was watching her like a hawk, as though he expected her to take to her heels and run, there and then.

'Very well,' Julia said steadily. 'May I have my money now, please?'

'Money?' He stared at her.

'It is customary in my society, when freeing a slave, to give them a purse of money so they can start their new life. I need to buy a slave myself, and decent clothes. Or do you wish me to return to my father's house looking as though I have been dragged at a barbarian's cart-tail for all these weeks? How my life is from now on may depend on how I appear to my family.'

He nodded. 'That is true, and just. I should have thought of it. More than one slave, I think. Wait.' He climbed up into the wagon and took a key from his belt. Julia drew in a deep, searching breath that seemed to go down to her toes and found that Berig was watching her, head tilted, a glint in his eye.

'What?' she mouthed.

He shrugged. 'Good luck.'

He knows I am up to something and he is not going to say... Julia got her expression under control as Wulfric jumped down and handed her a leather pouch. The weight told her it was as much as she had hoped for and more.

'Thank you,' she said with all the dignity of a young Roman matron, and tied the bag to her girdle under her cloak.

'Come.' Wulfric put one hand under her elbow and drew her towards the back of the wagon, into a little privacy. 'You are no longer mine. I find I regret that.'

'So do I. I told you so.' A small spark of hope began to flutter. Was he going to tell her that he loved her?

'You regret what you find are the freedoms of this life. You regret our lovemaking. You regret the people you tell me you love. But I do not think you will regret not being my possession.'

She looked up at him, up into the implacable green eyes, the strong face that showed a man ready to fight all his own desires in order to do what was right. She looked up into the face of the man she loved and who, it seemed, was not ready to hear how she felt. She could not make him listen.

'No,' she agreed steadily. 'I will certainly not miss being a possession. Will you kiss me goodbye? I doubt we could do it on Decius Marcus's doorstep.'

Wulfric took her in his arms and brushed his lips across hers, then he straightened and put her away from him. 'Goodbye, *miens liufs*.' My what? She did not know the word, and he did not translate. He swung her up beside Berig before striding off to mount his horse, and she almost asked the boy. Then she realised he would guess it was something Wulfric had just said to her, so she locked it away in her memory, along with the touch of his lips, so fleeting, yet so tender.

It was like walking out onto a battlefield in the certainty that you were going to die. A dreadful thing, but an honourable one and the right choice. To liken a man's honour in battle to his feelings for a woman just showed how far he had fallen into love with this brown-eyed Roman, Wulfric pondered as he turned aside from the road north and led his two wagons down into Rhegium for the last time.

He had made hard decisions before, but the knowledge that they were the right choices had made the hardship or the arguments easy to bear. Now this choice was twisting a knife in his guts and filling his mind with uncertainty. She wanted to stay, and she was wrong. A woman did not understand these matters of honour and duty, not as a Visigoth warrior did. He would simply have to do the right thing for both of them and bear the pain of that because he loved her.

'We are here.' Berig's voice jerked him out of his thoughts. This preoccupation with his emotions was making him weak; they could have been ambushed, set upon by footpads while he was dreaming about a pair of wide brown eyes, a pair of soft lips inciting him to passion.

'Good.' Wulfric dismounted and hammered on the door. The speed with which it was opened showed they were eagerly expected, or that Decius Marcus and his wife were desperate to get the embarrassing barbarians away before the neighbours noticed, he thought grimly.

The chief magistrate had done Julia the honour of coming to the door himself to welcome her, his wife at his side. Wulfric exchanged greetings, trying not to loom over the wife, who stared at him in wide-eyed horror. Berig was out of the wagon, lifting down Julia's meagre sack of belongings while she sat there demurely on the box, waiting to be assisted.

She was managing the shy Roman virgin act very well, he thought wryly, recalling the girl who had stood up to her knees in mud helping clear up the camp after the storm, or her grim determination as she had sewn up his arm.

Then he met her eyes and saw the anger that almost, but not quite, hid her fear and distress and all humour left him. This was it, these were his last few seconds with her. On impulse he unfastened the broad gold-and-garnet band that clasped his right wrist and pushed it over her hand. It was so large it slipped up her arm to her elbow.

'Oh! No, I cannot, it is too precious,' she protested, trying to slip it back down again.

'I wish you to have it.' Suddenly it was desperately important that she had something tangible of his. 'It was my grandsire's, and it was ancient before he had it. They are the old gods depicted on it. He would have told you it was a protection against harm. Keep it.'

'But, you have taken it from your sword arm.' She caught up his hand in hers, staring down at the white mark where it had covered the skin.

'So superstitious?' he chided gently to hide how touched he was by her alarm. 'I rely on technique, not upon talismans.'

Behind him he was conscious of her new hosts becoming restless and lifted her down, still protesting. She was so light in his arms for the seconds he held her, yet he felt somehow unsteady when he had released her.

'Julia Livia Rufa, you have met the chief magistrate, Decius Marcus,' he said formally, obviously startling the wife, who seemed to expect him to speak in grunts.

'My dear, welcome to our house.' The man was handling this with some aplomb, even if his wife was not. 'This is my wife, the Lady Lucia Cornelia Macula.'

Julia produced a composed smile. 'Thank you, sir. Lady, I am most grateful for your assistance—' She broke off as a furry body pressed itself between them. 'Smoke, no, you cannot come in.'

'A wolf! You have a tame wolf?' Lucia Cornelia slid nervously behind her husband.

'You do not tame a wolf, Lucia Cornelia,' Julia said calmly, her eyes locked with Wulfric's. 'Nor can you understand one. They are with you on their own terms, always.' *I am not talking about this animal,* her eyes told him. 'And this one is not mine, he is Wulfric's.' She crouched down and pulled Smoke's ears, then hugged him, getting a wet lick across the ear for her trouble. 'Good boy, now go back to Berig.' She produced another gasp from her hostess by hugging the boy, then mounted the steps and stood, eye to eye, with Wulfric.

The urge to reach and drag her back was almost a physical force; he felt his nails dig into his palms. 'Goodbye, Wulfric, son of Athanagild, son of Thorismund,' she said. She no longer stumbled over the long names. They sounded gracious from her mouth.

And then she had turned and gone.

Chapter Seventeen

Julia stood blinking at the back of the heavy door as the porter dropped the bar across it and waited deferentially for his master and mistress to usher their guest through. She closed one hand around the gold bracelet, feeling it truly was a talisman.

'Well, you have had an adventure, haven't you, my dear?' It was Lucia Cornelia, trying to sound bright and breezy and as if large barbarians dropped off kidnapped Roman girls of good breeding on her doorstep on a regular basis.

'Indeed, yes,' Julia agreed politely, following her hostess through into the peristyle.

'I expect you would like to use the bathhouse and to change before the noon meal. I have allocated you a slave and given her some of my clothes to tide you over until we can go shopping.' She seemed brisker and more confident the further she got from the front door.

'Thank you, Lucia Cornelia, you are most kind. I do hope I may take the slave with me around the town—I would not wish to inconvenience you to come with me.'

'We will see. It would not do for you to venture out without a retinue. Now, here we are, this is your room, and that is the girl who will look after you. We will see you later in the dining room.'

She smiled graciously and swept out, leaving Julia confronting a skinny girl of about fifteen, with a mass of russet hair tied back severely, a sprinkling of freckles across her nose and wary hazel eyes. She looked achingly familiar, then Julia realised why. The girl was a Visigoth.

'Hwa aithei izos?' she asked. It was suddenly very important to know her name, the memory flooding back of Wulfric's face when she confessed not knowing the name of the little slave girl killed when he had rescued her.

The wary look was replaced with one of burning eagerness and, instead of the requested name, a torrent of rapid Gothic that left Julia gasping. 'I do not speak much,' she explained. 'Tell me your name.'

'Ingunde, Lady. I am your slave.'

'How did you come here?' Julia asked, the girl's simple statement giving her an idea.

'I am not certain. I was hit on the head when Roman soldiers come to our camp, three years since. I woke up and I am in the slave market. My lady here bought me when she is in Rome.' She shrugged. 'Here I must stay.'

'Why did you not run away when the Visigoths came and camped outside the town?' Julia glanced around the luxurious room and the pile of clothing. 'You had better help me in the bathhouse while we talk or I will offend Lucia Cornelia by being late.'

The girl nodded and picked up towels, oil flask and strigil. 'The mistress had me locked up,' she said with simple acceptance. 'As soon as we hear they are coming.'

'Do you know of a man called Wulfric?' Julia asked as Ingunde led the way along the corridor.

'But yes. Everyone knows him, he is a great warrior like Willa and Athaulf and Alaric the king.'

'Are you of his kin?' The bathhouse was only a small suite—it was obvious why the master of the house preferred to go out to the masculine environs of the public baths.

'No. I have never seen him, only heard much of him.' Julia realised that Ingunde, like doubtless everyone in the household, had no idea why this lone woman had arrived to stay.

'Let me tell you why I am here,' she began as she untied her girdle and began to undress.

It took until they were back in her room and Julia was trying on one of Lucia Cornelia's spare tunics for her to get to the end of the story. 'And I want to go back, you see. I was much happier with the Goths than I was at home.' She pushed the bracelet firmly up her arm; it seemed to retain Wulfric's body heat.

'Me too,' Ingunde agreed sadly. 'But how, Lady?'

'I have a plan. Do you know anything about horses?'

'But yes. I ride very well, because I always run away from my mother and go to the horses with my brothers. I am in trouble all the time, but I do not care.'

'So, if you had the money, you could buy a good horse? One strong enough to carry us both?'

'Oh, yes, Lady!' The hazel eyes were dancing now. 'When?'

'I have another purchase to make first,' Julia said thoughtfully. 'Now, which way do I go for the triclinium?'

She found Lucia Cornelia already there, but the chief magistrate absent, called away, his proud wife announced, to the city council. 'And do you find your room comfortable?'

'Yes, thank you, it is such a relief after weeks in a tent,' Julia gushed, accepting a dish of pickled fish to make her choice from. In truth, she was already feeling uncomfortably claustrophobic, but instinct told her that the more revulsion she showed for her recent captivity, the better it would be. 'And the slave you have allocated me is such a good girl.'

'Really?' Lucia Cornelia sounded surprised. 'I confess I have always found her slow and dull, and I am sorry I had to give her to you, but I really do not have anyone else suitable—I sent my best girl to my daughter during her confinement.'

'No, really, she suits me excellently. I prefer a slave who does not chatter and keeps herself unobtrusive. In fact, if it would not be a great inconvenience to you, I wonder if I might buy her? I shall need a slave on my journey home, and I feel certain my mother would be much happier if I bought one from a respectable family where I know the history.'

'My dear, you may borrow her for as long as you wish!'

'No, I would prefer to purchase her. I am determined not to presume upon your hospitality.' Julia kept the winsome smile fixed on her lips and gritted her teeth. 'I have sufficient funds.'

'How so?' Lucia Cornelia put down her goblet and stared at Julia.

'Why, I insisted that Goth gave me gold when I left. I told him that I would have expenses on my journey back, and it was the least he could do after I had cooked for him and that boy, and washed their clothes.'

'And he gave it to you?'

'But yes. I was assertive, naturally—one has to be, don't you find, with non-Roman peoples? They respond well to firm direction.' The thought of Wulfric's response to *firm direction* was so amusing she had to bite the inside of her cheek to keep from giggling.

'And…' Lucia Cornelia glanced around her, was obviously satisfied that no one of any importance was within earshot—she could discount five slaves as non-existent—and whispered, 'He took no liberties beyond treating you as a household drudge?'

'Good Heavens, no!' Julia had no trouble looking appalled at this line of questioning. How was she going to answer without sounding either evasive or shifty? Then she had an inspiration. 'There was the er…boy, you understand.'

'No! How shocking.' Lucia Cornelia sounded intensely titillated by this revelation. Julia just hoped neither Berig nor Wulfric ever had any inkling of her stratagem. She found her fingers were stroking over the embossed animals entwined on the bracelet for comfort.

She did her best to look embarrassed, and to her relief her hostess changed the subject by recommending a dish of eggs. But there was no doubt that, reassured by the illusion of Julia's intact virtue, she was feeling much better about her uninvited guest.

'So, might I buy the girl?' Julia persisted.

'Of course. You may have her for what I paid.' Lucia Cornelia named a price, well within Julia's resources, and fell to gossiping about her daughter's latest baby, the relief that the invading throng had left the town and the inconvenience caused by the storm. 'With hardly any boats, trade is hampered and we are getting little good fish in the markets,' she lamented.

'And such a dreadful loss of life.' Julia felt quite shocked to have to make that point, the more so when she realised that the magistrate's wife was probably as sheltered from the daily reality of ordinary people's lives as she had been, only a short while before.

'Well, yes, that as well, of course.' Her hostess yawned slightly. 'Now, would you like to rest, or should we go out and buy some fabrics for your gowns?'

'There is no need for you to trouble yourself, I will take the girl,' Julia said, smiling. 'I would appreciate being able to do some shopping, and I would not want to bother you on such a hot day.'

'Well, if you are sure, dear. Tell the porter to give you one of the male slaves to carry things.'

'Thank you so much.' Julia kept the winsome smile fixed on her face as she slipped from the couch and made her way out. 'Is there anything I may get for you?'

Lucia Cornelia waved a languid hand in refusal and Julia took to her heels down the corridor to her room where Ingunde was patiently waiting.

'Ingunde, I have just bought you from Lucia Cornelia.'

'You have?' The girl's hazel eyes sparkled. 'So I will not be a runaway if I come with you?'

'No. But you must choose. You do not have to come at all, Ingunde, because I am giving you your freedom. Here…' Julia opened her purse of coins and removed two gold *solidii*. 'If you want to go your own way, this will help.'

'I cannot come with you?' Dismayed, the girl ignored the money.

'If you wish, come with me and I will take you back to your people. But you have the choice.'

'I will come with you, Lady. Now we get the horse? And then we can go?'

'Not immediately,' Julia said thoughtfully. 'It will not take us very long to catch up with them, for they can only travel at the speed of the ox carts, and I do not want to be so close he can send me back again.'

'I would be very scared if it was me who disobeyed Wulfric, Lady,' Ingunde said solemnly.

'Call me Julia, when we cannot be overheard. He *is* going to be angry, you are right.' Julia tried to tell herself that she was not afraid—after all, what could Wulfric do to her? But the more she thought about it, the queasier she felt. He wouldn't beat her, she did not believe that for a minute, but she had no desire at all to see what happened when he lost his temper. 'I will just have to manage as best I can,' she concluded. 'Wulfric has got many other things to worry about, besides me.

'Now, let's go and buy a horse.'

In the end, with Ingunde's sharp eye and withering comments on every minute fault in the animals they looked at, and Julia's patrician attitude to bargaining, which effectively cowed the dealer, they bought two horses with the harness thrown in. The dealer agreed to keep them until the next day and the young women went off to complete their shopping.

Buying the horses left the purse a little light, especially after they had bought boy's clothes for Ingunde, a pair of wicked knives for their belts, water flasks and blankets to act as bedrolls. But there was enough for Ingunde's slave price and to buy food for the two days Julia thought it would take them to catch up with the Visigoths on their slow march north.

They slipped out the next morning after the first meal. Julia left a wax tablet with an apologetic note in her room. She did not say where she was going, or how, in case the chief magistrate felt impelled to send riders after her. What they would think, she could not imagine, and she felt sorry for the worry she was sure she would cause them, but what else could she do, she reasoned, except write to them from the next town she came to and put their minds at rest?

In the public bathhouse they changed into male attire and hurried out before anyone saw them. Their hair was a problem. Julia bundled hers into an unflattering knitted cap and Ingunde plaited hers and dropped the plait down the back of her jerkin out of sight. They wouldn't convince anyone who gave them a second look for a moment, but then, Julia had no intention of getting close to anyone who might be a threat.

Ingunde went to get the horses, then gave Julia a leg up in the privacy of a back alley. After she had slid off the other side twice, she managed to get the hang of balancing, but it was very obvious that any thought of doing anything other than walking would lead to immediate disaster.

'You'll get the knack soon,' Ingunde promised her, leading the way through a network of back streets to the northern gate. They rode out under cover of a number of incoming goods wagons and soon were on the Via Popilia heading north in the wheel tracks of the Visigoth army.

At the end of that day, when Julia slid groaning off the back of her horse, she swore she would never be able to straighten her legs again, would never be able to get back on the horse again and would probably never be able to walk again either.

Ingunde, who had rapidly lost her awe of her companion, and with it her reserve, just laughed and led the horses to drink in the stream they had found. Julia hobbled off to find firewood, and they made a simple camp, well out of sight of the road. Over bread, cheese and cold meat washed down with water, Julia told Ingunde more about her adventure, carefully keeping to the main events and avoiding talking about Wulfric whenever possible.

'So,' Ingunde observed as Julia stretched out on her blanket, still grumbling about her stiff legs, 'you are in love with him.'

'Hwas? Hwa?' Julia sat bolt upright in shock. They had been chatting desultorily in Latin; for some reason, Ingunde's sly statement had jerked her straight into Gothic. 'What do you mean? Who?' She could think more clearly in Latin, and it seemed she needed to.

'Wulfric.' Ingunde sat up and curled her arms round her bent knees, resting her pointed chin on top. 'It is all right, I would never tell. I would never do anything to hurt you, you rescued me,' she added fiercely.

'I…yes, I am.'

'And you carry his child?'

'No!'

'Oh, I wondered if that was why you want so much to be with him again.'

'I just want to be with him,' Julia said flatly. 'He doesn't love me, and in any case he has to make a political marriage if he wants to be king. Or even to continue to lead the allies he has now, I suppose.'

'But Alaric is king.'

'He is not well. They are beginning to measure each other, the strong men, the ones with power, you can see it when they talk.' She had not realised it, being so close, but now she recognised the same political manoeuvring running under the courtesies of everyday life that she had noticed when her father had entertained men he wished to influence or to bend to his will.

By coming back, she was walking into the middle of this silent struggle for power, and if Wulfric was going to win it, she must recognise the precise moment when she must step back, open her hands and relinquish him. And then what was going to become of her?

Wulfric walked back from Alaric's tent, rubbing his hand through his beard and trying not to radiate anxiety. The king was ill and it was more than exhaustion, more even than the heart strain that turned his lips blue. This was an ague, a fever that had him sweating and shuddering in his bed, unable to stand, and none of his physicians' remedies were having the slightest effect on it.

He made himself put his hands at his side and stroll, stopping to speak reassuringly to anxious groups as he passed. They had tried to keep the king's condition quiet, but his very absence raised suspicions, and the sight of his Council disappearing into his tent for hours at a time and re-appearing solemn-faced was not helping.

They had stopped their journey north fifty leagues from Rhegium, just outside the town of Consentia, and were doubtless causing the townsfolk considerable anxiety by their lack of action.

'A fever, probably one of those marsh agues picked up when we were near Rome,' he repeated for perhaps the sixth time. 'The king is weak, as you would expect, but his mind is alert.' That was just about true, for minutes at a time, anyway.

Thank God he had left Julia behind in Rhegium. His left

hand curled around the leather wrist guard on his right wrist and rubbed it absently as he used to do with the gold bracelet. Was she wearing it now? Was she still angry with him, or had a few days of familiar Roman luxury made her realise how right he had been to leave her?

How long had it been? Six days, he realised. The ache of missing her was no less: he found he was waking, hard with desire, sweating from dreams where she danced, just out of his reach. But it was not simply lust, he knew that. He missed her for herself, for her courage and her temper and something he had no word for, but which made him feel whole when he was with her.

Wulfric saw Hilderic approaching and veered away. He recognised that he was not just neglecting to get on with the marriage negotiations for Sunilda's hand, he was positively avoiding it, and that was foolhardy when the battle for the inheritance might be almost upon them and he would need every ally he had, whatever action he decided to take.

He skirted round and approached his own tent from the back. They had pitched camp properly, in unspoken recognition that they might be there longer than anyone wanted to admit. Berig was sitting in front of the open door flap, grooming Smoke, whose tongue was lolling out in an absurd grin of pleasure.

'Is that my comb again?' Wulfric asked, resignedly.

'One of them.' Berig regarded him from under lowered brows. He was still upset about Julia, knew that he shouldn't be sulking and should obey his master, and couldn't quite work out how to get back on to terms with a man he was angry with. 'Julia used to groom him, he likes it.'

At the sound of her name the wolf whined. Wulfric grimaced in sympathy and leaned down to pull his ears. 'Look, I miss her too, but it was the right thing to do.'

'Suppose so.' Berig got to his feet and stretched. 'Hey, look, strange horses.'

Wulfric turned to look where the boy was pointing. If Berig, who seemed to know every horse in the camp, said these were strangers, then he was probably correct. But how had they got past the perimeter guards? Two animals, neither of them large, and ridden by two slight riders, no more than youths. He shaded his eyes against the sun, just as the rider on the bay turned to speak to his companion.

No! It cannot be, I am missing her so much I am imagining things. Then the rider pulled at his cap and a mass of glossy brown hair tumbled free. 'Julia!'

'What?' Berig scrambled up on the wagon. 'It is! Julia! Julia!' He was jumping up and down, waving both arms, and Smoke took off at a lope towards the riders, making both horses, unused to a wolf at close quarters, rear.

The other rider clung to their mount's neck like a limpet, but Julia simply slid off and landed with an audible thump on the ground.

Wulfric found he was running, his heart in his mouth.

She was all right, sitting winded on the hard earth, her hands behind her to brace her, her long legs clad in scandalous boy's clothes sprawled out in front of her.

Wulfric hauled Julia to her feet and began to shake her by the shoulders. 'You fool! You disobedient, wilful, immodest lunatic! You deserve that I should beat you, you deserve that I should lock you in a cage, you deserve that I send you straight back.' Her eyes widened in shock; he felt like a brute and that simply deepened his anger. How could she do this to him? 'In fact, I'll do just that, I'll get an escort together and back you go to Rhegium.'

Chapter Eighteen

Julia sagged dizzily in his arms. Her legs ached, her bottom hurt from contact with the hard ground and her head was spinning from the shaking Wulfric had just given her.

Then he let her go, still glaring at her.

'I am sorry—' she began, and got no further.

'Sorry? I'll make you sorry, so sorry you'll be begging me to send you back even sooner,' he threatened grimly, taking her by the shoulder and turning back the way he had come. She found Berig and Ingunde staring at them with identical expressions of horrified fascination on their faces. 'Who is that?' Wulfric demanded.

'Ingunde. She is a freed slave of the magistrate's house. She is a Visigoth.'

'I can see that. A pity she did not have more sense than to accompany you on this fool's errand.'

'She wanted to get back to her people,' Julia managed to gasp as she was hauled unceremoniously along towards the tents.

'That is natural, at least. Why you do not feel the same, I fail to understand.'

'Of course you do.' Julia managed to dig in her heels. Short of picking her up bodily, Wulfric was forced to stop. 'You are going back to Rome—I want to return on my own terms.'

'You will do as I tell you. How long did it take you to get here?'

'Four days. I kept falling off the horse if we went any faster,' she admitted sulkily. It was a sore point, both for her dignity and for her anatomy.

'Four days? Out in the open with no bodyguard? Do you realise how much danger you were in?'

'We were careful.' Ingunde spoke for the first time. 'And we are armed.'

'Armed? With that toothpick?' He gestured angrily at the knife in her belt. 'You at least should have had more sense.'

'Don't speak to my friend like that,' Julia snapped. 'Must you stand here ranting at us? Half the camp is staring.' It was a wild exaggeration, but they were certainly attracting attention.

'No,' he said slowly, his face grim. 'No, I don't have to stand here, we can have this discussion elsewhere.' Before she could resist he scooped her up, marched back, threw her face down over her horse's withers and mounted behind her, urging the weary animal away from the camp and up into the woodland that clothed the valley slopes.

It was undignified, uncomfortable and hideously embarrassing. When he finally let her slide off she was red in the face and her legs would not hold her. For the second time that day, Julia sat down with a painful bump.

Wulfric swung down off the horse and stood over her, hands fisted on his hips. He was wearing a leather wrist band on his right wrist, she realised; all the details of his appearance seemed starkly clear. 'What am I going to do with you?' he demanded.

'You said you would send me back. I will run away again if you do, I swear it.'

'I suppose you will.' He closed his eyes for a moment and she saw with a pang that he was looking tired once he let his guard down. 'Alaric is dying.'

'Oh, no! Poor man. How long?'

'I have no idea. Julia, you could not have come back at a worse time. There is danger from the Roman army, there is danger within the camp, and I have no time to look after you.'

'I do not need you to look after me.' She grimaced at his expression as he dropped down onto the grass beside her. All the anger seemed to have drained out of him, which made her feel even worse. He was tired, burdened with cares and she was adding to them. Now was the time, if there ever was one, to be strong, to be honourable and to do the right thing. Why was that never the easy path? she wondered bitterly.

'I know I am a worry to you, my timing could not be more wrong, but you do not have to concern yourself with me. Ingunde is going to seek her family. She is resigned that her parents were killed when she was captured, but she is certain she must still have some kin living. We will stay with them.'

'No,' Wulfric said flatly. 'You stay with me. I took you. Whatever happens, you are my responsibility until you get back to your father's house.'

'It will not be very popular with your new wife,' Julia pointed out, trying to ignore the hurt thinking about that gave her. 'And I am not going to stay with you once she is on the scene, believe me. If I am not your slave, then what am I? She will want to know, and I cannot blame her.'

'I have begun no negotiations for a marriage.' Wulfric was

sitting, knees drawn up and hands clasped round them, looking down the sloping glade towards the river and the camp below them.

'Well, you had better start,' Julia said tartly, making him look at her, surprise on his face. 'If the king is dying, then you need to have all your allies lined up with you. I will wager Willa and Athaulf have.'

'The argument is strong for Athaulf. Alaric will name him, he is kin.'

'Is he the king you need?'

'I am not certain. He would be a king in the old mould, but sometimes I feel we need something different. A new way of looking at the world.' His face was still and serious. There was more behind his words than uncertainty.

'To even think of going against Alaric's will makes you uncomfortable, does it not?' she prompted. 'It makes you feel disloyal. He must mean a lot to you.' He nodded. 'But your people perhaps need someone who thinks like you? Someone who wants to find a way to blend our two worlds into something new and strong?'

'Like me—or like Willa.'

'Oh!' Julia shifted round to face him, exasperated. 'You are so fair, so balanced, so reasonable! Do you have no personal ambition at all to be king? You know what to do with power, you can wield it, you can lead. Take it—be the king your people need in a new world.' She was grasping his hands, trying to pour some of her urgency and belief into him.

'Would you have me kill to reach that throne?' Wulfric asked her, his eyes suddenly bleak. 'I think Willa would do so. If the will of the people is overwhelmingly for Athaulf and Willa tries to overthrow that, I have told him he will do it through me.'

'If that happens and Athaulf cannot stop him, then he is not fit to be king,' Julia said robustly. 'Take it for yourself, or leave it. To risk your life for an ageing king for whom you have loyalty is one thing, to do it for a contender who cannot defend himself, even in his prime, is madness.'

'That is your advice is it, my Roman councillor?' He was smiling at her now, the amusement lifting the lines of strain from around his eyes.

'Yes, it is,' Julia said. 'Negotiate for a wife—it had better be Sunilda, I suppose, or you'll alienate Hilderic now. Make a claim on the throne—and stop being so fair about the competition!'

'You are a kingmaker—your Roman senator will need to watch out when you get home or he will find himself emperor,' Wulfric teased. He did not appear to suffer the slightest pang at the thought of her as another man's wife.

'Antonius Justus is in no danger of my interfering in his life. He would not have me now, I am sure, and I do not want him.'

'No?'

'No. He kisses like a wet fish.'

Wulfric snorted with laughter, closed his hands on hers and pulled her towards him. 'How do I kiss?'

'Like sin,' Julia said wistfully. 'Like sin and the taste of Heaven combined, and we should not, ever again.'

'Never?' He was very close, very male, very, very tempting. She could feel the pull of the charisma he was trying so hard to deny. He would, she knew in her heart, make a great king, if he could only overcome his scruples and believe that to reach for the crown was not arrogance and personal ambition, but his fate.

'Once more.' Julia said it on a sigh, knowing she should

be stronger than this. 'Just once.' She closed her eyes as Wulfric took her in his arms, kept them closed as her lips opened under his and she tasted him for the last time, feeling the sensual slide of his mouth across hers, the restraint with which he held her, his strong hands still on her body.

She knew he was aroused, that he wanted her. She could feel it in the tension of the long muscles that wrapped her to him and the hard stroke of his heart against her breast, but he honoured what she had said and when he lifted his mouth from hers he set her back away from him, his eyes smoky with passion.

She would never feel anything like that again; as long as she lived there would never be another man like this one. For a moment Julia let herself imagine what it would be like to be loved by him, to be his wife, and then she shut that dream away and felt her heart break as the key turned in the lock.

For a minute or two she wondered if either of them was ever going to speak again, or whether they would turn to stone there in the shade, gazing at each other. In a hundred years shepherds would tell the story of the lovers petrified by a spell…

'So, my councillor, where are you going to set up your tent? You will not live with me, I will not have you the other side of the camp with some family I do not know.' Wulfric's voice was husky with an emotion beyond simple desire. Julia watched him from under her lashes, but she could not read his face.

'By Una's, then. Will you find me a tent of my own?'

'You are expensive to keep,' he observed. 'I suppose you will want cooking vessels and plates and beakers.'

'Everything,' Julia agreed, grateful for the move away from tension and sensuality and the reality of loss. 'I could borrow from you, though, until we reach Rome. That would be an economy.'

'It would.' Wulfric flopped backwards as though sitting up was suddenly too much effort. Julia allowed herself to lie, propped on her elbows, an arm's reach from him. The air was hot and still, the birds had stopped singing in the heat and the scents of bruised grass and crushed herbs rose from where they lay. 'How is it,' he observed, 'you are so practical and give me so much good advice, yet you do such a foolish thing as to flee from Rhegium with only that scrap of a girl at your side?'

'I was stifled. It felt like being in a locked box after just one hour in that house.' She wrestled with her conscience and added, 'But I had planned to run away before we got there. I had the idea when Una gave me Berig's clothes to return to him.' Wulfric turned his head and regarded her quizzically. 'Yes, I know it was foolhardy. Before you took me I would have shrivelled with horror at the thought of acting independently, doing something so bold. Now, I cannot bear to be constrained.'

'I noticed. But four days on the road! Whatever possessed you?'

'I had no idea I would be such a bad rider and it would take so long,' Julia confessed. 'I thought it would be easy— not to ride well, but to stay on, at least. Ingunde tried to teach me, when she wasn't doubled up laughing at the spectacle I was making of myself.'

Wulfric sat up again, his energy apparently restored. 'I could teach you.'

Julia looked up and met his eyes. 'Better not, don't you think? And anyway, I am sure these trousers are considered quite indecent.'

'As you say.' He shrugged, then with a wicked spark grinned at her. 'The trousers are beginning to grow on me, though. You have very nice legs.'

'You have seen them without any trousers,' she pointed out, amused despite herself by what seemed to arouse the male libido.

'That's different. There is something about half hiding that is more exciting.' He uncoiled his long body and got to his feet, holding out a hand to pull her to hers. 'Come, let us get you back and respectably clothed and then we can find your companion's family for her.'

But when they got back to the wagons Berig and Ingunde had gone, leaving only Smoke on guard. Wulfric shrugged and went in search of Una, who returned, followed by Sichar hauling a bundle of canvas, and threw herself into Julia's arms.

'I am so glad to have you back! But what foolishness— and those trousers! How improper!' But the scold was spoiled by her wide smile and the tears in her eyes. 'Here's a tent for you, Berig can put it up. And there is a big sack to make a mattress. Can you borrow everything else you need from Wulfric? What about clothes?'

She rattled on, thinking out loud, occasionally breaking off for a hug, making Julia feel like one of her small children, returned from a prank. She was still talking, and Wulfric and Sichar had given up waiting for Berig and were putting up the tent themselves, when he reappeared, Ingunde at his side.

'What is it?' Julia saw Ingunde's face, pale and wide-eyed as she had been when she had first met her. 'Was it bad news?'

'They have all gone,' Berig explained, standing protectively close to the girl. 'People could remember the family, but no one has seen them since the attack when Ingunde was taken.'

'Then you stay with us,' Una said firmly. 'There is room in Julia's tent. I am Una, this is my husband, Sichar. Berig you have obviously met.' She cast a shrewd glance at the youth. 'And this is Wulfric.'

'I know.' Ingunde shot him a darkling look. 'I hope you have finished shouting at my friend Julia. She does not deserve it.'

Taken aback by the attack, Wulfric answered her seriously, although Julia could see the tell-tale signs of him suppressing laughter. 'I have finished shouting, yes. But the sooner the pair of you get into decent clothes, the better. Welcome to my kin.'

'I…you mean that?' Ingunde's face lost its pinched look. 'I did not truly expect to find anyone close of my own, but I did not realise what it would feel like to have no family.'

Una sniffed loudly. 'Bless you, child, you come with me. And you.' She grimaced at Julia's legs. 'The sooner you are both out of those clothes, the better.'

Wulfric tossed the mallet to Berig, who fumbled the catch. 'Finish off those tent pegs can you?' The boy stared at the tool, then at the tent. 'Julia's tent. What's the matter with you? You look half-witted.'

'Isn't she beautiful?' Berig appeared to have been hit over the head by more than a mallet.

'Who? Julia?'

'Ingunde.' Berig sighed gustily. 'That hair, those eyes…'

'Oh, for goodness' sake, boy, this is no time to go falling in love.' *And I have no time to put up with you mooning about like a lovesick sheep. One of us in that state is more than enough; at least I've the experience to hide it.*

'Isn't it?' Berig asked, his gaze suddenly focused and meaningful.

Hell, not as experienced as I thought after all. 'She's had a shock,' he said mildly. 'And she's young. Don't go hurrying her.'

Berig looked shocked at the very thought, then blushed. Wulfric, feeling about one hundred and ten, shook his head, added a few more well-chosen words on the subject of innocent virgins and hot-blooded youths and went to check on the king's condition. His previously tranquil tent was becoming a hotbed of emotion and suppressed passion; an hour in the company of grown men was what he needed.

As he walked down towards the cluster of tents arranged around Alaric's great pavilion, something in the movement of the crowd of people milling in the open space stopped him, one hand moving instinctively to his sword hilt.

The guards were not facing out as they should be, but inwards, spears tilted at all angles. The men waiting for news had turned as one and were staring at the doorway of the pavilion as if frozen.

Then there was a thin wail, the sound of earthenware crashing to the ground and a man appeared, ducking under the hangings. Alaric's physician. Wulfric broke into a run.

He reached the nearest guard, pulling his arm to swing him round. 'Damn it! Face out, what is the matter with you?'

Stumbling, the man did as he was told, his face white under his helmet. Confronted by Wulfric's anger, he pulled himself to attention and grounded his spear. *'Sa thidans diwith,'* he stammered. *'Sa thiudans sauk jah daw.'*

'The king has died,' Wulfric repeated blankly, even as his mind grappled with what must happen now. Why was he so shocked? They had expected this for days. He raised his voice and the other guards turned. 'Then show respect, do your duty and do not stand around like a lot of gossiping women at a well. Stand like warriors around the body of your king!'

They sprang to obey, their faces stark under their helmets, and Wulfric pushed past and into the pavilion. Inside was a sort of hushed chaos. A woman was sobbing in one corner, others gathered round her. The physician was holding forth to the group gathered round him about how he had done all he could and by the bedside stood a row of tall men, shoulder to shoulder, heads bowed.

Even from the back Wulfric could recognise Willa, Athaulf, Hilderic, a half-dozen more of the inner Council. He went to stand by Willa's side, facing down the length of the bed, and finally saw the face of the man who had held his loyalty for almost twenty years.

With the faded blue eyes closed, the trembling hands stilled and clasped around the hilt of his sword, he did not look his age, only as if he was sleeping and would rise shortly and stride out of the tent, refreshed after a short sleep.

The priest was finishing his business with oils and candles at the head of the bed and moved aside, head bowed in prayer to make way for the warriors.

'He died,' Hilderic observed, his voice neutral in the hushed space, 'before he named who he wished for his successor.'

Athaulf's head turned, as though jerked by a string and the look he sent the older man was inimical. 'We know who he favoured, it must be confirmed.'

Beside him Wulfric felt Willa square his shoulders. The whole group was braced, ready for an explosion of violence, either spoken or actual.

'No,' Wulfric said clearly into the fraught silence. 'No, that is not how it will be done.'

The faces, bearded, scarred, experienced and hard, turned as one to him—and Athaulf's blade sang as he drew it from the scabbard.

Chapter Nineteen

Across the dead king's body Wulfric faced the long, unwavering blade, then he drew his own and brought it up into the salute. 'As you show us, Athaulf, we draw our swords to honour Alaric our king one last time.'

Beside him Willa drew, followed by all the others in their turn and only Athaulf was left, his sword at the angle of attack, while his companions solemnly raised their own. Face flushed with anger, he brought his own blade up, seconds behind the others, then, as Wulfric sheathed his sword, followed suit.

Wulfric let his breath out in a long, inaudible sigh. 'Masterful,' Willa murmured. 'And what do you suggest we do next?' he added more loudly.

He had no clear idea, all he had wanted was to stop a confrontation over the deathbed. 'We should retire to the Council tent while the women and the priest prepare the body,' he said, 'and decide what is to be done next.'

They stood, instinctively, in a circle of equality in front of the great, empty chair. His first aggressive reaction thwarted,

Athaulf made no move to mount the steps. 'You have the floor, Wulfric, son of Athanagild, son of Thorismund,' Hilderic said with ponderous emphasis on the genealogy.

He sees himself as a kingmaker, Wulfric thought, his eyes thoughtful on the older man. *He sees his daughter as my queen and himself the power at my elbow.*

'It is unseemly to speak of the succession with Alaric unburied,' he said to a murmur of agreement. 'Let us carry out the funerary rites with all due honour and respect and then, and only then, will we be without our king. The first blow of grief will be accepted and we will debate the more calmly and wisely for it.'

'Where shall we bury him?' That was Euric, always stolidly practical.

'Here.' Athaulf was definite. 'There is flat land to raise a mound. It is fitting to lay him to rest where he died.'

'Under the walls of a Roman town? They would desecrate the grave and pillage its treasure the moment our rearguard was clear of the valley,' Willa said.

'What do you suggest, then?' Athaulf sneered. 'Cremation? Embalming and we carry the body with us?'

'Either is unseemly,' Wulfric said. 'We need a fitting location where his bones will not be disturbed. But I freely admit, I do not know where. We should go and break the news to our people and think on this. I vote we return at sunset and discuss it further.'

It took a long time to make his way back, passing the news, stopping to comfort the grieving, or to placate the anxious questioners with promises of more information soon.

'They feel insecure,' Una said, wiping the tears from her cheeks. She poured wine for them all as they sat in a subdued group around the fire, which seemed to give comfort, despite the heat of the day. Wulfric was conscious of small groups gathering, watching him, but not intruding. He had always been treated with respect as a leader; now he sensed a new distance being set around him: there was something different in the way people were standing, waiting patiently for his attention.

He got to his feet and walked over. 'Go back to your own fires, my friends, and grieve, there is nothing to be told yet.' They nodded and went, obedient, but with lingering, backward glances.

'What's to be done about the burial?' Sichar asked, passing the wine flask to Berig.

'We need to find somewhere that will not be disturbed the minute we are gone.' Wulfric ran his hand through his hair as he racked his brains. The ends were almost straight, he noted with part of his mind; he had been too preoccupied with Julia to remember to plait it. 'Somewhere we can bury Alaric with respect and with grave goods in the old manner, but somewhere secret.'

There was a thoughtful, but unproductive, silence. Then Julia cleared her throat. He had been trying, very hard, not to look at her and achieving some success. But he was as conscious of her presence as if she had been touching him, and the grief of renouncing her still felt as fresh and raw as when he had left her on the chief magistrate's threshold. He schooled his face to neutrality and turned to her.

'You have a suggestion, Julia Livia?' he asked formally. 'Please, make it.'

Her eyebrows rose a little at his tone, and his use of both her names, but she said, 'I noticed, when we were following your tracks, Ingunde and I, how wide the swathe of countryside was that was trodden, and how disturbed the ground was. You could hide anything under that.' She shrugged, displeased with her thought, 'But that is not a sensible idea, it would not be respectful to bury him under a road.'

'No.' Wulfric realised he was frowning at her and smiled. He loved the way her mind worked, the way she observed things, the little crease between her eyebrows when she was puzzling over something. 'But it is a useful observation.'

In the back of his mind an idea was stirring, taking a vague shape, but grope after it as he might, he could not catch hold of it. He took a long draught of wine and got to his feet. 'I am going to walk and think.' Berig scrambled to his feet. Suddenly he could not bear to have anyone near him—the weight of their questions and hopes and worries seemed crushing. 'Alone. I will be back for Council at sunset.'

They all sat down as Wulfric left and Julia realised that, without any word being said, they had all stood when he did. She shivered. The assumption that he would be king was growing, and she could see nothing but trouble ahead.

Athaulf she had no particular feeling for, but she guessed he could be vicious if he saw a real rival. Willa was impressive and, quite simply, dangerous, both as a rival in people's eyes and as an opponent on a personal level. He was of the same calibre as Wulfric, but, she guessed, with an ambition that was beginning to eat at him.

'Go after him,' she said to Berig suddenly. 'And take your weapon.'

'He said he wanted to be alone,' the boy protested uneasily, but his eyes were still on Wulfric's retreating back.

'Then do not let him see you,' Julia said, giving him a push. 'We don't want any accidents, do we?'

He gave her a startled look, then nodded with sudden comprehension and ran, dodging behind wagons, able to keep out of sight while Wulfric's height made him easy to follow. Smoke whined, then lay down at Julia's feet.

With a frown Sichar got up and went to pick up a whetstone, then stood, leaning against his wagon as he sharpened his knife, watching the direction the other two had gone in.

'Do you think he really is in danger?' Ingunde asked.

'Only if he doesn't see the other man first,' Julia said wryly. 'I don't know, I just have a bad feeling about this. I sense someone, or something, watching us. I have felt uneasy ever since we arrived here.'

'It is just the mood of the camp. People were worried about Alaric, anxious about where we are going.' But even as she spoke Una was shifting on her stool, looking anxiously for her children.

'Do you want Wulfric to be king?' Ingunde persisted.

Julia stared into the fire, watching the flames consume a log like a hungry tongue. 'I want whatever he thinks is best, but I am not sure he knows yet what that is.' The charred wood collapsed in a shower of sparks. 'I am a Roman, it is not my place to say what I think about the kingship of the Visigoths.'

'Go on, tell us,' Una urged. 'I would like to know how it seems to you.'

'Very well.' Julia dragged her eyes back from the tributary valley where Wulfric had vanished. 'I think that Athaulf represents the old ways, and perhaps the comfortable, familiar ways. But that he will succeed any better than Alaric at securing your land from the emperor, I very much doubt. Honorius will see you all as still too different, too alien. You will still seem like a threat, even if he gives you what he wants.

'Wulfric or Willa would be less comfortable for you, they would make you more like Romans—but where they settled they would make the Romans more like Goths. I think they would be strong in their dealings with Honorius, yet they would reassure him too.'

'Wulfric *or* Willa?' Una queried. 'You have no opinion as to who is the better man?'

'You know I do. But Wulfric respects Willa, he would be a good second choice.'

'And you would give Wulfric up?'

'I have already given Wulfric up,' Julia said tartly. 'Whatever happens, I will leave you when we get to Rome.'

'He knows?' Una's pitying face made her want to cry. Julia bit her lower lip until the sting of pain steadied her.

'He knows. It is, after all, what he wants.'

'It is what he thinks is right,' Ingunde said suddenly. 'That does not mean it is what he wants.'

There was no answer to that, not one that would not expose every lacerated wound on her heart. They sat in near-silence, occasionally throwing wood on the fire, watching for Wulfric and Berig to return.

Restless, Sichar finished sharpening his knife and strode off, muttering about checking the horse lines. Julia could almost hear the swish of the grains through a sand clock, and still they did not return.

Finally, as the shadows lengthened, and she was on the point of suggesting to Una that they ask Sichar to go and look, Wulfric appeared, striding through the camp, Berig, red-faced, at his heels.

They reached the fireside, obviously in the throes of a continuing row. 'When I want a nursemaid I will ask for one,' Wulfric said to Berig, his face grim. 'I left you here, thinking you would help Sichar guard the women.'

'There was someone in hiding, watching you,' Berig protested defiantly.

'And he vanished like mist when you turned up, crashing through the undergrowth. I thought I had taught you stalking. Any game would be in the next valley by now, let alone anyone spying.'

'I think someone is watching us too,' Julia intervened.

'I know there is. Do you think I hadn't noticed?' Wulfric raised one arrogant eyebrow. 'It is probably simply some of the garrison from the town, worrying about what we are going to do next.'

'Or someone's man with a sharp knife,' Una murmured.

'Hades, woman! If someone wants to challenge me, they will do it to my face. They are all men of honour here—or do you doubt your own people?'

'We do not doubt Willa,' Julia put in, trying to divert his wrath from her friend.

'But you do doubt someone else we will not name? You may well be right that he is an opponent. But a secret assassin? And in any case, give me some credit for being able to look after myself. Why do you think I am sweating in chain mail on a day like this?'

'Because it makes you look even more impressive?' Ingunde asked sweetly. She had slid around the fire to stand near Berig. Julia spared a glimmer of admiration for the carefully judged way she was offering him support without making it look as though he needed it.

Julia held her breath, waiting for the explosion, then Wulfric grinned at the girl and the tension drained away. 'You have the same adder's tongue as Julia, young Ingunde. Have I taken a nest of snakes into my household?'

'They are part of my household now,' Una interjected. 'And should you not be at Council?'

Wulfric glanced at the sky. 'Aye, I should. Berig—stay here. I mean it.'

He strode off, leaving the four of them in various states of exasperation and anxiety. 'Was there really someone there, following him?' Julia demanded.

'Watching him, certainly,' Berig said, fidgeting uneasily about the fire. 'Whether he followed Wulfric, or whether Wulfric walked into something, I don't know. Whoever it was, was very good. And I was not as bad as he said,' he added resentfully. 'If I hadn't virtually trodden on a partridge, neither of them would have known I was there.'

'Did you see the watcher?'

'No. And it may have been more than one man. I think Wulfric may be right, I think they may be Romans. I don't know why, it is just a gut feeling.'

He glanced up uneasily at the valley sides enclosing them and Julia reached down and stroked Smoke's head for comfort. Someone was out there, and they did not mean good.

'Well?' Hilderic demanded as the Council members came back into the tent. 'Has anyone thought of a solution?'

He appeared to have appointed himself to lead the Council and Wulfric sensed the same tacit agreement amongst the others that this was a wise move. Better that someone not in contention for the throne took charge for the moment.

'Athaulf? Euric? Willa?' One after the other heads shook. 'Wulfric? Have you an idea?'

'Yes.' Heads swivelled. 'The river.'

'The river? How does that achieve what we need? Do you want to send Alaric's body off on a raft?' Athaulf scoffed.

'I want to dig the grave in the bed of the river. Despite the season, the Basentus maintains a good flow. Even if it drops later, the passage of water over the river bed will erase all trace of disturbance.'

'And you intend to part the waters like Moses, do you? Have you delusions not just of grandeur but of divine influence, Wulfric?'

Wulfric kept his temper—Athaulf's reaction was too predictable. 'I have been to look at the river. It has moved its course over the years as rivers do, and it has left an old channel silted up. If we dam the Basentus, just downstream of the old channel mouth, the waters will flow into it again and we can dig in the river bed.'

There was silence. He anticipated questions. Athaulf's sneers were only to be expected, but he had not expected silence. Perhaps he was mistaken to believe his influence was still strong in the Council now the king was dead.

'Inspired!' Willa broke the quiet. 'That is positively inspired.' He clapped a hand on Wulfric's shoulder and murmured, 'I really am going to have to watch you, am I not?'

'Like a hawk,' Wulfric murmured back with a smile that showed his teeth. Or was Willa watching already? He really could not bring himself to dislike the man, try as he might. Nor could he believe, in his heart, that he would stoop to assassination.

The others broke into a babble of agreement and questions. Hilderic banged on the table. 'It is agreed? Then let us plan.'

It was late when they split up to work through their kin groups, telling the head men in each family what was intended, sorting out the guards to take the high ground all around the valley so no spies would observe the king's final resting place, selecting the condemned criminals who would create the dam and dig the grave, deciding which treasures would go with Alaric to his grave.

When Wulfric returned to his own fireside, grateful now for the warmth of the flames, he found all of his family seated round it, patiently waiting. Una was dozing gently against Sichar's shoulder, his hand caressing protectively over the mound of her belly. Berig and Ingunde had their heads together, whispering. Julia was grooming Smoke.

As the wolf looked up and gave his sharp bark of greeting, Wulfric realised how he was thinking about these people. None of them was closely related to him, yet he thought of them now as family. He had only begun to think like that when Julia came into his life. He tried to imagine sitting beside a camp-fire with Sunilda and feeling this warm inside, this calm, this—he wrestled for the word—this *belonging*. He failed. Life with Sunilda was not going to be peaceful, whatever else it might be.

He dropped down to sit on the ground beside Julia and took the bone comb from her hand without speaking. Smoke grunted with pleasure as he began to groom him harder than Julia ever would.

Sichar looked across, nodded, and went back to holding Una. He was, except in battle, a placid man and would be content to wait until Wulfric told him what was going on.

Berig, engrossed in his first love affair—whether he realised it or not—hardly noticed his return. But Julia, so close that he could feel her quivering impatience to know what was going on, simply placed her hand on his shoulder and waited.

Wulfric fought with his instincts as he dragged the comb through the rough pelt, then gave in to them and let his head tip sideways until his cheek rested against the back of her hand. He felt her stiffen, then her hand twisted until his cheek rested in her palm, and with her other hand she began to caress his hair in time with the strokes of the comb through Smoke's fur.

All he wanted was to sit like this for a little while he went through the events of the day, ordered what he must do on the morrow. Then he wanted his supper, a beaker of ale, perhaps, a wash in the warm water from the pot in the ashes. And then he would lift Julia in his arms and carry her into his tent and…

Her lips were warm at his ear and her lithe body was pressed close. Wulfric heard the growl deep in his own throat and felt the way his body hardened at her touch.

'Wake up,' Julia whispered. And he came to himself to find her smiling, her lips so close he hardly needed to move to touch his to them. For a long, drugging moment hers clung, the sweet taste of her like everlasting temptation, then she straightened, her cheeks flushed, and he realised she was as tired as he was, and as much off her guard.

'Is there any supper?' he asked, waking Una, who sat up with a gasp. Berig and Ingunde, who had managed to creep back into the shadows, strolled out again, attempting not to look self-conscious and Sichar sat bolt upright, trying hard not to look like a man who had just woken up.

'Yes, yes, there is a very good stew,' Julia said hastily. She was flurried and flustered and the realisation gave him a warm glow of satisfaction before common sense brought him back to reality. She was not his, she could never be his and the sooner he admitted it—really admitted it—the better for both of them.

She served up the food, broke the bread and poured the ale and they ate where they sat. Wulfric changed his position nonchalantly so he could watch her as she moved with grace around the dying fire. There was the feel of being on the cusp of some great change, that this evening was the end of something and they would never sit around like this again, casual and sleepily at ease.

'Well,' Berig said at last, predictably the one whose patience and curiosity had the shortest leash, 'what is happening?'

'We bury the king in the bed of the River Basentus,' he said, watching to see how they took it. 'It was Julia's idea about the passing of the great throng of people obliterating the signs on the earth that made me think of it.' He bowed slightly to her, making her blush. 'We start work tomorrow.' There was an awed silence. 'Never was a king buried in such a way,' he said quietly. 'Never will one's resting place be so secret.'

Chapter Twenty

Julia was stunned with the speed with which the burial plan was carried out. She realised she should not be—the heat of the autumn days that far south, the risk of attack at any time, made haste essential. Nor should she have been surprised at the organisation that had a cordon thrown around the area by dawn, the guards supplied with food and water by the older children acting as runners up and down the valley slopes.

Strong men, used to leadership and to improvisation and a people long practised at working together, were elements that produced an atmosphere far different from how she imagined the militaristic Roman response would be.

She worked alongside Una, preparing food for the guards now, and for the feast later, and watched for Wulfric. He passed often, not on horseback as she imagined he would, but on foot. That way he could speak more easily to people, both to organise and to reassure. He seemed tireless, she thought as she and Una flopped in the shade for a rest, mopping their brows after an hour spent by the fireside and the cooking pots.

Bare-headed, his hair golden in the sunlight, he stood out

even amidst the groups of large men around him. Julia watched as he paused and stopped an argument dead, just as the disputants were reaching for their knives. Wulfric did not seem to do very much, he simply interposed his broad shoulders into the narrowing space between the two men and said something quietly.

'Natural authority,' Una observed, following the direction of Julia's gaze as he turned away, heading for the next problem.

'More than that, he has charisma. I understand what Berig means when he says Wulfric is king-worthy. I thought at first he meant he had the right bloodlines to be considered, but it is more than that, isn't it?'

'Oh, yes—oh!' Una broke off as one of the men, just as his knife neared its scabbard, jerked it up again and made a lunge for his opponent.

Wulfric spun round, his hand already reaching for the man's knife arm, apparently acting on sound alone to guide him. He forced the wrist over until the sharp blade fell to the ground, then followed the move up with a square blow to the jaw. The man went down as though poleaxed. Wulfric spoke a few curt words to the onlookers and strode off.

'Phew!' Julia sank down again on her stool. 'Charisma *and* an amazing right fist.' This was the man who had made love to her, she mused. At times he had been so tender, at others urgent, dominant, yet she had never lost the sense that they were partners in some erotic journey of discovery.

There was a distant rumble, and a drift of dust, like smoke on the side of the valley amidst the trees. 'They must be blocking the river—shall we go and look?'

'Are we permitted?' Julia got up and brushed down her rumpled skirts. 'I thought no one was allowed.'

'We can go and look at the river and see if they have succeeded in diverting the flow.' Una led the way down to where it curved round a bend. Upstream, on the shore, guards stood, hands on their spears, eyes watchful. 'Yes, look, it must be working.' She pointed and Julia saw the swirls of muddy water and the definite slackening of the flow.

'I suppose it will stop and then start again as the old channel is filled,' Julia said, fascinated, as the river gradually ebbed away to a trickle.

A crowd gathered around them, watching and waiting. Small boys dashed daringly down to the muddy bed to snatch up floundering fish, until at last, in a wave of mud, dead foliage and tumbled branches, the river came to life again, swirling past them.

'Look.' Una pointed and there was Wulfric, mounted now, riding out of the valley and stopping to speak to the guards on the bank. Another man reined in beside him, then they turned and vanished up towards the site of the dam. 'Willa. Too friendly by half,' Una said as they turned and went back to their cooking pots.

'Wulfric likes him,' Julia pointed out, wondering if she could put off milking the goats, one of her least favourite tasks, until after the noon meal. 'It would be easier all round if he did not—at least he would feel more comfortable standing for the kingship.'

'I don't know what is the matter with him.' Una put her hands in the small of her back and grimaced. 'This baby has six feet and they are all kicking. Are you going to milk those goats?'

'Yes, all right.' Julia picked up a bucket and a stool and warily approached the oldest nanny goat. Their dislike of each other was mutual, and she watched warily for its yellowing teeth. 'The matter is, I *think,* that whereas Athaulf and

Willa want to be king because they want it for themselves, Wulfric is only considering it because he thinks it is his duty.'

'Hmm. He didn't think like that before you arrived.' Una did not say it unpleasantly, but Julia shifted on her stool, her conscience pricking her. 'He might not have thought seriously of the crown, but he was certainly ambitious enough to want to lead as many spears as he could draw into an alliance with our kin.'

'Well, the sooner the funeral is over and they are forced into a decision, the better,' Julia said, slapping the fidgeting goat firmly on the hindquarters. 'And the sooner we will get to Rome. Then I will leave and he can marry Sunilda.'

'I am sure Sunilda would agree with you,' Una said wryly.

Guards stayed at their posts throughout the night and the men did not come back to the wagons. There was activity at the burial site, the flares of the torches uncanny as they flickered amongst the trees in the wooded valley sides, and there was much going on around the king's encampment.

Berig appeared, unloaded a wagon, harnessed the oxen and led it off. 'For the burial goods,' he explained, looking harassed. 'We need four of them, all in good enough condition to jolt over the river bed.'

The women of Alaric's household would be laying him out, dressed in his finest clothes, Una explained, as the three of them had their evening meal.

'May we watch the burial?' Julia asked. 'I do not know the custom. Are women allowed?'

'Normally, yes. But this time, no. It will just be the Council, the priests and the men who will fill in the grave and unblock the dam.'

'How can they be trusted to keep the secret?' Julia wondered aloud.

'They are all condemned men. Criminals. This is their one act of grace before they die—they will not leave the valley alive.'

'Oh.' Julia tried to imagine the scene. The rough river bed with its pools and trickles of water reflecting the torchlight. The grim-faced guards, the exhausted men who would see the dawn one last time. It was like some sacrifice from the days of the old gods, the blood of the men mingling over the grave of the king as the sun rose.

Wulfric and Berig came back before first light and woke them. 'It will be at dawn,' Wulfric said, stripping off his filthy, wet clothing with his usual lack of self-consciousness. Una and Ingunde modestly effaced themselves as Berig lugged water, but Julia made no pretence of looking away.

She knew his body so well now, by touch, by scent, by sight. His muscles moved in the firelight, his skin gleaming like silk, cut here and there by old scars. She wanted to go and stand behind him and run her hands down his back, her thumbs dipping into the valley of his spine, feeling the taut dip of his waist, the flexible twist of his hips as he turned to take her in his arms.

And then she would be able to caress downwards through the felt of hair to where it narrowed, darkened, into the intriguing tangle of curls that shielded his sex and...

'Julia, do you know where my fine linen tunics are?' He was standing there—trousers on, thank goodness—waiting for her to come out of her trance. Julia fought for some composure. He must have known she was staring at him. Had he guessed what she was thinking? The firelight reflected in his eyes made his gaze seem as hot as the touch she was longing for.

'In the trunk behind here.' She hastened to open it, thankful for the excuse, searching by touch in the feeble dawn light. When she came back, holding out a choice of three for him, he had unlocked a small chest and was laying out pieces of jewellery, far finer than any she had seen him display before.

'Berig!' He handed the youth arm clasps and a heavy belt buckle, then took out a cloak pin and passed it to Ingunde, who gasped and ran her fingers over it, holding it up to the light to admire the twisting gold wire-work. 'Una may have borrowed you, but my household will be properly dressed for the occasion.' Despite his serious tone, Julia saw the corner of his mouth lift at the girl's pleasure. 'I shall want them all back in the chest by the end of the day,' he warned the youngsters, provoking earnest nods.

He laid aside more clasps, a circular cloak pin and a magnificent buckle in the form of a coiled serpent, then turned to Julia.

'What will you be wearing?'

'The dark red gown of Una's and the long gold-and-red scarf over my head.'

'Here, then.' There was another clasp to match the one he had given her in Rhegium, a necklace of twisted gold chains and a brooch heavy with garnet studs. 'I do not expect these back,' he added quietly.

'I cannot!'

'Why not? Why do you want to deny me the pleasure of giving you something that enhances your beauty?'

'Because…' She stumbled over the words, then made herself say them plainly. 'Because they should be Sunilda's.'

'Garnets would not suit her, she would look better with blue or green stones, I think.' He must have seen from her expression that this was a less-than-tactful answer. 'If I contract to marry Sunilda, *then* the bride price will be agreed, and the jewels I will give her will be selected. Not before.'

Wulfric turned away and began to clasp the bracelets at his wrists. 'Let me.' Julia closed the right-hand one by encircling it with both hands. 'I am glad you have a proper talisman on your sword arm again.'

'The priests would chide you for superstition,' he observed, smiling down at her as she reached for his left wrist and pressed that clasp closed also.

He changed the buckles over on his sword belt and settled the glittering scales of the serpent low on his hips. Julia handed him his cloak and, when he had swung it over his shoulders, she reached up to fasten the pin over his left breast. 'Another talisman,' she murmured, pressing her palm flat on it for a moment to feel the beat of his heart beneath. 'I wish I did not feel you needed them.'

'The watchers have gone.' Wulfric threw one side of his cloak back to free up his sword.

'Only because of the cordon of guards. They are still there, I can feel them.'

'So can I.' Wulfric lifted her chin in his hand. 'No wandering beyond the boundaries. Tomorrow we will send out sweep riders to draw their attention, and some scouts on foot I hope they will not notice, and then we will see what we can find.'

Julia twisted her head to kiss the long, calloused fingers. 'Go safely, Wulfric, son of Athanagild, son of Thorismund. I will see you at the feast.'

Then he and Berig were gone, outlined against the sky, which was just beginning to turn milky rose with the first hint of dawn.

* * *

The women lined the banks of the river and waited, covered heads lowered. Higher up, close to the bend that hid the burial site, the men stood in silent ranks.

They had wept, both men and women, as the wagon had creaked past with Alaric laid out upon a raised platform draped in rich purple-and-scarlet cloths, his helm on his head, his sword in his hands. The treasure wagons followed with their tribute of glory to go with him into the darkness.

It was pagan, yet the priests followed close at either side, and prayers were said, with no sense that they were seeing something from the past, the last of the kings to come out of the forests of the east.

When the cortège had passed out of sight, many of the women began to sing, very softly. Julia could not make out the words, but the swelling wave of sound seemed to carry their grief and make it tangible. She found there were tears in her eyes as she stood there.

How long it was before they heard the horns blaring, the sound echoing from side to side of the valley like the summoning of a great army to battle, she had no idea, but the sun was climbing now, staining the scene with light. The weeping became louder, drowning the soft singing, and there was a cry as first one, then a dozen bodies came swirling down on the current. The condemned men who had dug the grave had been executed, their blood had been spilt over the dead king's resting place.

His ancestors would have approved of the sacrifice, Julia thought bleakly, averting her eyes from the last of the bodies. And the temporary dam must have been breached, for the water ran first muddy, then clear again.

'It is done,' Una said quietly. By her side Ingunde wiped

the tear tracks from her cheeks. 'It will never be the same again.'

No one seemed to want to move. 'Look,' Una murmured, 'the king's household.' There was a tall woman, no longer young, her face bleak with grief. Around her, her tirewomen and, slightly to one side, also surrounded by servants, someone Julia recognised.

In formal Roman clothing, her head veiled, was a slender woman whose dark brown hair flowed down below the edge of her head covering. 'Galla Placidia. She looks very calm.'

'She thinks she is going to marry the next king,' Ingunde observed. 'Do you think it is a love match, her and Athaulf?'

'I do not know,' Julia said drily. 'It has been known to happen.'

Ingunde flushed, and seemed on the point of apologising for her lack of tact when the waiting women finally began to move away from the water's edge.

Julia, Una and Ingunde drew back a little to allow one group to pass. 'You! What are you doing here, you Roman? It is a sacrilege.' Sunilda, magnificent in dark blue, her eyes flashing, her arms laden with heavy bracelets, confronted them.

'I am here out of reverence to the memory of your king,' Julia said as calmly as she could manage. She did not care what Sunilda thought of her, but she did not want any of the onlookers to believe she was here in any spirit other than one of utmost respect. 'Galla Placidia is also here. I mean no disrespect, any more than she does. In Rome it is normal for visitors to attend state funerals.'

'Princes, ambassadors, persons of status and worth, I am sure,' Sunilda sneered. 'Not slaves, not whores.'

Julia gasped. Heads were turning. Ingunde stepped forward and Una put a hand on her arm to hold her back.

'I am neither, Sunilda. And it is you who are showing disrespect to speak so, just moments after the funeral. You do not like me, I can understand that, but this is neither the time nor the place to discuss it.' Julia knew her cheeks were burning under the scrutiny of so many watchers. A murmur of voices rose around them and she realised that they were the centre of a circle now. She struggled for dignity and control. It was difficult in the face of the tall woman's powerfully angry personality.

'This is exactly the time, without any of the men here to be seduced by your witchcraft, you whore.'

'Stop using that word. I am no such thing.'

'You deny you lie with Wulfric?' Sunilda spat, her veil whipping back in the breeze. 'You would swear on the relics to that, would you, Roman slave?'

'No, I do not deny it.' She would go far to evade an answer, but Julia knew she could not put herself in the position of having to swear falsely, or to be seen to be forced to an admission. 'But to be the lover of a man does not make a woman a whore. I lay with Wulfric out of joy, not for payment.'

There was a gasp at her brazen admission, but not, she sensed, an entirely critical one. Many of the encircling women appeared to approve her statement.

'Really?' Sunilda drawled, leaning forward to flick at the brooch on her breast and the gold at her neck. 'You bought these then, did you, you lying trollop? Or did you steal them?'

The sneering face seemed to swim in front of her eyes. Julia ignored Ingunde's gasp of outrage. 'Wulfric gave them

to me as a gift so that I might wear them today and be fit-
tingly dressed for the occasion.'

'Liar! You have stolen them. They are mine, for I will be
his wife.' Sunilda spoke with utter confidence. Out of the
corner of her eye Julia could see some heads begin to nod. *Yes,
that is what they believe will happen. And of course they are
right.*

'When Wulfric negotiates with your father for your hand,
then no doubt such things will be agreed. But he has done no
such thing yet, has he? And until he does, then he may do
what he wishes with his possessions.'

Sunilda was very close now. Julia could see the way her
pupils had dilated so the blue eyes seemed almost black. She
was a tall woman, wide shouldered, long limbed like most of
her race and Julia fought the instinct to step back. Instead she
tipped up her chin and returned the look of fury with one of
calm superiority. It was her mother's best expression for
dealing with other wives attempting to rise above their own
place in society and it had always made her wince. Now she
allowed her mouth to curve, very slightly, into a patronising
smile and waited for Sunilda's retort.

'You little slut!' As Julia had expected, it would be more
of the same insults. Sooner or later the blonde was going to
tire of it and flounce off.

'But it must be worrying that Wulfric is taking so long
about it,' she added with provocative sympathy.

Then she saw the set of the other woman's mouth, the way
her hands had flexed into claws, and realised, too late, that this
was not a world where the game was won with verbal knife
play. In Sunilda's world, fighting for what you wanted meant
just that.

She heard Una's cry of warning as Sunilda lunged, then

she was reeling back, her head ringing from the violence of the blow to her cheek. Julia staggered, regained her balance and saw her rival leap for her, the small eating knife from her girdle flashing in her hand.

Chapter Twenty-One

'For God's sake, put that down!' Julia backed away, her hands held up, palms outwards. Sunilda showed her teeth and kept coming. 'Someone is going to get hurt—'

'That is my intention, Roman whore.' Julia whipped round, looking for escape. She had not the slightest desire to stand her ground, not against an enraged Goth a head taller, wielding a knife. But the women had formed a circle around them, backing away, to be sure, but only to leave them room. It was just as it had been when Wulfric had fought Rathar: a personal duel was taking place and that was accepted. Both Ingunde and Una were white-faced, but neither intervened.

Wulfric's fight had ended in a death—was that what they expected now? Her hand went to her waist, but, dressing in Una's borrowed finery this morning, she had not thought to tie her own eating knife to her girdle. And, even if she had, could she have used it? Could she really knife another woman, even in self-defence?

Sunilda was circling, teasing her with little flicks of the blade. Julia edged round warily. 'What do you want?' she asked, hating the way her voice cracked.

'I want my jewels, slut. And to show that you are not fit to even be the whore of a Visigoth warrior, of a king.'

Oh, thank goodness, she just wants to humiliate me, not to kill me, Julia thought with a frantic attempt at some sort of steadying humour. 'Then put the knife down,' she challenged, managing to keep her voice steady this time. 'Or do you need it to fight an unarmed woman who is half your weight?' It was a random insult, and a wild exaggeration, but slenderness was prized amongst the women of her own social class—it might goad the taller woman into unwise action.

She succeeded rather better than she had hoped. Sunilda flung the knife away, making the circle of watchers shriek and lurch backwards as it landed amongst them, then she launched herself at Julia with a snarl of fury.

They went down in a tangle of limbs and fine linens. Julia twisted as she fell, hit the hard ground with her shoulder and rolled away, feeling her veil tearing out of the pins as it caught under their bodies. Sunilda's hands were clutching at the heavy brooch on her shoulder. Julia went limp, pretending to be stunned, let her tear it free, then bit the other woman's hand with a viciousness she had no idea she possessed. With a shriek Sunilda let it go, Julia snatched it and tossed it awkwardly across her prone body towards Ingunde.

She just had time to see the girl catch it before Sunilda's fingers closed on the gold chains around her neck. This time she did not make the mistake of trying to unfasten them, or dragging them over her opponent's neck: Sunilda tightened the links in her fists and twisted them into a noose.

Julia forced her chin down, instinctively protecting her throat, and fought desperately to dislodge the other woman. She reached up and clawed at her wrists, but Sunilda was wearing wrist clasps of wrought gold, studded with turquoises, and Julia's nails broke and tore against them.

They rolled, clawing and kicking. Julia, desperately dragging air into her lungs, was almost stunned by how much it was all hurting. Watching fights, she had always imagined somehow that the flame of battle dulled all sensation until the fight was over. How else had Wulfric fought on with his sword arm slashed to the bone? With sheer courage and endurance, she realised, making a determined effort to bend one of her opponent's fingers back to break her grip on the choking necklace.

Sunilda snatched her hand away, fetched Julia a stinging slap on the side of the head and renewed her hold. It was becoming a dirty, frantic, chaotic fight, a battle not of trained moves and skill, but of simple hatred, pain, fear and desperation.

Leverage, try and throw her off... Julia dug her fingers into the earth, scrabbling for a position where she could force her tiring body upwards, but the other woman's weight was too much for her. She felt one of the strands of the necklace break, then another; the dry earth crumbled in her fists and, with a cry of fury and determination, she hurled both handfuls of dust and grass into Sunilda's face.

The Visigoth woman shrieked and clawed at her own eyes. Julia uncurled herself violently and thrust the other body off. Something gave with a sharp pain in her shoulder, but she ignored it. She rolled, scrambled to her feet and dragged the broken necklace over her head. 'Here.' Ingunde was at her side, reaching for it. Julia pulled off the arm clasps and piled those into her hands as well. 'I can't believe this is happening,' she panted, her voice raw in her throat. She would never have enough air in her lungs again, never. 'Why isn't anyone stopping it?'

'But this is a matter of honour.' Ingunde appeared shocked she should ask. 'Afterwards, if we had stopped it, you would have been very angry, shamed, believe me.'

'I'm very angry now,' Julia said grimly, throwing aside the remains of her cloak and dragging off her girdle so she could remove what was left of Una's beautiful gown. Underneath she wore her own plain shift. With the weight of cloth gone, the blood surging through her veins, she was suddenly back in the yard at the women's baths, exercising with her girl-friends, her limbs strong and free. She could move, use the advantage of her size and lightness.

Sunilda, her face streaked with dirt and perspiration, her eyes red from the dust, turned towards her like an avenging Fury. Julia ran straight at her, ducked under the grasping arms and hit her with both hands flat on the chest. The other woman staggered, shaken by the direct attack, and Julia hooked one ankle round her leg, jerked and she was down, Julia on top of her, kneeling on her arms.

'Stop it! Do you hear me! Just stop it! The jewels have gone, I will be gone soon, you can have him,' she shouted into the furious face below hers. 'Just stop it,' she repeated quietly as she felt Sunilda go limp. 'Just stop.'

'You do not want him?' The woman was incredulous.

'More than my life,' Julia said softly. 'More than my honour. But not more than his.'

Julia wondered vaguely if she was going to faint, about how she was going to find the strength to climb off the prone body beneath her, about how it was possible for her entire body to be hurting as badly as it was.

With a sigh she managed to topple over sideways and collapse onto her back on the scuffed grass. She lay there and another hand slid into hers, clasped it. 'I believe you,' Sunilda whispered. Julia turned her head with an effort that made her back ache and found she was looking into her opponent's bloodshot-red eyes. 'It was a good fight.'

'If you enjoy that sort of thing,' Julia conceded, fighting an insane urge to laugh. It would probably come out as hysteria and complete her utter humiliation. She was a patrician Roman lady, yet she had stooped to a cat fight in the dust of a barbarian camp and now she was lying in her shift, exchanging conversation with a woman who had tried to knife her moments before.

There was noise behind them, raised voices; she ignored them, her eyes locked with Sunilda's. The voices died away into silence. Then someone was kneeling beside her, hauling her up into a sitting position. Wearily she looked up to see who it was. Wulfric. *Of course, it would be. This is a momentous day for him, a day of mourning, a day of destiny. Look at him,* she told herself wearily, *look how beautiful he is, how powerful, how gorgeously dressed. A king in the making. And he has to come and rescue his ex-slave, his ex-lover, his far from ex-problem in the face of hundreds of witnesses whose opinion will mean everything to him.*

She turned her head away so she could not see the disgust she knew she would find on his face. She loved him so much she was not going to add to his shame for her by betraying that now, in front of everyone. She saw that Hilderic was helping his daughter to sit up, her finery in tatters about her. And saw that he was smiling. *Smiling?* 'A hard-won truce, I see,' he commented.

'I wish we could have seen the fight that led to it,' Wulfric said, his voice deep, with a streak of amusement buried in it.

'You…you *what?*' Julia turned back to him, making the world spin with the unconsidered movement. 'You do not mind that this has happened, and now of all times?'

'I am flattered,' he admitted. She was close enough to see the way his mouth quirked, the darker green flecks in his irises that always seemed more pronounced when he was excited or aroused. 'And I am impressed.' *So close I can see each individual hair of his beard, every lash of his eyelashes, every...* 'Don't faint.' His breath was warm in her ear. 'You are going to walk away now.'

'I cannot.' Presumably two of the parts of her body that hurt so much were her legs, but she was not sure which.

'Yes, you can.' He was lifting her to her feet, steadying her with an arm around her waist. 'You are Wulfric's woman, and you do not faint in front of everyone.'

'No, I am not your woman. We have just settled that,' she said. But she forced herself to stand and pushed his hand away. Doing that hurt as much as Sunilda's blows had. Someone had come with a cloak for Sunilda, who was walking off on her father's arm, a group of friends surrounding her, talking and laughing. Julia put one foot in front of the other and somehow made it to where Ingunde was pushing forward with a cloak.

'That was wonderful,' she proclaimed, grinning broadly at Wulfric. 'She saved all your jewellery, did you see?'

'*My* jewellery,' Julia said between clenched teeth. 'She can have his, for all I care. And stop smirking.' She turned on Wulfric, bolstering her own resolve with feigned anger. 'You have no cause to feel flattered. When a large woman insults me, attacks me and attempts to rob me, I am going to fight.' She limped round the back of a wagon. 'Now, please, will you put all those impressive muscles to some practical use, and carry me?'

Wulfric scooped her up in his arms, his heart contracting with the lightness of her. She was so small compared to

Sunilda's long-limbed, big-boned magnificence. 'I am not smirking,' he said, knowing perfectly well he had been. He still wanted to. Julia had more than enough sense to avoid Sunilda, or to avoid her wrath if it had simply been a clash of personalities. But they had been fighting over him, and over the jewels he had given her. Her gruffness did not fool him.

He thought he understood her well enough to know she would not use violence to defend them simply because she coveted wealth. She had fought to defend them because they were his gift. But now she was hurt and she was not used to that. Sunilda had grown up in the rough and tumble of camp life, had reached womanhood in a society that expected its women to fight the enemy to defend their hearths and children, and each other if necessary to settle insults.

'You should have warned me,' she grumbled, her head on his shoulder. 'I would have carried my knife if I'd known I would find myself in that sort of situation.'

'Knife? She threatened you with a knife?' The warm glow inside turned ice-cold.

'Mmm.' The tangled brown hair bobbed as she nodded. 'After boxing my ears and before attempting to strangle me with the necklace.'

'Are you wounded?' he demanded, trying to keep the panic out of his voice. There had been no sign of blood on her, but a small, deep wound would not necessarily show at once.

'No. Just battered. I made her throw it away. Are we nearly there?'

'Yes, almost there. *How* did you make her throw it away?'

'I shamed her for attacking someone without a weapon. Besides, she wanted the satisfaction of getting her hands on me. I annoy her very much.'

'My clever darling.' He set her down in front of her tent, trying to school his face into some semblance of neutrality. He wanted to crow because she had fought for what he had given her, he wanted to kiss her out of sheer relief that she was alive and because he was so proud of her, he wanted to fuss because she was hurting and he wanted to take her pain to his own body. 'Now show me where you are hurt.'

'No.' She was suddenly shy. 'Ingunde will look after me.'

'Miens liufs…'

'No, don't call me that.' Sweetheart—she had discovered what it meant. She tried to push him away. Smoke appeared on silent feet and pushed his nose into her hand, grumbling anxiously.

Gentleness was getting them nowhere. It was making her bashful and him soft. 'Get into that tent, now,' he ordered. 'Take off everything and lie down.' Julia gave a gasp of surprise at his tone, but did as she was told. 'And leave the tent flap open, I need the light,' he added. 'Smoke, guard.'

'What is the matter with you?' he demanded a few minutes later as he ducked into the tent, a basin of warm water in his hands, linen bandages under one arm. She was curled up at the head of her bed, naked as he had ordered, but in a tight knot of embarrassment. 'Let me see. Julia, for Heaven's sake, I have seen you naked often enough now.'

'That was different. We were lovers. Now…now, I just don't know.'

Now you sense that I still want to make love to you, stretch out over that slender body marked with purpling bruises and caress you until you can think of nothing but the pleasure of my lovemaking. Do you sense that I love you, Julia Livia? Do you sense that every breath you take makes it harder and harder to face the fact that I am losing you?

She did not love him, that was obvious, he thought as he took one foot, ignoring her wriggles of protest, and began to wash it, checking for cuts and scrapes as he did so. He had always known it, but some foolishness kept the flicker of hope alive, kept him looking in vain for some clue. The intensity of a fight like that was enough to knock all inhibition, all pretence out of you. If he had lifted her in his arms and she had loved him, she would have turned to him, she would not have been able to hide how she felt.

Her loyalty, her friendship, were both his. She would fight for his interests, fight for what he had given her, worry herself sick if she thought he was in danger. But she would do the same for any of her new friends, he told himself. He was nothing special, except that he had taken her virginity, and he supposed that would always affect the way she thought about him.

Wulfric forced his mind to blankness as he worked his way over Julia's naked skin, cleaning the small cuts, smoothing on one of Una's salves where the skin was bruised. He had done this often enough for Berig when he had come back, battered after a scrap with a bigger lad, or hurling himself with his friends into yet another dangerous adventure. All he had to do was to mentally substitute this soft, rounded flesh for the scrawny limbs and scabbed knees of the boy.

He failed utterly. And, apparently, obviously. Her fingers brushed his forehead as he was wrapping a bandage around her ribs under the sweet swell of her breast. 'You are sweating,' she said.

'I do not like to think I am hurting you.' He made himself continue.

'Then I have my revenge for you making me sew up your

arm. How do you think I felt?' Her fingers slipped into the
fall of his hair and combed through it. Wulfric forced himself
not to close his eyes.

'I am a man. I am supposed to be able to withstand pain.'
Her fingers were playing now, pushing back his hair, experi-
menting by tucking it behind one ear. *I am even supposed to
be able to withstand torture,* he thought grimly, tying off the
end of the bandage. *Not the most ingenious enemy could be
as inventive in that field as Julia is.*

'And women aren't? What about childbirth? And, in any
case, you approved of us fighting, so you are being inconsis-
tent by worrying about me now.'

'Don't use logic on me, woman,' he growled. 'Let me see
your throat.' He was fighting not to take her in his arms, but
her glib retort steadied him. This was hard enough, without
exposing himself to her pity by a stammering declaration of
his feelings. What she wanted him to show her, it seemed, was
his strength and his ambition and that was what he wanted
too. Of course it was.

Julia let Wulfric doctor her sore body and tried to hide her
reaction to the touch of his hands. He was gentle, but he was
firm, and he was as detached as if he had been tending Berig's
cuts and bruises. More so; he would probably have been lec-
turing the lad on how he could have avoided various blows.

She was still shaken by his reaction to the fact that she had
been fighting. What would Antonius Justus have said if he had
witnessed such a scene? She shuddered to imagine. But deep
inside, fighting the upbringing that told her that a patrician
woman should shun such behaviour, was the beginnings
of pride that she had stood up to Sunilda, that she had
fought back.

The admiration in Wulfric's eyes had been dangerously exciting. For a few heady moments she had imagined herself at his side, a fit queen for a barbarian warrior. Then common sense had crashed down, sweeping the dream away. If nothing else, that clash had proved how necessary it was for her to leave. In that exhausted, unguarded moment of bonding with Sunilda she had betrayed how she felt about Wulfric. It was hard to believe that the other woman would throw it back at her in his hearing, it would be too much of a risk to her own position, but, even so, too many people knew that she loved him.

That feeling was not returned, she thought sadly as his big hands checked carefully down the column of her neck, running over each vertebra, his eyes on her face watching for any wince of pain. She kept her expression tranquil; the pain was in her mind, not in her body. He was protective, as he had been almost from the beginning. But then he was with everyone he regarded as being his responsibility. He had been her first lover, and that, she suspected, would weigh with him, because he did not take lightly what it would mean to her. But when it all came back to basics, she was just an alien woman he had plucked out of her world on a whim, and he was a man with a destiny.

'Sleep now,' he said at last, drawing the covers up over her and tucking her in as though she was sick. 'I will get Una to bring you one of her draughts.'

'But the feast!' What would happen that evening? Was it the start of the process by which the king would be chosen? What would take place while she was not there to see? Julia struggled up on her elbows and was firmly pressed back down again.

'Rest, my anxious Roman councillor.' Wulfric smiled down at her. 'Nothing is going to happen other than the consumption of too much food and ale, the singing of songs, the making of speeches, the shedding of tears and the creation of many hangovers. Rest.'

Chapter Twenty-Two

Julia awoke from a deep sleep to find herself stiff, sore and one of the most clear-headed people in the camp. Everywhere she looked as she limped her way towards the latrine were red-rimmed eyes, pale faces and people ruefully rubbing their temples as they grimaced into the depths of herb-steeped potions.

Una, stirring porridge no one appeared to want, did at least seem to be suffering from nothing worse than a very late night. 'Hello, my love.' She smiled a welcome. 'How do you feel? Sore?'

'Very.' She looked down at the marks on her wrists and wondered if Sunilda was waking up this morning in the knowledge that her marriage to Wulfric was settled. 'Where is everyone?' Julia asked, lowering herself cautiously onto a stool and accepting ale in a beaker. 'Ingunde's bed wasn't slept in last night, unless she tidied up very quietly this morning.'

'Ingunde is sulking down by the waterside in an effort to make herself seem aloof and interesting. Berig is sulking in the horse lines, pretending to help Sichar, and also trying to look aloof and interesting. They were both up all night, making themselves thoroughly miserable.' Una poured some honey into the pot and stirred. 'Do you want some of this?'

'Please.' Julia cupped her hands round the warm bowl and blew on the surface. 'Have they had a row?'

'As far as I can gather,' Una said wearily, 'they both had rather a lot to drink. She tried to seduce him, he repulsed her, she called him a prig, he called her wanton, she slapped his face, he stormed off. Honestly, it is bad enough having small children to look after without those two.'

'How do you know all that, or were they yelling at each other? And are you sure Ingunde made the first move—after all, he's the male!'

'They both came separately and told me their versions and marched off when I wasn't sympathetic enough. And as for who started it—girls are always more advanced than boys, in my experience.' Una served herself some porridge and came to sit down. 'Ingunde knows what she wants, and that is Berig. He is scared witless of the way he's feeling, would be my guess—he wants to have sex with her, but he wants to protect her. He wants her on a pedestal as a virgin goddess, but he wants to impress her with his lovemaking. And she's his first, so he is terrified of making a mull of it—and on top of all that, Wulfric's read him a lecture on respecting female purity.'

'*Wulfric* has?'

'Quite.' Una grinned. 'Men are endlessly fascinating, aren't they?'

'Where is Wulfric? Did anything happen at the feast?'

'Nothing more than you would expect. A lot of speech-making, endless toasts. There were no incidents, thank God,' she added piously. 'Hilderic tried to get Wulfric alone, presumably to start negotiating over Sunilda, but he managed to avoid him.'

'Why?' Julia found she was suddenly surprisingly happy and enormously hungry and delved into the pot for a second helping.

'Because he's got more sense than to get into discussions with that old fox when he's had as much to drink as he had last night.' Una frowned into her porridge. 'I've never seen him drink that much before. Reckless, almost.'

'But not so reckless he would commit himself to Sunilda.'

'No. Odd, that.'

They were both still eating porridge and frowning in thought when Wulfric walked in. 'You look awful,' Julia said encouragingly. Although she wanted to hide her feelings behind a façade of teasing, he did look less than his usual healthy self, she realised. His face was grey under the golden tan, his eyes slightly bloodshot and there were shadows under them. 'Have some porridge,' she added helpfully, wishing she could cradle his head in her breast and soothe away his headache with cool fingers.

'Thank you. You, I assume, are quite revived.' He did not wait for an answer, but took the food and leaned against the wagon, spooning it down with the determined air of a man taking unpleasant medicine. 'Where is Berig?'

'In the horse lines, brooding on his hangover, his sore cheek and your lecture on female purity,' Una said.

'What?' Wulfric looked startled.

'There was no need to make the poor boy any more anxious about girls than he is already,' she chided. 'Go and talk to him, he needs some masculine advice and I don't expect he'll confide in Sichar.'

With a muffled oath Wulfric pushed himself upright, put down his bowl and turned to climb the hill. He turned back after two strides. 'We leave tomorrow. Two days' journey north is a place we camped at on our way down. It is a good site, and one that is easy to defend. We will stay there until the decision is made.'

Julia watched his back as he walked away. 'I suppose there is no need to ask what it is that will be decided.' *The kingship. The destiny of one man and of a people.*

'No,' Una agreed. She gave herself a little shake. 'Now, do you want some witch hazel for those bruises?'

There was a new tension about the camp. Julia felt it like the warning of an approaching thunderstorm, prickling under her skin and making her edgy and aware. The watchers were back, she was sure of it, although the sweep riders and the scouts had failed to find them.

'It does not mean there is nobody there,' she had heard Wulfric cautioning as he sent out the dawn riders to patrol the perimeter. 'It means we haven't found them yet. They are good.'

Nor was it just the presence of the unseen watchers, or the lingering physical and emotional effects of the funeral and feast. There was the knowledge amongst everyone in the camp that a decision was about to be made that would change their lives for ever, for better or ill.

'We move as though expecting battle,' Wulfric said curtly as they began loading the wagons. 'In groups with the remains of the royal household and Galla Placidia in the centre. We—' he swept one hand around the gathering of his kin group who surrounded him '—we take the rearguard. All men mounted. Everyone armed, children in the carts.'

Una was packing the smaller children into the back of their

wagon, making a game of joining them. Ulf, her middle son, was beside himself with delight at being allowed to sit up beside Gunthar, his brother, and to help drive. Neither of them seemed to notice that their mother had laid their father's bundle of boar-hunting spears casually within arm's reach in the back.

Ingunde took the wagon Berig normally drove, managing not to look in his direction as he checked over the yoke and the oxen's harness. He had Wulfric's second sword hanging from his belt, his own long knife, and a shield strapped to his back.

No longer a boy, not quite a man, Julia thought as she watched him, her heart aching for him: so young, so proud of riding out with a sword at his side, and so painfully conscious of Ingunde ignoring him. She walked across, and climbed up beside the girl. 'Stop it. Speak to Berig. Go to him, touch him, don't leave unsaid something you might regret later.'

Ingunde turned her head away. 'He doesn't want me, he thinks I am a wanton, that all I want is…*that*. Prig. I am not going to humiliate myself by crawling to him. He can go off and get tonsured and be a monk after this for all I care.'

'I am not suggesting you crawl,' Julia said tartly. 'Just be civil.'

'Not until he apologises to me.'

'Oh, for goodness' sake! Does it not occur to you that he isn't very experienced at this either?' Ingunde turned her shoulder. 'Stew in your own misery, then.' Julia jumped down and stalked back to her own wagon, passing Berig leading his horse away as she did so.

'You look so fine.' She smiled at him, then ran a hand over his shiny new chain mail. 'Can I give you some advice? You do not have very much experience of women yet. Just remember they might be as frightened of you as you are of them. And sometimes, when you are frightened, it is easy to make mistakes, be clumsy.'

She walked away before he could answer her, but when she glanced back, he was looking at Ingunde's averted head, a slight smile on his lips.

'What are you doing?' Wulfric reined in beside her, his face unreadable beneath the iron and gilt of his helmet, the straight nose-piece shadowing his eyes so he seemed to be regarding her from behind bars.

'Knocking heads together, or, at least, trying to.'

'Huh.' He shot a glance at Berig's retreating back. 'Make sure you keep up today.' He handed her the iron-shod goad. 'Keep this to hand at all times. There is a pass through the hills, that is where there will be trouble if it is going to come.'

'Yes, I will keep up.' He turned the grey's head. *Speak to him, touch him, don't leave unsaid something you might regret later.* Her own words swam in her mind, burned on her tongue. 'Wulfric—'

'Yes?' He swung the animal around on its haunches, his mail bright in the sun, his hair flying with the sudden movement, and the words dried up on her lips.

'Be careful.' *I love you. I love you, my magnificent Goth.*

They drove through the long hot day, riders always in movement on their flanks, cantering back and forth down the length of the column. Gradually the slopes closed in; the oxen began to labour against the yoke as the way steepened.

'That must be the pass ahead,' Julia called across to Una's sons and Ingunde. 'See how narrow it is. We must not slow down.'

The oxen lowed and shook their heads as she prodded them, but they were well rested and kept up their speed.

'The head of the column must be through now,' she said, pulling up alongside Ingunde and shading her eyes to stare ahead. 'It is more a defile than a pass. It looks as though there has been a rock fall, that is why everything is going so slowly. Now we are stopping.'

Berig rode back to them. 'Rocks and soil keep rolling down. There was quite a big fall after the last group of wagons. We are going to clear it, it should speed things up in the end. Close up.'

There were perhaps thirty wagons left, twenty or so riders at their backs. Ahead men were dismounting, pulling mattocks from the backs of wagons and walking into the defile. Julia could see Wulfric as he rode back and forth, scanning the scene, urging haste.

The shout, when it came, echoed round the narrow valley so she could not tell at first where it was coming from. Then the men at the mouth of the defile scattered, she saw Wulfric's grey rearing as he fought to bring its head down, and another horseman burst through.

'A trap, a hundred or more armed men on the hillside—' It was Willa, spurring his horse viciously, and behind him as he burst through men poured down the slopes on either side, the gleam of plate armour, the red of helmet crests, the orders in Latin and the bursts of trumpet blasts unmistakeable. They were Roman troops and the Visigoth rearguard was in their trap.

'To me!' Wulfric yelled and men ran or galloped to his side to form a line protecting the wagons as the Roman infantry crashed to a halt, regained their order and began to advance.

'Behind us!' Ingunde screamed and Julia stood and turned. Cavalry was wheeling out of the trees.

'Form a line, protect the men's backs.' Julia hauled on the reins, shouting at the oxen until they swung round, presenting the side of the wagon to the oncoming riders. The women and boys followed suit.

'Get the children underneath!' That was Una, herself already down despite her pregnant bulk, lifting children, pushing them under the wagon. All along the line the other women were doing the same, then, instead of joining them, lifting the long boar spears and turning to confront the cavalry with a bristling wall of iron. It would give the horsemen pause if they had any sense, Julia thought grimly; the women were protecting their children and would be as vicious as cornered cats with kittens if the soldiers got close.

She stood up and started to scramble back to find the spears Wulfric had laid in the wagon beside his spare shield. The thought that she would be threatening her own troops crossed her mind, only to be dismissed. It was an unprovoked attack.

Her hand was closing around the shaft of a spear when she saw Wulfric. He was standing back to back with Willa, the pair of them using their swords to hold back a knot of infantry. Berig was beside him, the youth dwarfed by the broad-shouldered, mail-clad warriors towering over him.

The three shifted and turned as one, in what must be a long-practised tactic, presenting a constantly changing front to the attackers. They all appeared to be unhurt, but the Goth line was under serious pressure, outnumbered and with the cavalry at their backs held at bay only by the line of carts and the determination of the women.

Julia looked back; the women's line was holding, the thirty or so cavalry riders were weaving back and forth, apparently unwilling to engage and assessing whether to try for the flanks. She picked up three spears, as many as she could hold one-handed, and started to climb back.

'Wulfric!' It was Berig's voice. Julia spun round and saw Wulfric down on one knee, his shield split from top to bottom by a tremendous sword stroke. As she watched, frozen with fear, he regained his feet and instead of using his sword, hurled one half of the shield at his attacker. It caught the legionary full in the chest, felling him.

In their small group now only Willa and Berig had shields. Julia hefted the one at her feet. It took all her strength to manage it, but she dragged it to the side of the wagon and jumped down, stumbling towards the fighting men, dodging the individual battles all around her. A Goth staggered back, a javelin in his chest, and crashed to his feet in front of her. She feinted round the fallen body and looked for a way through to Wulfric past the shifting wall of struggling fighters.

Then a gap opened, just as Willa dodged to one side and Wulfric turned with him, his sword swinging up to drive back the soldier lunging for Berig.

'Wulfric!' She pitched her voice loud and high above the shouting and the clash of swords, and he heard her.

'Get back!'

'Here, catch!' She pushed the shield as though she were rolling a wheel and it ran true and fast, through the gap, straight to his hand. He caught it, slid his arm through the straps and lifted it, bringing his sword up in a fleeting salute to her as he turned back to the fight.

Tell him now, you may never get another chance! 'I love you,' she shouted, and saw his face as her voice arrested him. *Did he hear?* His lips moved, just as a blast on the Roman trumpet blared around the field. *What did he say?* Her lips moved, trying to recreate the glimpse she'd had of his. *I love you?* or *Go back?*

The thunder of hooves had her spinning round. The cavalry had outflanked the women's line and were attacking between the Goths and the front of the wagons. Julia scrambled backwards towards her wagon, shifting one of the spears to her right hand as she went. She had never tried to throw a javelin in the exercise yard, now her hand was already shaking with the strain of holding the heavy hunting weapon as she tried to find a target in the shifting, chaotic mêlée.

The horses parted and there was a centurion, magnificent in his uniform and armour, scanning, not the fighting men, but the women. 'There, that one!' he yelled, pointing straight at her. Two riders at his side spurred towards her. She began to run, dropping all but one spear, frantic to regain the wagons before the pounding hooves reached her.

One stride from the wheels a hand fastened on her arm and she was dragged, kicking and screaming, up towards the saddle of the soldier who held her. She dangled, her feet a perilous hand's span from the thrashing hooves and tried to swing at him with her spear. With almost contemptuous ease he knocked it from her grasp just as a dark furry body launched itself up.

The cavalry horse snorted and shied and the wolf fell back, then crouched to leap again. With a grunt of effort the rider swung his sword across and stabbed downwards as Smoke began to rise. Julia did the only thing she could, rolling her body across so she blocked the stroke.

For a heart-stopping moment she thought the soldier could not pull the blow in time, then the blade whistled past her and with the momentum of her own movement he hurled her across the saddle bow, the pommel knocking the breath out of her.

She choked, ducked her head and buried her teeth in the bare knee in front of her. The man cursed, cuffing her ear. She tried to roll free, and as she did so she saw Wulfric.

He had seen her. As she twisted, frantic to keep him in sight, he broke away from the man he was fighting, threw down his shield and began to run towards her. 'Julia!' He cut through the battlefield like a hero from the pages of the myths, she thought hazily, desperately dragging the air into her aching lungs, too winded to do more than hang over the saddle. Broad shouldered, a giant in gleaming mail, his hair flowing behind him as he ran, his teeth bared in a snarl of primal fury, he fought his way towards her like a man possessed, sword in one hand, long knife in the other, and men fell back before him.

'Look out!' She saw the javelin, he did not. She doubted her scream even reached him before the weapon took him in the left shoulder. She saw him stagger and fall and then the cavalryman had whipped his horse around and was spurring off the field, away from the fight. His elbow hit Julia's temple as he dragged the reins round and she saw stars, heard a roaring sound and everything went black.

Chapter Twenty-Three

'This is not Galla Placidia, which, considering the state she is in, is something we must be thankful for. I doubt Honorius would be grateful to us for returning his sister covered in bruises and hit on the temple by some idiot cavalryman's elbow.'

The drawling, patrician voice echoed in her ears, making no sense at all. Used to very different accents, to a mixture of tongues, Julia fought to focus. *Where am I?* The words would not leave her mouth. Perhaps opening her eyes would help. She did so, and found herself blinking in the subdued light of a cool room.

'Must be the other one, sir. Definitely younger, answers to the description we were given.' This speaker had clipped, authoritative tones. Julia fought the nausea that was rising in her throat and made herself think. Military. Respectful, yet not subservient. A senior officer talking to a senior magistrate or a local governor, then?

She tried to remember where she was and why and it suddenly came back with a rush. 'No!' She struggled up, managing to get to a sitting position before the room began to move and she had to shut her eyes and stay still.

'No.' Wulfric, running for her. His image was all she could see, slowed as though time had stretched, his gaze fixed on her even as his sword beat back the soldiers, his arms, muscles bulging with the effort, throwing off every obstacle, the soundless flight of the spear as it took him down. Such a small thing to kill such a big man.

'Oh, God.' It was a prayer and she expected no message of hope. What she got was the sight, as she opened her eyes again, of a middle-aged man, his hair severely cropped, his austere expression at odds with a richly embroidered silk tunic.

'Are you Julia Livia Rufa, daughter of Julius Livius Rufus and affianced bride of Antonius Justus Celsus?' he demanded.

'Yes.' The admission was out before she could deny it. 'Where am I? What has happened to the Goths? I must go back!' She struggled to put her feet on the floor and found herself respectfully, but very firmly, held by two women who appeared from behind the couch she was lying on. 'Let me go!'

'You have had a very terrifying experience, Julia Livia,' the man said. 'Your mind is confused, which is only natural. The emperor sent Gaius Octavius here to locate and rescue his beloved sister, and he was good enough to extend the remit to finding you, as you are the daughter of such a prominent senator.'

'I do not need rescuing,' Julia managed. 'I was on my way back to Rome. But never mind that, that is the least of it— what happened to the Goths you attacked? Where are they?'

'Where we left them.' The soldier moved into her line of sight.

Very senior, I can't remember how to tell rank, why do I feel so dizzy... Oh, yes, my head... 'They are all dead?' *Wulfric, Una, Berig, Ingunde... No!*

'Some, all men. Once we had you, and established that we

had missed the emperor's sister, we pulled back.' He frowned at her. 'I have no intention of risking my troops on that rabble unnecessarily.'

'They are not a rabble.' She sank back against the pillows. Not all dead, then. Just some…just Wulfric. *Oh, my love.* 'I must go back to them.'

'Poor child, she is quite unhinged by the experience.' It was one of the women. 'I am Titia Gracia, wife of Gnaeus Arminius Albus, governor of this area.' The tall man inclined his head. 'I will look after you until you are able to travel home. Dear girl, what you must have suffered.' She began to pat Julia's hand, an irritating distraction from her circling thoughts.

Julia tugged her hand free. 'You do not understand. I must go back!'

'But why?' The patrician stared at her down his long nose, good manners obviously at war with the sheer irritation of having to deal with a battered, uncooperative female who showed not the slightest gratitude for her rescue. 'You said you were coming back to Rome—what has changed?'

'Your unprovoked attack on my friends,' Julia snapped.

'My dear Julia Livia.' He smiled at her coolly. 'It is a well-known fact that captives, if they are forced to live for any length of time with their captors, will become irrationally attached to them. I can see that in your case this pretence of belonging would have made things easier, given you more freedom, but you can cast that affectation aside now. You are safe and in civilisation once again.'

'Civilisation?' She stared at him, the comprehensively patronising tone almost taking her breath away. 'I have been living with civilised people these past months, sir, and I can tell you, there is more than one kind of civilisation in the world.' The beautiful handicrafts, the skills that produced them kept alive despite the dangers and difficulties of a nomadic life. The sophisticated interweaving of family and alliance, kingship and loyalty, the laughing children and the dignified women, having their say, fighting alongside their men. Was that not civilisation?

Julia looked around her at the coolly perfect interior, the silent slaves standing to attention at the sides of the room, the rich silks that adorned her hosts. She knew they would not believe her for a moment if she told them that those long-haired warriors, preserving their way of life even if they had to load it into ox carts and drag it across a continent fighting every inch of the way, aroused more respect in her breast than either of the two *civilised* men standing before her.

'Please let me go,' she said calmly. 'I do not wish to be here.'

All four faces reflected shock. 'Dear child, you must do as your father commands,' Titia Gracia said soothingly. 'She is confused by the blow to her head,' she explained to the men. 'Leave her with us, we will tend to her. You will see, she will be more rational tomorrow.'

'Very well, Domina.' It was the cavalry officer. 'But one vital question before I go. Julia Livia, where is Galla Placidia? Our scouts could not find her in the days we have been watching.'

Julia stared at him. What to say? Would the emperor's sister welcome rescue, or was she, as she appeared and everyone said, in love with Athaulf and willing to marry him? And even if she were, these men would try to snatch her back and more killing would ensue.

More or less bloodshed if she told them where Galla Placidia was? Her head spun with the effort to decide. In the end she did the only thing she could think of and collapsed back onto the couch with a little moan. 'She has fainted,' Titia

Gracia said. 'I must insist you do not question her until tomorrow, Gaius Octavius. We will leave her to sleep. I am certain she will be in a calmer and more rational state when she awakes.'

Julia heard the door close behind them and lay, pretending limp unconsciousness until she was certain they had not left a slave in the room with her. Then she turned her face into the silken cushions and wept.

The rest of the day passed in a blur. They came back to see her in the late afternoon, pressed food she could not eat upon her, escorted her firmly, but kindly, to the bathhouse, spoke soothingly to her, but all she could do was to drift with them, outwardly compliant—except that she could not force food between her lips—but inwardly focussed on just one thing.

I have to find the strength to hope, I have to find the cunning to escape. Wulfric might not be dead, he might simply be wounded, and, if that were the case it might have saved his life by stopping him fighting on. They might all be alive, all her friends—and Galla Placidia would be unaware that her brother had sent a rescue party after her.

If she was told, and she wanted to escape, then all she had to do was to get to the perimeter of the camp and the hidden scouts would snatch her to safety without anyone being hurt. If she did not want to, if she wanted to stay with her lover, then at least they would be warned that troops had been sent to take her.

But whether or not her warnings could help the other woman, Julia knew she could not live with this uncertainty. She had to know who had lived and who had died. She had to know what those words were on Wulfric's lips as he had faced her across the chaos of the battlefield, even if she then had to turn and walk away from him.

It should be easy, she told herself. She was not the indecisive, sheltered woman she had been when he had taken her. She felt a strength, a ruthlessness in herself that these involuntary hosts of hers would not expect. She simply had to pretend to be grateful to be in their custody, feign helplessness and she could slip away, steal a horse… Her scheming stuttered to a halt at that point. Having stolen it, could she stay on it? Probably she would be better on foot, and less visible. At least they had left her old clothes when they had dressed her in these silken tunics.

Accordingly Julia allowed herself to recover from her faintness, to appear to be confused, grateful and biddable and sweetly distressed that she had spoken so. Titia Gracia petted and made much of her, tempted her with the best delicacies from the dining table and bade her goodnight with a smile and the promise of discussing plans to return her to Rome in the morning.

She had also, as Julia discovered when she tried to open her door well past midnight, locked her guest in tight and left a slave outside the room. A large male one, by the sound of his gruff voice when he enquired if the lady required anything in response to her rattling the latch.

Julia muttered every bad word she had picked up from Berig's unguarded lips, and dragged a stool to the high window. It proved to have bars on the outside. She collapsed back on the sleeping couch, all the nervous energy and optimism she had summoned up to escape knocked out of her. Now all she could do was hope and pray and watch like a hawk for any opportunity on the journey back to Rome. And worry.

'My darling daughter!' Her mother embraced her in a flutter of veils, pretty tears and smiles. 'You are safe!' She smiled graciously at the optio and the two foot soldiers who had been sent to escort Julia and two female slaves home. 'Thank you so much.'

'Domina.' The optio snapped off another smart salute and handed over a scroll. 'With the compliments of Gnaeus Arminius Albus.'

'Of course. Now, you must go and take refreshment while we prepare a letter of thanks for you to take back.' Vibia Octavia fluttered a hand at her husband. 'Could you see to that, dearest?'

Alone with her mother and her usual accompaniment of expressionless slaves, Julia stood silent, not expecting the sweet maternal effusions to endure once they were without witnesses.

'Look at you, Julia! You look like a wild thing—your hair, your nails and those clothes!'

'I was dragged off a battlefield by a cavalry trooper,' Julia said mildly. 'I have just had a four-day journey without my own clothes.' It was pointless to feel either distress at this welcome or to waste her energy in being angry.

'And what were you doing there?' Vibia Octavia demanded petulantly.

'I was captured by the barbarians during the sack of the city,' Julia said patiently, sitting down without being invited to. Her store of filial duty was running very low. 'As I assume you know.'

'Marcus Atilius told us he saw you at the Forum. How could you have been so careless?' Vibia Octavia threw herself down in a decorative flutter of embroideries. 'I was frantic.'

'If you had sent me out with an escort of male slaves, I would have been a lot safer—and that poor girl you did send with me would still be alive,' Julia retorted.

'They murdered her! How shocking.' Her mother did seem appropriately appalled, Julia was glad to see, then had to bite back her anger when she added, 'And she was so expensive. The best embroiderer we had. And those barbarians—to think that people have been saying since that they were not as bad as they might have been. It just goes to show.'

'She was murdered by the respectable citizens who were attempting to rape me when the Goth rescued me, Mother,' Julia interjected.

'Rape.' Vibia Octavia's eyes opened wide. 'Oh, my God! Ruined…'

'I said attempting.' Not, *how horrible*, not *were you hurt?*, but *ruined. For what exactly?*

'Then you are still a virgin?'

Julia knew she should have been prepared for that question. Now, she did not know whether to lie or to be honest. It was either her face or her hesitation that gave her away. 'Those barbarian monsters!' Vibia Octavia raged, jumping to her feet and beginning to pace. 'And I suppose you are about to tell me you are with child? How can we explain away some blond, blue-eyed bastard?'

'Green-eyed,' Julia said between rigid lips. 'But you need not worry, he was a very careful barbarian monster, you are not about to become a grandmother.'

'Insolent child!' Her mother's slap rocked Julia back on her couch. She was half on her feet, not certain whether she was going to flee the room or shout back when her father entered.

'Some Goth has had her,' Vibia Octavia wailed. 'The only blessing is that she says she is not with child.'

'He is not—' *Oh, my God, I almost said* was. Julia blinked back the tears and made herself go on. 'He is not *some Goth.*

His name is Wulfric. He is so well born that he may well be their next king.'

'Not well born enough, it seems,' her father said. 'I have just heard, the new king is Alaric's brother-in-law Athaulf. And he has married Galla Placidia.'

Julia hardly heard her mother exclaiming in horror at the dreadful fate of the emperor's favourite sister. Her legs gave way and she sat down with a thump. Not Willa, not Wulfric, but Athaulf, who had been safely ahead of the ambush. If it had been Willa crowned, then she could have hoped that Wulfric was still alive, but Willa had been at his side in the fight. Now she had no way of knowing if they had simply both lost the contest for the kingship—or their lives.

'Is what your mother says correct?' Julius Livius planted himself in front of her. 'You are not with child?'

'I am not.'

'Then all is not lost. Antonius Justus is still willing to marry you, I believe. I may have to increase your dowry under the circumstances, but it will still be worth it to avoid the scandal. I can well do without that just now.'

'The Goths did not pillage all your wealth, then, Father?'

'No. Between my banker's secure vaults and your mother's skill in hiding the household silver, we lost nothing.'

'And why should Antonius Justus still wish to marry me? You do not think I can hide my lost maidenhead from him, do you?' Julia got up and began to pace angrily. 'Mind you, he is such an inept lover, perhaps he will not notice after all.'

'Oh! Such coarseness! How can you compare Antonius Justus with this savage of yours? Besides, do not tell me he ever took liberties with you,' her mother flashed.

'He kisses like a wet fish. I have no wish to experience any other contact with him.'

'You will marry him, my girl, and do your level best to remember you were raised in a respectable patrician household. He needs my support in the Senate, I need his backing for new trade ventures with the Eastern Empire. I have no intention of that good relationship being disturbed because of your vapourings. You will stay confined to your room until your mother's women can at least make you look like a lady again. Then you will receive Antonius Justus, behave with becoming modesty and accept his offer. And be grateful.'

'Or what?' Julia demanded.

'Or nothing.' Her father's face was white with anger. 'You agree, you behave or you stay in your quarters until you do.'

'I will never agree,' she flung at him passionately.

'Then I suggest you resign yourself to having a great deal of time to remember your lover in.'

They stood glaring at each other for a long moment, then Julius shook his head in exasperation. 'Confound it, Julia, you were willing enough to marry him before. Do you think I wish to be harsh? We were beside ourselves with worry until we learned you were safe.'

'You have a fine way of showing it on my return,' she said bitterly. 'And I accepted Antonius because I knew no better. I have loved a warrior, a leader—do you expect me to settle for some prig of a politician?'

'Brute strength and muscles? Is that what it is?' her mother demanded, finding her voice again. 'Do not show her any weakness, Julius. She is no better than those strumpets who lust after gladiators. Deny it if you can.'

'Deny that Wulfric is magnificent? Deny that he is built like a god? Deny his muscles and his golden skin and his green eyes and his strength in battle? Deny that it arouses me just to speak of him? I will do none of those things.'

'Oh!' Vibia Octavia clamped her hands over her ears. 'Wicked girl! Go to your rooms at once and do not come out until your father says you may. The slaves have been told you may not set foot over the threshold, so it is no use trying to persuade any of them to let you out. Now go!'

'Gladly.' Julia swept her skirts around her with as much dignity as she could muster. 'And if you send Antonius Justus to me, I will catalogue every physical attribute of my lover to him with detailed comparisons to his own endowments!' She closed the door behind her on her mother's shriek of rage.

Celebrate 100 years of pure reading pleasure with Mills & Boon®

To mark our centenary, each month we're publishing a special 100th Birthday Edition. These celebratory editions are packed with extra features and include a FREE bonus story.

Now that's worth celebrating!

4th January 2008

The Vanishing Viscountess by Diane Gaston
With FREE story The Mysterious Miss M
This award-winning tale of the Regency Underworld launched Diane Gaston's writing career.

1st February 2008

Cattle Rancher, Secret Son by Margaret Way
With FREE story His Heiress Wife
Margaret Way excels at rugged Outback heroes…

15th February 2008

Raintree: Inferno by Linda Howard
With FREE story Loving Evangeline
A double dose of Linda Howard's heady mix of passion and adventure.

Don't miss out! From February you'll have the chance to enter our fabulous monthly prize draw. See special 100th Birthday Editions for details.

www.millsandboon.co.uk

2 FREE

BOOKS AND A SURPRISE GIFT!

We would like to take this opportunity to thank you for reading this Mills & Boon® book by offering you the chance to take TWO more specially selected titles from the Historical series absolutely FREE! We're also making this offer to introduce you to the benefits of the Mills & Boon® Reader Service™—

- ★ **FREE home delivery**
- ★ **FREE gifts and competitions**
- ★ **FREE monthly Newsletter**
- ★ **Exclusive Reader Service offers**
- ★ **Books available before they're in the shops**

Accepting these FREE books and gift places you under no obligation to buy, you may cancel at any time, even after receiving your free shipment. Simply complete your details below and return the entire page to the address below. You don't even need a stamp!

YES! Please send me 2 free Historical books and a surprise gift. I understand that unless you hear from me, I will receive 4 superb new titles every month for just £3.69 each, postage and packing free. I am under no obligation to purchase any books and may cancel my subscription at any time. The free books and gift will be mine to keep in any case.

H8ZED

Ms/Mrs/Miss/Mr ....Initials ....
BLOCK CAPITALS PLEASE

Surname ....

Address ....

....

....Postcode.........................

Send this whole page to:
UK: FREEPOST CN81, Croydon, CR9 3WZ

Chapter Twenty-Four

Three weeks confined to a suite of three rooms and a small courtyard with the highlight of the day an escorted visit to the bathhouse gave Julia long hours to dwell not only on Wulfric's physical attributes, but, more dear, more precious, his mind, his words, his character.

She could not believe he was dead, yet all she had to base that hope upon was hope itself. No news was transmitted to her, although she clung to the comfort that her parents would not hesitate to tell her if word of his death was received. Inside was a constant, sore ache of worry, of loneliness and of love.

Defiance had got her nowhere. Julia sat on the stone bench in her little garden, drew up her knees, wrapped her arms around them and brooded. It was chilly outside now, but she missed the open sky over her head and defiantly wrapped herself in her cloak to stay out.

She was in no doubt that she would stay in these rooms until either she agreed to marry Antonius or she faded away. Wisely her father had, so he informed her, told her putative betrothed that she had been deeply distressed by her harrowing rescue, that her face had been badly cut and bruised and she could not cope with a meeting until her looks and spirits were restored.

Julius was gambling on her capitulation. Julia was slowly coming to realise that her only hope of escape lay in appearing to yield. The household was in a turmoil, preparing for a banquet her parents were giving to celebrate her mother's birthday. She could hear the bustle from where she sat.

'Minia.' The slave whom her mother had sent to serve her, and, she was convinced, to spy upon her, looked up from her sewing.

'Yes, mistress?'

'Who is invited to the banquet tonight?'

'Why, everyone, mistress.'

'Including Antonius Justus?' She managed a soft, regretful sigh. 'I had hoped he would come and visit me…'

'You want to see him, mistress?' The slave put down the mending.

'Oh, I don't know.' Julia sighed again and rubbed the back of her hand across her eyes. 'I have been so…perhaps my parents… Oh, I don't know, I am so miserable, living like this.'

'I will go and bring you a posset, mistress, it will help settle your spirits.' Minia hurried out, although Julia did not risk a triumphant grin. For all she knew, there were spy holes in the courtyard walls.

Her suspicions about Minia were confirmed when her mother drifted in half an hour later. 'How are you, Julia?' she asked, more pleasantly than she had spoken for many days.

'Well enough. Mother, is Antonius Justus coming to your party tonight?'

'Yes, he is. Why do you ask?'

Julia shrugged. 'I…I had thought he would come to see me before now.'

'Your father did not wish it until he felt confident of your modest and compliant behaviour,' Vibia Octavia said severely. 'Are you telling me you are willing to receive him in a proper spirit?'

'Yes… Mother, being back, living in a proper Roman household again…I realise how very different things are from the Goth camp. I can understand clearly what is important.'

'I see.' Vibia Octavia frowned. 'And if Antonius comes to you, you will say all that is proper?'

'Oh, yes, Mother,' Julia said fervently. 'But…it is going to be hard enough to have such a discussion, let alone with witnesses. May I speak with him by myself?'

'I do not see why not.' Vibia Octavia looked thoughtful. 'I think it is best if we fix his affections quite firmly now. I see no reason why, if he visits your rooms after the meal is over and the other guests are watching the entertainers, he should not stay for quite a while. Long enough to fully commit himself.' She sent her daughter a very direct stare. 'You understand what I am saying?'

'Yes, Mother.' Julia dropped her eyes modestly to her linked hands and did her best to look both flustered and gratified. It could not be better. Even Mother would not expect her to make love to Antonius Justus with half a dozen slaves in attendance, and the house would be in such a bustle, no one would notice a cloaked and veiled figure slipping out with the entertainers.

That supposed she was capable of immobilising one substantially built senator. Julia began to run through possible weapons in her mind. The small water amphora behind her bedchamber door seemed the best bet for something she could lift and which was hard enough to knock a man out.

'Thank you, Mother,' she said earnestly. 'Thank you for giving me another chance.'

Bathed, perfumed, painted and dressed in fine amber and gold silks, Julia fidgeted about her room. She was hardly dressed suitably either for assaulting the unsuspecting Antonius, or for an escape disguised as an acrobat or musician, but she sensed that making at least a pretence of seduction was the best way to lull her suitor into complaisance.

The noise level from the main part of the house was considerable now. The guests were arriving, being greeted, chattering and drinking before being ushered into the banquet. Julia tried to make herself relax and plan the best way to hit Antonius.

By the time she judged the final course to have been served she had already rearranged her room three times. Now the couch sat in the middle of the room, surrounded by flickering lamps. The eyes of anyone entering would be drawn to it at once and the light would dazzle as they came in from the poorly lit courtyard. She hefted the amphora standing just behind the door one last time. Perfect. She sent up a last, heartfelt prayer for herself, for Wulfric and, as an afterthought, for the unfortunate Antonius, and set herself to wait.

It did not take long. She heard the catch on the gate into the courtyard click open, then the faint creak as the gate opened and shut. Footsteps, cautious, but obviously male, on the pavement.

She pushed the door ajar so the light spilt out onto the design of peacocks and vine leaves and called softly, 'In here.'

Standing in the narrow space between the door and the wall, looking through the gap at the hinge end, she could see a figure, see a large male shadow of a man in a tunic thrown across the courtyard. There was the rustle of heavy silks as he put his hand on the door, then he was stepping inside.

Julia glimpsed a sandaled foot, the hem of a lavishly embroidered green tunic, then she swung up the amphora and stepped out of cover, just behind him as he entered. The vessel blocked her view of his head, but she judged her blow by his shoulders and swung down, just as her senses started to protest. *He is too big…*

The man spun round, caught the earthenware vessel in both hands, wrenched it out of her grasp and threw it away to shatter on the floor. The door banged shut, the lamps guttered and smoked, half went out and Julia found herself seized in a ruthless grip.

'Oh, my fierce Roman girl,' said a voice she had feared never to hear again and she was crushed in an embrace so tight she thought her ribs would crack.

'Wulfric? I thought…' The rest of her words were lost as he took her mouth. He was not gentle. It was a kiss of possession, of weeks of fear and loss, of desperate claiming. His tongue swept her mouth, testing, tasting, and she answered with the thrust of her own.

It was him. His taste, his scent, the feel of his skin under her hands, the thud of his heart against her breast. He was here, it was a miracle. Then, as the first intensity slipped into something else, and his arms relaxed and his hands slid up to her shoulder blades to hold her more gently and his lips moved across hers in a tantalising, silent question, she realised that something was different.

The mouth that was worshipping hers was not surrounded

by the softness of a moustache, the prickle of newly clipped beard did not graze her cheek as he turned his head. Julia reached up, pressing her hands to either side of his face. He was clean-shaven. And that shadow glimpsed in the courtyard in the light spilling from her door… She had thought it was Antonius. Why?

Ice clutching her heart, she raised her hands to his head and found the ruthless crop of the patrician Roman male, felt the bare tendons at his nape, the curl of his ear. Her fingers closed and short hair slid from her grasp.

'No!' She said it against his mouth, but he heard her and lifted his lips from hers. Then he opened his hands and stepped back, watching her.

The man in front of her would have fitted in perfectly in the banqueting room just the other side of the wall. Not an Italian, or an Iberian, obviously, but perhaps a wealthy visitor from Britannica. Blond, broad shouldered, impeccably groomed in his rich silks, the tasteful glint of gold at his neck.

He looked almost like a man she knew: the green eyes watching her steadily, the long lashes, the imperious nose that had once been broken, the sensual, expressive mouth. But this man had a strong chin, wide cheekbones, a broad forehead that she had never seen before, only felt under caressing fingers or glimpsed as the wind caught his mane of hair. His sacred hair. The hair of a king.

'What have you done?' she whispered. His words came back to her, it seemed from years before. 'You said *no man whose hair is shorn can lead, let alone rule. His only role can be as an outcast or a priest.'*

'I have no intention of becoming a priest.' His eyes on her were watchful, measuring. Was he expecting her to reject him, as presumably his people had?

'Your hair,' she said helplessly. 'Who cut it?' Had he been defeated, had it come to a fight and had Athaulf taken a dreadful revenge on his rival?

'I did. Or at least, Berig did.'

'What? You did this of your own free will?' He must not think she was spurning him as the others must have. She took his hands in hers. 'Why?'

His mouth twisted in amusement. 'Can you imagine me strolling into Rome, let alone this house, looking like a Visigoth come to call?'

'You did that just to find me? Oh, no, Wulfric, I would never have asked it, you know I would never have.' The tears were pouring down her face. He lifted his, still trapped in hers, and cupped her wet cheeks.

'I know.' His thumbs wiped gently under her eyes, catching the tears. 'I had to make a decision, not only about you, but about what I wanted and about what I should do. Come, come and sit down and I will explain.'

Still trembling with reaction, she let him lead her to the couch and sat beside him. 'We regrouped after the ambush. All your friends are safe. So is Willa. We went on to the place we had chosen for the decision and there was a long debate. I listened to Willa and heard my own thoughts, my own ambitions for our people, echoing back to me from his lips. There is nothing I can do as king that he cannot.'

'You are *you*,' she protested loyally. 'You are the better man.'

'He is more ruthless, more ambitious. I threw my vote and my kin behind him, but it was not enough. People were scared, they were unsettled by the loss of Alaric—the ambush was the final straw. They wanted continuity and I think they saw in Athaulf's marriage to Galla Placidia the hope that Honorius will deal fairly at last. He is king now.'

'I know—I thought it meant that you and Willa must be dead.' Julia curled her arms around his shoulders and buried her face in the angle of his neck, so strange without the fall of hair to mingle with hers.

'Oh, sweetheart.' His big hand pressed her against him. 'I was free to come for you. I discussed it with my kin, my nearest advisors, and I told them what I planned to do, both to find you, and then afterwards.

'Julia, I want to go north into Gaul, not wait for Honorius and Athaulf to talk endlessly for years. I want to buy land, not wait for it to be given. I want to settle, learn to live with my Roman neighbours. I told my kin that, and said that if that is not what they wanted, then I released them from their fealty. Either Athaulf or Willa would welcome them. Most said they would go with me.' His lips twisted wryly. Julia found herself fascinated by them, naked. She had learned to read them despite his beard; now she could see how cleanly sculpted they were, how expressive.

'Then I told them what I had to do to come for you and told them that they would need to chose another leader, for I would no longer be eligible.'

'What did they say?'

'That they would follow me anyway. They conceded that a king must keep his hair, but, it seems, in this new world, a leader need not.'

'I think,' Julia said gently, reading in his eyes how moved he was still by that loyalty, 'I think that it very much depends on the leader.'

She saw his Adam's apple move convulsively as he swallowed, but his voice when he spoke was gently teasing. 'Do you mind?'

'The beard, no,' she decided, finding it almost impossible

to stop running her fingers down the planes of his cheeks, along his jawbone. 'I like to see your face. But the hair, yes, I do miss that.'

'Typical woman,' he pretended to grumble, pulling her onto his lap. 'You leave me the chore of shaving and my hair—' His head came up sharply. 'There is someone at the gate.'

'Oh, lord! Antonius Justus. He is coming to seduce me.'

'What?' How Wulfric managed to thunder in a whisper she had no idea. Stifling a hysterical giggle, Julia watched him slip behind the door and gesture her to call out.

'Antonius? I am in here.'

'Julia, my dear.' The senator stepped through the door, smiling widely. *Father has been plying him with drink,* Julia guessed, holding out her hands as if in welcome.

'Antonius.' His face as he felt the tap on his shoulder was a picture of incredulity. He swung round and met Wulfric's right fist, which lifted him off his feet to land with a crash at Julia's feet.

'He'll be fine,' Wulfric said in answer to her gasp of alarm. 'What do you mean, seduce you?' He began to drag the unconscious man through the door. 'Is there another room we can lock?'

'Yes, that one there. He was coming to propose, and my parents thought, as I'm not a virgin, it would be best if he, er, committed himself.'

'He's taken long enough about it.' Wulfric snatched a linen cloth from Minia's mending basket, tore it into strips and began to bind Antonius hand and foot. 'There, that'll keep him quiet.' He added a gag, pulled the door shut, put the stop through the latch and led her back into her bedchamber.

'At first I was not very cooperative,' Julia confessed. 'When my father told me I had to receive him, I said I would catalogue my barbarian lover's attributes and compare them with Antonius's for his education.'

Wulfric choked back a gasp of laughter. 'On my soul, I do love you, my little Roman.'

'You do?' He had never said it before; the doubts shook her again, then she saw his eyes.

'More than my life I love you. Can you doubt it?'

'It is easy to be unsure, when you are in love and cannot face the thought of being wrong,' she murmured.

'Did I read your lips aright, just after you sent me my shield?' His hands had slipped down to cup her rear, pulling her against him, the evidence of his arousal very clear.

'Yes. I love you. Oh, I love you. Oh—and that javelin! It went right out of my head when I saw you, realised about your hair! I thought you were dead.' She linked her hands behind his neck and stared up into his face, searching.

'It caught in the links of my mail. It penetrated a little, made a mess with the mail, but it is almost healed. I am in reasonably good condition to be a bridegroom.'

'Is that a proposal?'

'Yes, it is, my love. At least, provided you can convince me that your intentions tonight were not to seduce that senator.'

'No. I meant to hit him on the head with the amphora, escape disguised as one of the entertainers, change into some simple clothes I found in the servant's room and walk until I found you all.'

'Not steal a horse?'

'No.' She flashed a provocative glance up from under her lashes. 'And how do *you* plan to get us out?'

'Berig has been scouting around. It took us some time to find where you lived. He has been delivering your vegetables

for a few days, waiting for news of some function I could in-
filtrate. I thought we could simply walk out together, provided
you have a modest veil to wear. Otherwise we'll need to go
over the wall.'

'Not in this tunic.' She let her palms slide down his ribs,
enjoying the feel of the thick silk over his muscles.

'Julia.' His voice was husky. She let her hands stray
between them, then wander down. 'Stop it! When is the best
time for us to leave?'

She listened. 'Another half-hour, I think. The first guests
will be going, but there is less risk of my parents coming out
of the triclinium at that stage.'

'Excellent.' He began to unfasten her girdle. 'Plenty of time.'

'For what?' Her voice came out as a gasp. It was all too plain
as first her overtunic, then undertunic and shift were whisked
over her head. He stripped off the gorgeous tunic as though it
was sackcloth, wrenching off his sandals impatiently.

'This.' It was a growl as he swept her up and down onto
the couch, his weight coming over her to cover and possess
her as he took her mouth. Julia arched under him, cradling
him between her thighs, tipping her pelvis to incite him
shamelessly. He surged into her and she felt her body accept
him as a scabbard accepts the sword it was made for.

'Mine,' he said fiercely. 'My love, always.'

'Mine,' she echoed, pulling his head down again so she
could kiss him, nibbling along the edge of his lips, teasing
the sensitive skin with her tongue. But he was impatient for
her, moving hard already so her head began to thrash on the
pillow and all her words became a moan of desire.

She had waited too long for him, the shock of his presence
was too intense for her to withstand her own body. Her cry as
he took her over the edge into ecstasy was swallowed up by his

kiss, then he threw back his head and his cry of triumph filled the room, echoing in her ears as he collapsed into her embrace.

'I love you,' she murmured, savouring the feel of his body, still within her.

'I love you,' he answered, nuzzling her neck. 'The bliss of being able to say it!'

She smiled, turning her head to give him better access. 'No, don't,' she murmured as she felt his thigh muscles tense as he began to lift himself away from her.

'We must go. Sooner or later your parents are going to conclude that your senator has been delayed by more than your charms.'

'I want to stay like this for ever,' she murmured, sighing as he slipped from her body and stood up, naked and glorious and golden in the lamplight.

'Come.' Wulfric held out a hand and pulled her to her feet to stand beside him. 'I love the way your skin looks next to mine.' She snuggled up and he laughed. 'No! We must stop this before we wake up and find the cocks are crowing. Get dressed, Julia. Time to leave your father's house.'

She slipped on a different tunic, one she had not worn since she had been back, and draped her stole modestly over her head, holding it across her face like any well-bred matron about to emerge onto a public street. When she turned from her mirror, Wulfric was fastening his sandals.

'So, Domina, shall we go?'

It was so easy, slipping out amidst slightly tipsy guests. The slaves were scurrying back and forth, calling for chairs, finding ladies' cloaks. Wulfric sauntered through the middle of it all, Julia at his side, and they were out onto the street in moments.

'Round the corner. Don't hurry.'

There was a wagon, its bulging load sheeted, two figures

apparently asleep on the driver's box. At the sound of their sandaled feet one looked up. 'It's them. Julia!' There was a gruff bark and a cold, wet nose pressed into her hand.

'Hush, Berig, Smoke.' Ingunde, her face just shadow with the flash of teeth in the darkness of the unlit street. 'I am so glad you are safe!'

They embraced, scrambling into the seat together. Julia felt their warm bodies, the fierceness of their hugs, the pressure of their lips, clumsy in the gloom, and knew she was home.

'Let's go,' Wulfric said. 'We will be at the gate for dawn and then we will meet the others. Una and Sichar will travel with us, the rest in small groups of not more than five wagons. We will be inconspicuous, unthreatening and blend in.' He leaned forward to prod the oxen and Julia spared one last glance at her old home.

'I'm not cutting my hair,' said Berig, obviously pursuing an old argument as Ingunde began to tease him softly.

Julia turned on the cramped seat and slipped her arm through Wulfric's. 'I love you,' she whispered fiercely. 'And now I am home.'

'So am I. Do you know, I thought I would never have one until we found a place to settle. I did not realise all that I needed was to be where my love was. So simple, so hard to find. You are my home, Julia, my love.'

She pressed against his side, letting her other hand rest on the flat plane of her stomach in a soft rustle of silk. Somehow she knew that tonight they had created the future, the child she craved so much. She would not tell Wulfric yet. She knew he would believe her, however improbable it seemed that she could tell already—only he would fuss over her so.

Wulfric turned his head and she could sense his smile in the darkness. He took the reins in one hand and slipped the other to lie over hers. She had forgotten his incredible hearing. 'I love you both,' he whispered as the wagon rumbled slowly into the night, out of Rome and into a new world.

* * * * *

Historical Footnote

Alaric, Willa, Athaulf, Honorius and Galla Placidia were all real people, and I have tried not to take liberties with the known facts of their lives.

The Sack of Rome by Alaric and the Visigoths did occur on the 24th of August, AD 410, lasted three days and by all accounts was a remarkably restrained and relatively bloodless event.

I have followed the movements of the Visigoths after the Sack as accurately as the scanty records allow. The journey south, the towns taken along the way and their eventual arrival in Rhegium (Reggio di Calabria) are as the histories relate, as are the storm, the loss of the fleet, the return north and Alaric's death. The river-bed burial in the Bastenus at Consentia (Cozenza) is a persistent legend that no one has ever disproved.

After the burial the records falter and fall largely silent. Athaulf married Galla Placidia and was made king. The movements of his people for perhaps eighteen months after that are uncertain. Then he died and Willa succeeded. At last, it seems, here was a man with whom Honorius would come to terms. The long-sought grant of land was confirmed and the Visigoths settled in the part of Gaul we now call Aquitaine. Eventually they moved over the Pyrenees and founded the great Visigoth kingdom of Spain.

The Visigoths were known, well into the early Middle Ages, as the Long-Haired Kings. One simple and relatively painless way of clearing rivals out of the succession was to kidnap them and cut off their hair. Wulfric's reaction to Julia's attempts at cutting his would have been completely predictable.

In large part it is the Goths who founded the Europe of the Middle Ages and the basis of the Europe we live in today. Their blending of Roman civilisation with their own was my inspiration for the love story of Wulfric and Julia, and I think I know where their villa lies: in the shadow of Mont Ventoux in southern France. Perhaps their descendants live there still....

On sale 1st February 2008

THE UNWILLING BRIDE
by Margaret Moore

Promised to Merrick of Tregellas when she was but
a child, Lady Constance was unwilling to wed a man she
remembered only as a spoiled boy. Convinced he had
grown into an arrogant knight, she sought to make
herself so unappealing that Merrick would refuse to
honour their betrothal.

Yet no sooner had this enigmatic, darkly handsome
man ridden through the castle gates than she
realised he was nothing like the boy she recalled.
And very much a man she could love…

MILLS & BOON

Historical

On sale 1st February 2008

RUNAWAY MISS
by Mary Nichols

Alexander, Viscount Malvers, is sure the beautiful girl on the public coach is not who she says she is. Her shabby clothing and claim of being a companion cannot hide the fact that she is Quality. He's intrigued. This captivating Miss is definitely running away, but from what – or whom?

MY LADY INNOCENT
by Annie Burrows

As the nobility jostles for the new King's favour, Maddy is all alone. So she accepts a bridegroom she has never met. Fiercely loyal to the King, Sir Geraint cannot trust his Yorkist bride – but neither can he resist her innocent temptation!

THE COMMANDER
by Kate Bridges

Julia O'Shea is fast reaching the limit of her patience caring for her young son alone. Her pragmatic solution? To advertise for a husband. Her plans go out the window when Ryan Reid – the man who loved and left her ten years ago – comes back to town. Julia can't hide her attraction to this bad-boy-turned-surgeon, especially when he swears he's reformed…